The
SWEETGUM LADIES
Knit for Love

**Center Point
Large Print**

Also by Beth Pattillo
available from Center Point Large Print

Heavens to Betsy
Earth to Betsy
The Sweetgum Knit Lit Society

**This Large Print Book carries the
Seal of Approval of N.A.V.H.**

The SWEETGUM LADIES *Knit for Love*

Beth Pattillo

Center Point Publishing
Thorndike, Maine

This Center Point Large Print edition is published in
the year 2009 by arrangement with WaterBrook Press,
an imprint of The Crown Publishing Group,
a division of Random House, Inc.

The text of this Large Print edition is unabridged.
In other aspects, this book may vary
from the original edition.
Printed in the United States of America.
Set in 16-point Times New Roman type.

ISBN: 978-1-60285-544-1

Library of Congress Cataloging-in-Publication Data

Pattillo, Beth.
  The Sweetgum ladies knit for love / Beth Pattillo.
    p. cm.
  ISBN 978-1-60285-544-1 (library binding : alk. paper)
  1. Knitters (Persons)--Fiction. 2. Knitting--Fiction.
  3. Book clubs (Discussion groups)--Fiction. 4. Female friendship--Fiction.
  5. Women--Southern States--Fiction. 6. Domestic fiction. 7. Large type books.
  I. Title.

PS3616.A925S95 2009b
813'.6--dc22

2009014823

For the ladies of Pursuit—
You know who you are,
and I know how fabulous you are.
Thank you for the love and support,
but most of all,
thank you for the bling.

One

Every Tuesday at eleven o'clock in the morning, Eugenie Carson descended the steps of the Sweetgum Public Library and made her way to Tallulah's Café on the town square. In the past, she would have eaten the diet plate—cottage cheese and a peach half—in solitary splendor. Then she would have returned to her job running the library, just as she'd done for the last forty years.

On this humid September morning, though, Eugenie was meeting someone for lunch—her new husband, Rev. Paul Carson, pastor of the Sweetgum Christian Church. Eugenie smiled at the thought of Paul waiting for her at the café. They might both be gray haired and near retirement, but happiness was happiness, no matter what age you found it.

Eugenie entered the square from the southeast corner. The antebellum courthouse anchored the middle, while Kendall's Department Store occupied the east side to her right. She walked along the south side of the square, past Callahan's Hardware, the drugstore, and the movie theater, and crossed the street to the café. The good citizens of Sweetgum were already arriving at Tallulah's for lunch. But Eugenie passed the café, heading up the western side of the square. She had a brief errand to do before she met her husband. Two doors down, she could see the sign for Munden's Five-and-Dime. Her business there shouldn't take long.

Before she reached Munden's, a familiar figure emerged from one of the shops and blocked the sidewalk.

Hazel Emerson. President of the women's auxiliary at the Sweetgum Christian Church and self-appointed judge and jury of her fellow parishioners.

"Eugenie." Hazel smiled, but the expression, coupled with her rather prominent eyeteeth, gave her a wolfish look. Hazel was on the heavy side, a bit younger than Eugenie's own sixty-five years, and her hair was dyed an unbecoming shade of mink. Hazel smiled, but there was no pleasantness in it. "Just the person I wanted to see."

Eugenie knew better than to let her distaste for the woman show. "Good morning, Hazel," she replied. "How are you?"

"Distressed, Eugenie. Thoroughly distressed."

"I'm sorry to hear that." Eugenie truly was dismayed, but not from worry over Hazel's discomfort.

"Yes, well, you have the power to calm the waters," Hazel said with the same false smile. "In a manner of speaking, at least."

Since Eugenie's marriage to Paul only a few weeks before, she'd learned how demanding Hazel could be. The other woman called the parsonage at all hours and appeared in Paul's office at least once a day. Although Eugenie had known Hazel casually for years, she'd never had to bother with her much. Eugenie couldn't remember Hazel ever having entered the library.

"How can I help you?" Eugenie said in her best librarian's voice. She had uttered the phrase countless times over the last forty years and had it down to an art form. Interested but not enmeshed. Solicitous but not overly involved.

"Well, Eugenie, you must know that many people in the church are distressed by your marriage to Paul."

"Really?" Eugenie kept the pleasant smile on her face and continued to breathe evenly. "I'm sorry to hear that."

"Oh, not me, of course," Hazel said and pressed a hand to her ample chest. "I'm perfectly delighted. But some people . . . Well, they have concerns."

"What concerns would those be?" Eugenie asked with measured calm.

Hazel glanced to the right and to the left, then leaned forward to whisper in a conspiratorial fashion. "Some of them aren't sure you're a Christian," she said. Then she straightened and resumed her normal tone of voice. "As I said, I'm not one of them, but I thought I should tell you. For your own good, but also for Rev. Carson's."

"I see." And Eugenie certainly did, far more than Hazel would guess. Eugenie wasn't new to small-town gossip. Heaven knew she'd heard her share, and even been the target of some, over the last forty years. She'd known that her marriage to Paul would cause some comments, but she hadn't expected this blatant response.

"I'm mentioning it because I don't think it would be difficult to put people's fears to rest," Hazel said. Her smug expression needled Eugenie. "I know you've been attending worship, and that's a wonderful start." Hazel quickly moved from inter-fering to patronizing. "The women's auxiliary meets on Tuesday mornings. If you joined us—"

"I'm afraid that's not possible," Eugenie answered. She was determined to keep a civil tongue in her head if it killed her. "I have to work."

"For something this important, I'm sure you could find someone to cover for you."

Eugenie tightened her grip on her handbag. In an emergency, no doubt she could arrange something. But this wasn't an emergency. It was manipulation.

"Hazel—"

"Particularly at this time," Hazel said, barely stopping for breath. "With all the losses we've had in these last few months . . . Well, our community needs leadership. Our church needs leadership." She gave Eugenie a meaningful look.

Eugenie paused to consider her words carefully. "It has been a difficult summer," she began. "Tom

Munden's death was so unexpected, and then to lose Frank Jackson like that. And now, with Nancy St. Clair . . ."

"So you see why it's more important than ever that you prove to church members that their pastor hasn't made a grave mistake."

"I hardly think that my attending a meeting of the women's auxiliary will offer much comfort to the grieving." Nor would it convince anyone of her status as a believer. Those sorts of people weren't looking for proof. They were looking for Eugenie to grovel for acceptance.

Hazel sniffed. "Don't be difficult, Eugenie. You're being unrealistic if you expect people to accept you as a Christian after forty years of never darkening the door of any sanctuary in this town."

"I've always felt that faith is a private matter." That was the sum of any personal information Eugenie was willing to concede to Hazel. "I prefer to let my actions speak for me."

"There are rumblings," Hazel said darkly. "Budget rumblings."

"What do you mean?"

"People need to have full confidence in their pastor, Eugenie. Otherwise they're less motivated to support the church financially."

Eugenie bit her tongue. She couldn't believe Hazel Emerson was standing here, in the middle of the town square, practicing her own brand of extortion.

"Are you threatening me?" Eugenie asked, incredulous.

Hazel sniffed. "Of course not. Don't be silly. I'm merely cautioning you. As a Christian and as a friend."

Eugenie wanted to reply that Hazel didn't appear to be filling either role very well, but she refrained.

"I'll take your concerns under advisement," she said to Hazel with forced pleasantness. "I'm sure you mean them in the kindest possible way."

"Of course I do. How else would I mean them?"

"How else, indeed?" Eugenie muttered under her breath.

"Well, I won't keep you." Hazel nodded. "Have a nice day, Eugenie."

"You too, Hazel." The response was automatic and helped Eugenie to cover her true sentiments. She stood in place for a long moment as Hazel moved past her, on her way to stir up trouble in some other quarter, no doubt. Then, with a deep breath, Eugenie forced herself to start moving toward Munden's Five-and-Dime.

She had known it would be difficult, stepping into this unfamiliar role as a pastor's wife. Paul had assured her that he had no expectations, that she should do what she felt was right. But Eugenie wondered if he had any idea of the trouble Hazel Emerson was stirring up right under his nose.

True, she hadn't attended church for forty years. After she and Paul had ended their young romance, she'd blamed God for separating them. If Paul hadn't felt called to the ministry, if he hadn't refused to take her with him when he went to seminary, if she hadn't stubbornly insisted on going with him or ending their relationship . . .

Last year she and Paul had found each other again, all these decades later, and she'd thought the past behind them. But here it was once more in the person of Hazel Emerson, raising troubling questions. Threatening Paul. Forcing Eugenie to examine issues she'd rather leave unanswered.

As the head of the Sweetgum Knit Lit Society, Eugenie had taken on responsibility for the well-being of the little group several years before. Since Ruthie Allen, the church secretary, had left for Africa last spring to do volunteer work, the group had experienced a definite void. It was time for an infusion of new blood, and after careful considera-tion, Eugenie had determined that Maria Munden was just the person the Knit Lit Society needed. What's more, Maria needed the group too. The recent loss of her father must be quite difficult for her, Eugenie was sure. And so despite having had her feathers ruffled by Hazel Emerson, Eugenie walked into Munden's Five-and-Dime with a firm purpose.

"Good morning, Maria," Eugenie called above the whine of the door. For years she'd been after Tom Munden to use a little WD-40 on the hinges, but he had insisted that the noise bothered him less than the idea of a customer entering without him knowing it.

"Eugenie! Hello." Maria straightened from where she stood slumped over the counter. She had red marks on her forehead from resting her head in her hands, and her nondescript shoulder-length brown hair hung on each side of her face in a clump. Eugenie had come at the right time. Maria was in her early thirties, but her father's death seemed to have aged her ten years.

Maria came around the counter. "What can I help you with today?"

"Oh, I'm not here to buy anything," Eugenie said, and then she was dismayed when disappointment showed in Maria's eyes. With the superstores of the world creeping closer and closer to Sweetgum, mom-and-pop shops like Munden's were living on borrowed time. Even if Tom Munden had lived, the inevitable day when the store closed couldn't have been avoided.

"What did you need then?" Maria's tone was polite but strained.

"I have an invitation for you."

"An invitation?"

Eugenie stood a little straighter. "On behalf of the Sweetgum Knit Lit Society, I'd like to extend an invitation to you to become a part of the group."

Maria's brown eyes were blank for a moment, and then they darkened. "The Knit Lit Society?"

"I can't think of anyone who would be a better fit." Eugenie paused. "If you don't know how to knit, one of us can teach you. And I know you enjoy reading." Maria was one of the most faithful and frequent patrons of the library. "I think you'd appreciate the discussion."

Maria said nothing.

"If you'd like some time to think—"

"I'll do it," Maria said quickly, as if she didn't want to give herself time to reconsider. "I know how to knit. You won't have to teach me."

"Excellent," Eugenie said, relieved. "Our meeting is this Friday."

"Do I have to read something by then?" Lines of doubt wrinkled Maria's forehead beneath the strands of gray that streaked her hair.

Eugenie shook her head. "I haven't passed out the reading list for this year. This first meeting will be to get us organized."

Relief eased the tight lines on her face.

"We meet at the church, of course," Eugenie continued. "Upstairs, in the Pairs and Spares Sunday school room. If you'd like, I can drop by here Friday evening and we can walk over together."

Maria shook her head. "Thank you, but that won't be necessary." She paused, as if collecting her thoughts, then spoke. "I'm not sure why you asked me to join, Eugenie, but I appreciate it."

"I'm delighted to have you. The others will be as

well." Mission accomplished, Eugenie shifted her pocketbook to the other arm. "I'd better be going. I'm meeting Paul for lunch at the café."

Like most of Sweetgum, with the possible exception of Hazel Emerson, Maria smiled at Eugenie's mention of her new husband. "Tell the preacher I said hello." Maria moved to open the door for Eugenie. "I'll see you at the meeting."

Eugenie lifted her shoulders and nodded with as much equanimity as she could. After years of being the town spinster, playing the newlywed was a novel experience. She hoped she'd become accustomed to it with time—if she didn't drive away all of Paul's parishioners first with her heathen ways.

"Have a nice afternoon," Eugenie said and slipped out the door, glad that at least one thing that morning had gone as planned.

After Eugenie left, Maria Munden halfheartedly swiped her feather duster at the back-to-school display in the front window. Hot sunshine, amplified by the plate glass, made sweat bead on her forehead. What was the point of dusting the same old collection of binders, backpacks, and two-pocket folders? She'd barely seen a customer all day. She turned from the window and looked around at the neat rows of shelving. The five symmetrical aisles had stood in the same place as long as she could remember.

Aisle one, to the far left, held greeting cards, gift-wrap, stationery, office and school supplies. Aisle two, housewares and paper goods. Aisle three, decorative items. Aisle four, cleaning supplies and detergent. Aisle five had always been her favorite, with its games, puzzles, and coloring books. Across the back wall stretched the sewing notions, yarn, and craft supplies. Everything to outfit a household and its members in one small space. The only problem was, no one wanted small anymore. They wanted variety, bulk, and large economy size with a McDonald's and a credit union. Not quaint and limited, like the old five-and-dime.

From the counter a few feet away, Maria's cell phone buzzed, and she sighed. She knew without looking at the display who it would be.

"Hi, Mom."

"Maria, you have to do something about this." Her mother never acknowledged the greeting but plunged into a voluble litany of complaints that covered everything from the state of the weather to her older sister Daphne's management of the farm.

"Mom?" Maria tried to interrupt her mother's diatribe. "Mom? Look, I'm the only one in the store right now. I'll have to call you back later."

"Where's Stephanie? She was supposed to be there at nine."

"I don't know where she is." Maria's younger sister, the baby at twenty-five, was AWOL more often than not.

Maria heard the shop door open with a whine of its hinges, not too different from her mother's tone of voice. She looked up, expecting to see her younger sister. Instead, a tall, dark-haired man entered the store. He took two steps inside, then stopped. His eyes traveled around the rows of shelves, and his lips twisted in an expression of disapproval. The hairs on Maria's neck stood on end. The stranger saw her, nodded, and then disappeared down the far aisle, but he was so tall that Maria could track his progress as he moved. He came to a stop in front of the office supplies. Someone from out of town, obviously. Probably a traveling salesman who needed paper clips or legal pads. Maybe a couple of blank CDs or a flash drive. Maria had dealt with his type before.

"Bye, Mom," she said into the phone before clicking it shut. From experience, she knew it would take her mother several moments before she realized Maria was no longer on the other end of the line. Such discoveries never seemed to faze her mother. She would simply look around the room at home and find Daphne so she could continue her rant.

Maria tucked the cell phone under the counter and moved across the store toward the stranger. "May I help you?" Upon closer inspection, she could see that his suit was expensive. So were his haircut, his shoes, and his aftershave.

His head turned toward her, and she felt a little

catch in her chest. His dark eyes stared down at her as if she were a lesser mortal approaching a demigod.

"I'm looking for a fountain pen," he said. He turned back toward the shelves of office supplies and studied them as if attempting to decipher a secret code.

A fountain pen? In Sweetgum? He was definitely from out of town.

"I'm afraid we only have ballpoint or gel." She waved a hand toward the appropriate shelf. "Would one of these do?"

He looked at her again, one eyebrow arched like the vault of a cathedral. "I need a fountain pen."

Maria took a calming breath. A sale was a sale, and the customer was always right—her father's two favorite dictums, drummed into her from the day she was tall enough to see over the counter.

"I'm sorry. Our selection is limited, I know. Which way are you headed? I can direct you to the nearest Wal-Mart. You might find one there."

At her mention of the chain superstore, the man's mouth turned down as if she'd just insulted him. "No, thank you. That won't be necessary."

"Is there anything else I can help you with?" she said, practically gritting her teeth. She resisted the urge to grab his arm and hustle him out of the store. Today was not the day to try her patience. In two hours, assuming Stephanie showed up, Maria was going to cross the town square to the lawyer's office and do the unthinkable. At the moment, she didn't have time for this man and his supercilious attitude toward Sweetgum.

"I need directions," he said, eyeing her dubiously, as if he thought she might not be up to the task.

"Well, if you're looking for someplace nearby, I can tell you where you need to go," she said without a hint of a smile.

He looked away, as if deliberating whether to accept her offer. Honestly, the man might be extraordinarily good-looking—and wealthy, no doubt—but she would be surprised if he had any friends. He had the social skills of a goat.

The hinges on the door whined again. Maria looked over her shoulder to see another man entering the shop.

"James!" The second man grinned when he caught sight of the stranger at Maria's side. "You disappeared." The newcomer was as fair as the first was dark. "We're late."

"Yes," the stranger replied with a continued lack of charm. "But I needed a pen." He snatched a two-pack of ballpoints from the shelf and extended them toward Maria. "I'll take these."

Maria bit the inside of her lip and took the package from his hand. "I'll ring you up at the counter." She whirled on one heel and walked, spine rigid, to the front of the store.

"Hi." The second man greeted her with cheery

casualness. "Great store. I haven't seen anything like this in years."

It was a polite way of saying that Munden's Five-and-Dime was dated, but Maria appreciated his chivalry. Especially since his friend obviously didn't have a courteous bone in his body.

"Thank you." Maria smiled at him and then stepped behind the counter to ring up the sale on the ancient register. She'd pushed her father for years to computerize their sales—not to mention the inventory—but he'd been perfectly happy with his tried-and-true methods. Unfortunately, while he'd been able to keep track of sales and stock in his head, Maria wasn't quite so gifted.

The tall man appeared on the other side of the register. "Three dollars and thirty-two cents," she said, not looking him in the eye.

He reached for his wallet and pulled out a hundred dollar bill. Maria refused to show her frustration. Great. Now he would wipe out all her change, and she'd have to figure out a way to run over to the bank without anyone to watch the store. She completed the transaction and slid the package of pens into a paper bag with the Munden's logo emblazoned on it.

"Hey, can you recommend a place for lunch?" the blond man asked. He glanced at his watch. "We need a place to eat between meetings."

"Tallulah's Café down the block," Maria said. Even the tall, arrogant stranger wouldn't be able to find fault with Tallulah's home cooking. People drove from miles around for her fried chicken, beef stew, and thick, juicy pork chops. "But you might want to go soon. The café gets busy at lunch."

"Thanks." His smile could only be described as sunny, and it made Maria feel better. She smiled in response.

"You're welcome."

The tall man watched the exchange impassively. Maria hoped he'd be gone from Sweetgum before the sun went down. Big-city folks who came into town dispensing condescension were one of her biggest pet peeves.

"C'mon, James," the blond man said. "I have a lot of papers to go over." He nodded toward his friend. "James here thinks I'm crazy to buy so much land in the middle of nowhere."

Maria froze. It couldn't be.

"Oh." She couldn't think what else to say.

"We'd better go," the tall man said, glancing at his watch. "Thank you." He nodded curtly at Maria, letting her know she'd been dismissed as the inferior creature that she was.

"But I thought you wanted—" Before she could remind him about his request for directions, the two men disappeared out the door, and Maria's suspicions—not to mention her fears—flooded through her.

She should have put two and two together the moment the first man had walked into the store. A stranger in an expensive suit. In town for a meeting. Looking for a fountain pen to sign things. Normally Maria was good at figuring things out. Like where her father had put the quarterly tax forms and how she and Stephanie could manage the store with just the two of them for employees.

What she hadn't figured out, though, were the more complex questions. Like how she had come to be a small-town spinster when she hadn't been aware of time passing. Or how she was going to keep the five-and-dime afloat even as the town's economy continued to wither on the vine. And she certainly had no idea how she was going to tell her mother and sisters that she, as executrix of her father's will, was about to sell their farm, and the only home they'd ever known, right out from under them.

"Welcome to Sweetgum," she said to the empty aisles around her, and then she picked up the feather duster once more.

Two

Outside Maxine's Dress Shop on the north side of the square, the clock in the courthouse tower chimed the noon hour. Camille St. Clair paused to listen, then returned to hanging blouses on a rack marked fifty percent off. Normally she didn't put things on sale in September, but she'd made an error when she ordered the geometric prints. The local ladies weren't quite ready for clothes that would look more at home on Fifth Avenue than on Main Street. Camille was ready, though, for something different. Ready for anything that made her feel that, at twenty-four, she wasn't trapped in her hometown for the rest of her life.

Camille gave the blouses a final tweak just as the bell above the door jangled. She looked over her shoulder to see Merry McGavin entering the shop. Thirtysomething Merry was a fellow member of the Knit Lit Society, mother of four, and the peacemaker of the group.

"Good morning, Merry." Camille appreciated her coming into the shop. She would be among the first to appear and buy something, knowing that Camille's livelihood depended on the store's continued profitability. Camille had closed the dress shop for three days after her mother's death. One day so she could plan the funeral, one day so she could attend the funeral, and one day so that the other residents of Sweetgum wouldn't be shocked at how quickly she reopened the store.

"Hello, Camille." Merry hurried toward her, and Camille had no choice but to submit to the motherly hug Merry was determined to bestow. Still, Camille kept her defenses up and refused to give in to the weakness that threatened her knees.

"Thanks for stopping in." Camille forced a smile.

Merry laughed ruefully, her eyes filled with concern. "I know you're probably sick to death of people asking how you are, so I thought I'd just give you a hug instead."

"Thanks." Camille appreciated Merry's honesty as much as her presence. "I'm just ready for things to get back to normal"—her throat tightened—"if I can figure out what normal is anymore."

"Give yourself time." Merry patted Camille's shoulder, which again threatened her composure. At least there weren't any other customers in the shop. She jinxed herself with that thought, though, because the bell rang again. Camille stiffened as she recognized the young woman coming through the door. Natalie Grant. Rival, nemesis, and one of the biggest gossips in Sweetgum. At the same moment, Merry's cell phone rang from the depths of her purse. She murmured an apology and disappeared toward the back of the store as she answered it, leaving Camille to deal with Natalie.

"Camille! Did you hear about Coach Stults?" Natalie was out of breath, as if she'd sprinted across the town square to deliver her news. Her sleek brunette hair hung in chic layers and emphasized her high cheekbones and catlike green eyes.

Camille frowned, not bothering with a greeting since Natalie hadn't either. She'd learned long ago to be wary when Natalie appeared with one of her bombshells.

"No, I haven't heard anything. What about the coach? Is he okay?" Edward Stults had been the varsity football coach at Sweetgum High School for more than thirty years. He also taught senior year world history, so almost every adult in town had been a student in his class—including Camille.

"He's retiring to Florida. Mrs. Stults finally convinced him it was time."

"That's nice." Camille smothered a sigh of relief, glad that the news was good for once. She knew the town would miss the couple, but it hardly seemed the kind of topic to put Natalie in such a frenzy.

"Yes, but I haven't told you the most interesting part." Natalie's attention was caught by Merry's voice from the back of the store. "Hey, Merry," she called before turning back to Camille.

Camille was instantly wary. "What could be so interesting about Coach Stults retiring?" She couldn't imagine why Natalie would think the news worthy of bolting to the dress shop.

"The interesting part is who they're going to name as his replacement." Natalie looked like the cat that had gotten into the cream.

"And that would be . . . ?" Camille prodded, hoping to bring the conversation to a swift conclusion. She still had to pull together the information for the shop's weekly advertisement in the *Sweetgum Reporter*, and a shipment of winter separates waited in the back to be unpacked.

"The new coach is someone we know. Someone we went to school with."

Even though Camille was only twenty-four, her high school days seemed a lifetime ago. So much had happened since the beginning of her senior year—her father's desertion, her mother's long illness and recent death, the burial of Camille's own precious dreams of a glamorous life beyond Sweetgum.

"I can't imagine anyone our age being hired as head football coach," Camille answered. "Did I mention the new shipment I just got in?" she asked, hoping to distract Natalie. "There's a suede jacket I think you might—"

"Dante Brown. " Natalie's sharp features lit with a mixture of spite and glee.

Camille's jaw dropped for a moment before she remembered to close her mouth and maintain her composure. Merry reappeared from the back of the store and saved Camille from having to reply.

"Are you sure about Dante?" Merry asked. She'd obviously overheard Natalie's announcement. "I thought he was playing professionally some-where."

"He got sliced or whatever you call it by the Dallas Cowboys during training camp. His knee never was the same after that hit he took in the Alabama game."

Camille knew exactly which hit Natalie meant. It had been shown over and over on sports news channels. A chop block, the announcers had called it, with one man tackling Dante around the shoulders while another took him out from behind at the knees. The first time she'd seen the replay, Camille had rushed to the bathroom and thrown up.

Dante Brown. Beads of sweat broke out along her forehead. Dante. Back in Sweetgum.

"He's taking over the team starting tomorrow," Natalie said. "Cody says they're a shoo-in to win the state championship now." Cody Grant, Natalie's husband, had been the quarterback to Dante's running back. The two had been an unstoppable team.

A hard knot formed in Camille's stomach. Dante had made it out, escaped Sweetgum, left small-town life behind. And now he was coming back. Had evidently chosen to return of his own free will.

Well, he always had been a little crazy. About football. About his future.

About Camille.

She had refused to give him so much as the time of day in school. Not because he was black and she was white, as many people had whispered. She'd avoided him because of the way he made her feel just by passing her in the hall and saying hello. She'd switched lockers with her friend Jackie her junior year so she wouldn't have to see him any more than she could help.

And then her senior year, Camille had learned how fickle life—and men—could be when her father walked out, which only reinforced her decision to avoid Dante Brown. The intervening six years had done nothing to dim the truth of the lesson her father had taught her.

"Dante always did have a thing for you," Natalie said with a smile both teasing and malicious.

"Did he?" Camille's tone could have frosted ice. "I don't really remember." But she did remember. All too well. How she had cheered as hard as anyone when he scored the winning touchdown at the state football championships. How she'd turned down his invitation to the prom with a sniff and a lift of her chin.

"So, he's back in town already?" She couldn't stop herself from asking.

Natalie smiled in triumph at Camille's interest. "He was at Tallulah's awhile ago, eating chicken-fried steak. Or should I say a couple of chicken-fried steaks."

Camille remembered that too. Dante, a mountain of a fullback even in high school, could put away more food than a family of four. She resisted the urge to move closer to the shop windows and peek out at the square. Although the large Victorian county courthouse blocked her view of Tallulah's Café, people often parked wherever they could find a place on the busy square. Perhaps even now, at this moment, Dante Brown was passing outside of Maxine's Dress Shop.

Camille refused to let Natalie see the effect of the news on her. "I just got in some designer jeans, too, but I haven't put them out yet. If you're thinking of something for the homecoming game—"

"Oh, I don't need to buy anything today," Natalie said. "I just wanted to tell you the news."

Camille kept the smile pasted on her face, aware of Merry's knowing gaze. Of course her old rival wasn't there to shop. She was there to throw Dante Brown in Camille's face and see what kind of response she got. Natalie would never forgive Camille for being both homecoming and prom queen their senior year.

"You're taking the news very well," Natalie said with a teasing smile rimmed with malice.

"Well, I'm happy for the football team," Camille said. "I'm sure everyone will be. Dante has a lot of professional experience to draw on." Camille had followed his career as avidly as anyone in town, although she'd been careful to appear casual whenever anyone mentioned his name. But some people like Natalie knew enough—or could at least guess—about what had passed between them in high school.

"You'll probably see him before too long," Natalie added, hiking her designer handbag higher on her shoulder. "I wouldn't be surprised if—"

The bell above the shop door sounded again, and Camille's heart leaped to her throat. She gripped the clothing rack next to her, prepared to see—

But it was only Eugenie, the town librarian.

"Good morning, Eugenie," Camille said, stepping toward her and away from Natalie's poisonous darts. She smiled so hard it hurt her face, but she was determined not to let Natalie see her flinch. "It's good to see you."

"I'm on my way back from lunch," Eugenie said in her usual no-nonsense kind of way. Even her recent marriage hadn't softened her that much. While Eugenie was a kind person, she was also brusque. "I'm in need of a—" She broke off when she realized there were other customers in the shop.

"Good morning, Miss Pierce. I mean, Mrs. Carson." Honestly, Camille thought, Natalie's nose should be permanently brown from the way she was always kissing up to people.

"Good morning, um . . ." Eugenie looked to Camille for help.

"Natalie was just leaving," Camille said, taking a few steps toward the door. Flustered, Natalie followed. Camille suppressed a smile at Natalie's bewilderment.

"Yes. I was. I mean—" Natalie broke off when she realized that she was being hustled out of the store, but by that time Camille had ushered her into the warm September sunshine.

"I'll call you next week when the new cocktail dresses come in," Camille assured her with a smile and then slipped back into the shop, leaving Natalie on the sidewalk. When she stepped back inside,

Eugenie and Merry were deep in conversation.

"What are you two talking about?" Camille asked, trying not to bristle. She was tired of being the object of speculation and pity. She'd found that hard enough to take during her mother's long illness. Now that her mother was gone, it was time for the pity to stop. If it didn't, Camille feared she would break down completely.

Merry and Eugenie stepped apart, and the librarian looked decidedly guilty. Camille took a deep breath, ready to launch a preemptive strike, but she was stopped by Merry's staying hand.

"Before you say anything, we weren't talking about you," Merry said with a small smile. "Eugenie was just breaking some news to me. I think you'll want to hear this too."

Camille stepped closer to them, her chest tight with apprehension. She'd had enough news of any sort to last her for quite a while. Eugenie noticed her wariness, because she softened her expression and gave Camille an encouraging smile.

"I've invited Maria Munden to join the Knit Lit Society," Eugenie said. Merry nodded encouragingly, as if willing Camille to respond positively to the news.

"Sure. Fine. Whatever." Camille shrugged her shoulders. Like she cared one way or another. Maria Munden was a dour woman, but Camille didn't have any strong feelings about her. If Eugenie wanted to fill Ruthie's slot, did it matter?

After the events of the last week, did anything matter? She shouldn't even be reacting to Natalie's news, much less to the addition of a new member to the Knit Lit Society.

"It's okay with you then?" Merry looked worried. Camille was sick of people looking concerned every time they came into the shop. Or, before that, the funeral home. Or, before that, the hospital. Why were they worried now? It was over. Her mother was gone.

"Well, then." Eugenie hitched her pocketbook further up on her arm. "I'll let Esther and Hannah know about Maria. And I'll look forward to seeing you all on Friday evening."

"Can't wait," Merry said with a generous smile and a wave. "I'd better get moving. My mom actually volunteered to keep the baby for an hour, and I need to run some errands before the kids get out of school." She glanced at her watch. "I'll have to come back to do my shopping for the homecoming game."

Camille bid the two women good-bye and saw them to the door of the shop. Once it closed behind them, she turned and hustled toward the storeroom with long, determined strides.

She would get back to work. She would somehow manage to get herself through the day. And she would not think about her mother. Or how she would never be able to find a buyer for the dress shop now, given the current state of the town's economy. Neither would she think about Dante Brown. Or spending the rest of her life trapped in Sweetgum.

No use in brooding over things that could never be changed.

And no use wondering how at twenty-four she could feel as old as the antebellum courthouse across the street.

Three

"That's all?" Esther Jackson stared at the number on the piece of paper in shock. She kept her hands firmly in her lap, resisting the urge to grip the arms of the chair. "There should be more zeroes." It was all she could think to say. Frank had taken out life insurance when they were younger, and they had paid the premiums faithfully. "There should be more—"

"Your husband had a term life policy, Esther. That's different from universal life insurance." The sympathy in Alvin Fraley's voice was almost her undoing. She kept her eyes glued to the paper, afraid to look right or left, but mostly afraid to look at Alvin across the expanse of his desk. In all her fifty-five years, she'd never felt so awash with shame and anger. "It's not intended to leave you with a lump sum."

Esther did look up then and met Alvin's gaze.

The thin, bald man had handled their insurance for more than a quarter of a century. He would never lie to her, and he didn't make mistakes. Which only made the number on the piece of paper all the more distressing. And all the more real.

"You weren't expecting this," Alvin said. It wasn't a question but a statement. His watery green eyes were filled with sympathy. "I'm sorry, Esther. I thought you understood. With term life, the idea is to take the savings on your premiums and invest them for a better return. That's what I advise my clients to do anyway." He paused. "That's what I advised Frank to do."

But there was no stock portfolio. No mutual funds. No IRA or 401(k) or whatever other combination of letters and numbers meant she could continue to live her life in the way she had always lived it now that her husband was gone.

"And there's no other . . . ?" She couldn't bring herself to finish the sentence.

"I'm afraid not." He paused, cleared his throat, and looked over her left shoulder as he hammered the final nail in her financial coffin. "I should also tell you that your insurance premiums—house, cars, boat—are all overdue."

"Frank didn't—"

"No."

She'd known it would be difficult. Even before Frank's sudden death from a heart attack, she'd been aware that their financial state was precarious. There had been so many expenses along the way—their home, the country club fees, Alex's education and loaning him a down payment for his first home. They'd even paid for their son's wedding since his wife's parents could never have afforded the kind of event necessary for people of Frank and Esther's standing in Sweetgum.

"Esther, I hesitate to suggest this, but you may need to consider selling your home."

Her head shot up at Alvin's words. She couldn't possibly part with her house. What else would she have left then of her life with Frank? "What about the condo at Sweetgum Lake? I can sell that immediately."

Alvin sat back in his chair and shook his head. The movement caused a tight knot to form in Esther's stomach.

"I think you should consider selling the house and living in the condo." He crossed his arms over his thin chest. "Your expenses will be much less—utilities, insurance, upkeep, taxes."

Live in the one-bedroom condo? He couldn't possibly be serious. She might have lost her husband, but she refused to lose her dignity.

Fifteen years ago, developers had come in and tried to turn the lake into a resort area. She and Frank had purchased the condo for a song. But the development had never taken off. She and Frank had kept the condo only because they couldn't sell it.

"I don't think that will be necessary. I still have Frank's interest in the law firm."

Alvin nodded but looked unconvinced. "Of course. I'm sorry if I overstepped my bounds. I'm just concerned for you."

Esther straightened her spine and smiled with all the graciousness she'd cultivated as Sweetgum's social leader for the last thirty years. "I appreciate your concern. And I'll take your advice into consideration, of course." She didn't add that she had no intention of following it.

"You know, Esther, you might also think about—"

"I might think about what?" She tried to keep the chill tone out of her voice, with little success.

"You might consider finding a job."

Esther shrank back as if he'd slapped her. "I don't think there will be any need for that." She picked up her handbag from the floor beside her chair. "I appreciate your help, Alvin. If you'll have your secretary send me another invoice for the premiums, I'll pay them immediately." Although how she would accomplish that, she had no idea. Her bank account was very low, and now that there would be no life insurance settlement coming in . . .

"Just pay them when you can," he said, standing when she did. "That will be fine."

And there it was. In his voice. In his expression. The thing she'd hated the most since the moment the paramedic had looked up at her from where he'd been crouched over Frank's prone form on the eighteenth green.

Pity.

Esther Jackson had never been an object of pity in her life, and she wasn't about to start now. Head high, she bid Alvin good-bye, secured her Louis Vuitton bag more firmly on her shoulder, and headed for the door.

The life insurance was merely a temporary setback. Surely she would realize all she needed from her interest in Frank's law firm. She made her way from Alvin's office to her Jaguar parked at the curb outside. Her next appointment was with Frank's law partner, Lloyd Manning. Certainly he would have better news for her.

Matters simply could not be as dire as they seemed. Esther refused to allow it. Circumstances had never managed to thwart her before, and she wasn't going to allow them to do so now.

Two hours later, Esther wasn't feeling quite so positive. Lloyd Manning had broken the bad news that Frank had very little equity in the firm. He would be happy to buy out Esther's share, but the small amount of money was a pittance compared to what she'd hoped for.

Too agitated to go home and too upset to be around other people, Esther pointed the car west. The afternoon sun, low and piercing, made her squint as she raced down Old Lake Road toward the condo on Sweetgum Lake. Even with her over-sized Chanel sunglasses in place and the car's visor pulled down, she could hardly see the two-lane highway for the glare. She and Frank had learned long ago not to set off for Memphis in the late afternoon to see their son because of that very problem. Now, though, the bright light was complicated by the tears that filled Esther's eyes and streamed down her cheeks.

Dear Lord in heaven, what was she going to do? Fervent prayer had never been a part of Esther's spiritual routine. She and the Divine had been cordial but distant acquaintances for years, and that had seemed to suit them both. Esther knew her duty, she did her duty, and she expected God to do His. Why she still thought that the Almighty would hold up His end of the bargain, though, she had no idea. Any real hope of divine intervention in her life had died with her first child more than thirty years before.

The road curved sharply to the left, and Esther's foot pumped the brake. The piercing sun blurred her vision, and then a haze of brown and white streaked across the highway in front of her. She slammed on the brakes, her high heel catching beneath the pedal. The car skidded to the right, and Esther whipped the wheel in the same direction to correct her slide, but to no avail. She heard a sharp *thump* and then the car banged against the guardrail that separated the highway from Cooter

Creek ten feet below. The Jaguar jerked to a stop, the engine and her own blood thrumming in her ears. Her breath came in short gasps. The seat belt pressed against her chest, pinning her in the car.

She had hit something living. She knew it instinctively.

With shaking hands, she struggled to unfasten the seat belt. After several tries, she managed to release the catch and untangle herself from the restraint. She opened the car door and pulled herself out.

She'd hit some sort of animal, of course. Not a skunk, or she would smell it. And the fast-moving blur had been too small for a deer. Esther moved around the front of the car and saw a mop of fur lying motionless on the asphalt.

A dog.

More tears stung Esther's eyes. She knelt beside the animal and felt for a pulse at its neck. Did dogs even have a pulse there? A wave of nausea overcame her, for this was exactly how she'd knelt beside Frank when he'd collapsed that last fateful day.

"Come on," she pleaded, not sure whom she was addressing—the good Lord in heaven or the limp form of the dog. And then she felt a small movement beneath her fingers. It wasn't dead.

Relief washed over her but was quickly replaced by dread. What did she do now? She'd never owned a pet in her life. Her experience with animals was limited to shooing them away from her so they wouldn't put a run in her stockings or get paw prints on her designer suits.

The dog whimpered, and instinctively she reached to rub the animal behind the ears. His fur was wet and matted, and when she ran a gentle hand down his side, she could feel his ribs. She needed to get him to the veterinarian, but how?

Esther could arrange a seating chart for the Centennial Society luncheon in under fifteen minutes. She knew how to pressure the local florist into letting her buy wholesale. And she could motivate a caterer to stretch food for fifty to accommodate an extra ten people. But she didn't know how to get this pitiful animal off the highway and into her car.

The sound of an approaching vehicle caught her attention, and she looked up to see a battered pickup truck slowing to a stop on the shoulder of the road. At that moment, she realized how vulnerable she was, kneeling in the highway by the dog, but the animal looked up at her with huge, sorrowful brown eyes, and she couldn't bring herself to move to safety.

A tall, red-headed man, about ten years younger than Esther, emerged from the truck. His shirt was the same rusted gray as the pickup. "You all right?" he asked as he moved toward her. Then he saw the dog beside her. "Is he dead?"

Esther shook her head, beyond grateful that the

man had stopped. He looked like a farmer. Surely he would know what to do about the dog.

"He's alive, but he's hurt. I need to get him to the vet."

The man nodded. "I can help you get him into your car."

Her heart sank. She had hoped the man would offer to take over and see about the dog. "Thank you. Although . . ." She fixed a troubled expression on her face. "I don't really know anything about dogs."

"Not much to know."

He dropped to one knee and ran his hands over the animal, much as Esther had, but his motions were far more competent, experienced. He was oblivious to the damsel-in-distress signals she was sending out, but he was certainly solicitous of the dog. She wasn't as young as she used to be, but she was still the best-dressed, best-coiffed woman in Sweetgum.

He looked up at her. "He's not in any immediate danger, but he needs his leg set. Just take him to Doc Everton's. He'll know what to do."

"Oh. Of course." She hid her dismay, and the man turned back to his truck. He returned with an old army blanket that had seen better days and spread it on the ground next to the dog. Esther stepped back to give him room to maneuver. He lifted the dog and smoothly settled him on the blanket. The animal whimpered but otherwise didn't protest.

"You grab those two corners," he instructed Esther. She started to object—surely he could lift the dog by himself—but his look silenced her. She took hold of the corners of the blanket nearest her while the man did the same on his end. "All right. Lift on the count of three."

"Wait!" Esther glanced back at her car. "I need to open the door." She darted across the asphalt and opened the passenger door of her Jaguar, thankful for the blanket to protect the leather interior. She returned to the dog and gripped the blanket. "Okay."

Together, they maneuvered the dog around the front of her car. Trying to get the animal through the door, though, wasn't as easy.

"Slide in there," the man said to Esther, motioning to the space between the car frame and the open door. She did as he instructed, and he moved in behind her so they were both wedged into the small space. The dog whimpered when they gently swung him onto the seat. For a long moment, Esther thought the man wasn't going to let go of the blanket and step away. He was very tall, and he smelled like new-mown grass.

"There you go, pup." He settled the end of the blanket over the dog before moving away. Esther let out a sigh of relief. She wasn't used to being close to strange men. Or any man, for that matter. Even Frank had learned to keep his distance over the years.

"Thank you." Esther suddenly felt awkward. The man stood on the shoulder of the highway, and his green eyes met her gaze.

"No problem. I'd go with you, but—" He paused to glance at his watch. "I'm in a bit of a hurry. Must be the day for emergencies."

"If you'll give me your card, I'll return your blanket after—" She broke off. Given her recent run of luck, the dog would probably die, but she didn't want to say it out loud.

"I don't have a card." A smile teased at the corners of his lips. "And I don't need the blanket back. It's not good for much anyway." He paused and looked at her so closely it made her take a small step backward. "He's going to be okay. Just get him to Doc Everton's."

"Oh. Well, thank you again. For your help." Another step backward. He must not be from Sweetgum, because she'd never seen him before. She wanted to ask him his name, but something stopped her. "I'd better get to the vet."

"Drive safely." He lifted his hand, waved, and turned to jog back to his truck. He drove off in a spurt of gravel, clearly anxious to get to his unknown destination.

Esther watched him go with a mixture of trepidation and relief. And then a sound from the car, the dog's soft cry, turned her attention back to the problem at hand. She shut the passenger door and crossed back in front of the car. Esther slid behind the wheel and, after a quick glance over her shoulder, made a U-turn so that she was headed in the direction of town.

Straight back into the muddle that was her life, only this time with a broken dog in tow.

Four

Eugenie arrived earlier than usual for the Knit Lit Society's first meeting of the year. Tonight brought a fresh start—a new reading list and new knitting projects.

Under normal circumstances, Eugenie would have looked forward to this meeting, but the last few months had brought anything but normal circumstances. Camille's mother had died less than two weeks ago. Ruthie was off doing mission work in Africa, and in her place would be Maria Munden, whom all of them knew but none of them knew well. Esther's recent bereavement was not quite as fresh as Camille's, but no doubt just as painful. And now that Hannah, the youngest member of the group, lived with Eugenie and Paul as their foster daughter—well, Eugenie wasn't sure how their new relationship might affect these meetings.

The biggest problem, though, was Eugenie's trepidation about the reading list she'd chosen. She took the folder containing the lists from her knitting bag. What had she been thinking? They were all going to laugh at her. Maybe not out loud or to her face, but her choices could be the buzz of the Sweetgum grapevine by this time tomorrow.

"Good evening, Eugenie." Merry appeared in the doorway, baby carrier in tow. Her fourth child, Hunter, lay snuggled amid the padding and blankets, his head crooked at the impossible angle that only a baby can manage. "I can't believe I'm the first one here."

Since Merry was perpetually late, Eugenie couldn't argue with her. "It's good to see you. And this handsome boy." Eugenie smiled, although she couldn't help wishing Merry had left the baby at home. He was sure to be a significant distraction, even if he didn't cry. Eugenie had enough trouble as it was keeping the women focused on the discussion.

Merry took a chair on the opposite side of the table from Eugenie and proceeded to settle in. Eugenie wondered if she should offer to help Merry juggle the diaper bag, knitting tote, and other assorted paraphernalia, but just as she was about to do so, two more figures appeared in the doorway.

Camille and Maria must have come up the stairs together. They were talking politely, but both showed the strain of grief. The lines around Camille's mouth were pronounced for a twenty-four-year-old, and Maria had dark shadows beneath her eyes.

"Good evening, ladies." Eugenie waved toward

the other chairs. "Come in and make yourselves comfortable."

Maria looked hesitant, but Camille led the way, and they sat between Eugenie and Merry. A moment later, Hannah raced in, backpack flying. She dropped into the chair on the other side of Eugenie. "Sorry. I lost track of the time."

Eugenie bit her lip. She'd never imagined becoming a foster mother at sixty-five, but Hannah had come into her life last year as unexpectedly as Paul had reappeared. Eugenie had forced Hannah into the Knit Lit Society as penance for some minor vandalism of a library book, but the girl had stayed of her own accord. And when Hannah's mother took off and left the girl to fend for herself, Eugenie had taken her in.

"That's fine," Eugenie said. "We're still waiting for Esther." Hannah's presence in her life had challenged Eugenie to learn to be more flexible. Some days she was more successful than others.

Eugenie introduced Maria to Merry and Hannah, although that was mostly a formality. Anyone who'd spent more than a few days in Sweetgum had been in Munden's Five-and-Dime. In fact, Maria possibly knew more people in Sweetgum than Eugenie herself, because while not everyone read for pleasure or needed to use the Internet at the public library, every resident of Sweetgum stopped in Munden's Five-and-Dime for chewing gum, copy paper, and greeting cards.

"Well, we should get started," Eugenie said when she'd waited as long as she could for the still-absent Esther. Hiding her worry behind her usual formal manner, she opened a manila folder on the table in front of her and drew out some papers. "I wanted to keep this year's reading list a surprise. Here it is."

She tried to ignore the color that rose in her cheeks. The others passed the papers around the table while Eugenie watched their faces. Camille looked troubled, Maria looked surprised, Merry looked amused, and Hannah looked perplexed.

"As you can see, I've taken a different approach this year." Eugenie took the extra sheets from Hannah as they completed their journey around the table. "Our theme for the year is 'Great Love Stories in Literature.' " She couldn't quite meet the other women's eyes. "Instead of specific knitting projects, I thought we would focus on a different type of stitch to accompany each selection." She paused, cleared her throat, and continued. "You may pick your own project for each book, but you need to use the assigned stitch. I thought this would be a creative challenge."

Hannah snorted, which Eugenie had learned over the last few months was her way of downplaying the unexpected, so Eugenie didn't take offense. Camille's expression remained flat, but at least Maria looked intrigued.

Merry still looked amused. "It looks great,

Eugenie. *Pride and Prejudice, Gone with the Wind.* These are some of my favorites."

Why hadn't she just pinned her heart on her sleeve and been done with it, Eugenie thought as she fought the urge to wave a hand to cool her flaming cheeks.

"I'm glad to hear that, Merry. We won't get into *Romeo and Juliet*, the first selection, until next month, so I thought we might focus our discussion tonight on something a bit different. Since we're going to talk about love this year, I thought I'd ask each of you to share your definition of love. What it means to you personally."

Eugenie heard the *click-click* of high heels in the hallway.

"Sorry I'm late."

She twisted in her chair to see Esther hurrying into the room.

Merry glanced at her watch. "We were going to start worrying about you in a few minutes," she said, and the others nodded in agreement.

Esther's perfect hair was mussed, and she had smudges on her blouse. She perched on the last remaining chair on the other side of Hannah. Like Camille, she had deep lines carved around her mouth. "I'm afraid I got a little sidetracked this afternoon. But it's all taken care of now." She ran a hand over her hair, which did little to calm its disorder, and pasted a determined smile on her face. "What have I missed?"

"We're glad you made it." Eugenie slid a copy of the reading list across the table to her. "We were just getting started."

She thought Esther might offer further explanation for her tardiness, but the other woman simply picked up the list and skimmed its contents. Her lips thinned and then pursed as she scanned the titles on the paper.

"I was inviting everyone to think about your definition of love and share it with the group, if you feel comfortable." Eugenie drew a deep breath. "Who would like to start?"

For a long moment silence reigned, and with each passing second, Eugenie's apprehension grew. She'd wanted to challenge the other women this year, invite them to share their thoughts and feelings at a deeper level. Perhaps, though, she should have played it safe and not tested the new-found closeness of the group. Especially not with a new member in the mix.

Just as she was about to despair of anyone speaking up, Camille cleared her throat. "Love is what you do for other people." She folded one corner of the reading list and then smoothed it out again.

Eugenie noticed that the girl's nails, usually manicured into impeccable french tips, had been bitten to the quick. Eugenie waited for a moment to see if she would add anything else to her statement. Camille's gaze met hers then, and Eugenie could see the deep well of pain in her eyes.

"Yes," Eugenie agreed. "Service to others is an important part of love. We're all called to think about the needs of our neighbors."

"Not much of that thinking going on in Sweetgum," Hannah interjected. She popped her gum, a habit that drove Eugenie to distraction.

Eugenie tamped down the hurt that sprang up at the teenager's words. Since Hannah had come into her life, Eugenie had developed the habit of reminding herself several times a day that patience was the key to transformation. While Hannah had made a lot of progress, she still struggled to trust the adults in her life. More than thirteen years of parental neglect—and sometimes outright abuse— couldn't be undone overnight.

"Besides," Hannah continued between smacks of her gum, "when people are nice to you, it's usually because they want something."

The teenager's words were met with silence as the other women looked at each other, unsure how to respond. Hannah flushed when she realized the implication of what she'd said. "I didn't mean you, Mrs. Carson. I mean, Eugenie."

"I know that, Hannah." Eugenie thought it best to steer the discussion in someone else's direction. "Merry, how would you define love?"

Merry made a wry face. "Overwhelming." Her answer was as prompt as it was emphatic. The others laughed, as Merry had intended, but Eugenie could sense a thread of truth behind the humorous reply. With four children and a husband who had a solo law practice, Merry more than had her hands full. Eugenie had observed in the past that Merry's busy schedule left little time for self-care. Now, with the new baby, that wouldn't get any better.

"Anyone else?" Eugenie looked around the table. "Esther?"

"It isn't that complicated." Esther's attention was on the tangle of yarn on the table in front of her as she attempted to smooth out the knotted wool. "I agree with Camille. Love is sacrifice. You do for others because it's the proper thing to do. The Christian thing to do," she added for emphasis. "I'm sure we'll enjoy the books, Eugenie, but I'm not much of a believer in romantic love."

Eugenie hardly knew what to say. Those were the last words she would have expected to hear from a woman who'd been recently widowed.

"What should I do for my first project?" Merry intervened, and for once Eugenie was grateful to her for taking the conversation off in a new direction. She swallowed against the disappointment that gathered in her throat. When she'd made out the list, she'd been so sure the theme would be popular with the group. After all, who didn't like to read a good love story? She'd been so caught up in her own romantic happiness, she realized, that she hadn't given enough thought to how the reading list would be received by the others.

"*Romeo and Juliet* might be a challenge to come up with something. Can you knit a doublet?" Merry asked Eugenie with a smile. "That would be authentic to Shakespeare."

"You can make whatever you like. As long as you use garter stitch," Eugenie replied. "That's the assigned stitch for the book." She'd wanted to start simple since Hannah was still a beginner, and garter stitch was the easiest—the basic knit stitch back and forth with no variation. Hannah should be up to the challenge, at least when it came to the knitting. Eugenie looked around the group once more and wondered if any of them were up to the challenge of pondering the meaning and the mystery of love.

Time would tell, she thought, not without a fair amount of apprehension.

Maria pulled her mother's ancient Cadillac to the shoulder of the road and rolled to a stop beneath a stand of sweetgum trees. Night had fallen, but there was still the faint reminder of a sunset in the western sky. The two-lane road came to an abrupt stop a mile farther on. Fitting, probably, that her family's ancestral home sat on a dead end at the edge of Sweetgum Lake.

She opened the car door and stepped out into the night air. As always, she could breathe in the scent of the land and instantly feel calmer. Spending her days cooped up in the five-and-dime had never been her dream, but her father had chosen her for the job before she'd even finished high school.

Maria sighed. *Painful.* That's what she would have said if Eugenie had gotten around to putting her on the spot about her definition of love. It was painful. Whether the person you loved was alive or dead didn't make a difference. Presence and absence were different sides of the same coin.

Maria walked beneath the stand of trees at the edge of the road and then followed the rise until she stood at the top of the hill. Here, the trees fell away, and she could see a good distance in all directions despite the falling darkness. To the east, back the way she'd come, were the church steeple and the water tower. To the south, rolling hills dotted with the occasional house and barn. To the west, she could make out the dark curve of Sweetgum Lake. Faint lights pinpointed the windows of her family's home near the shoreline.

More than thirty years. She'd lived in the white two-story clapboard house all her life. Now it was sorely in need of a coat of paint, but in her childhood it had been pristine. In those days the five-and-dime had provided for the family—if not abundantly, then at least adequately. But those days, like her father, were gone. Her memories might as well be buried in the Sweetgum Cemetery alongside him.

Change was in the air, not only because of her father's death, but also because of the life-changing decision she had made in Jeff McGavin's law office.

Maria could handle change. Or at least she hoped she could. Daphne, her older sister, was far too gentle to take charge of the family and her mother too much of an overwrought hypochondriac. Stephanie, the youngest, couldn't even be counted on to show up at the store on time. With her father gone, the responsibility fell on Maria. All it required was the sacrifice of almost everything she loved.

She took a deep breath, drinking in the scents of the night. Eugenie's "Great Love Stories in Literature" might lure her into thinking that Prince Charming would arrive shortly and whisk her away, make all her worries disappear, but Maria knew that was impossible. She was too old, too bland, too late. Love and romance had passed her by. Responsibility was all she had left. She'd never shirked it before, and she wasn't about to now.

With a sigh, she turned away from the top of the hill and started back toward the car, wondering how and when she would tell her mother and sisters that their home was not their home anymore.

Five

Early Monday morning, Hannah slammed her locker shut and twisted the combination lock with a turn of her wrist. She squared her shoulders, preparing herself to face the hallways of Sweetgum High School. Only a few weeks into her freshman year, she had already learned that moving from class to class was like running a gauntlet of upperclassmen.

"Hannah! Wait up." Kristen came up behind her and grabbed her shoulder, almost jerking her to the floor. "Guess who just moved back to Sweetgum?"

Hannah shrugged. "No idea." She shifted her weight from one foot to the other, not wanting to be late for class but also not wanting to annoy Kristen. Her friendship with the other girl, if that's what you could call it, was on shaky ground as it was.

"Josh Hargrove is back," Kristen said with a teasing smile. "Weren't you guys like totally an item in fifth grade?" She smirked. "Maybe he's come back to sweep you off your feet."

Hannah rolled her eyes and refused to show the little spark of joy that flickered in her heart. "Whatever."

"Sure. Play it cool." Kristen laughed, but there wasn't much humor in the sound. Kristen was still mad at her for refusing to hang out at the cemetery after school with the slacker crowd. Hannah wished Kristen would just let it rest, but the girl didn't like to take no for an answer. "I bet you guys hook up by tomorrow." She laughed, but the sound had an edge that made Hannah nervous. Kristen had something up her sleeve. Something she wasn't telling her.

"Dang. The bell's about to ring." Kristen glanced at the time on her cell phone. "Later." She darted off, leaving Hannah in peace.

Josh Hargrove. Hannah swallowed hard, determined not to let her feelings show on her face. He probably wouldn't even remember her. And she could only pray he'd forgotten her mother, although Tracy Simmons showing up drunk for Field Day had been pretty memorable. As had the end-of-school picnic. Her mom had brought soft drinks for the kids and plenty of beer for herself.

Josh had always been a brainiac. He was probably a math genius or something. No way he would remember her. But if he didn't, it also meant he'd forgotten the good stuff—catching crawdads in Sweetgum Creek and buying Popsicles at the IGA. They'd hung out together every day that last summer, and then his mother had married her rich boss and abandoned the trailer next door to Hannah's. Josh and his mom moved to Birmingham. His trailer park days were over.

Why was he back? Hannah hugged her binder and math book to shield herself from the seed of

57

hope that took root in her chest. She turned right into the senior hall, careful to avoid the mustang logo in the middle of the tile floor. In the first few weeks of school, more than one freshman had made the mistake of stepping on the school mascot. She shouldn't even have classes here, but Eugenie had stuck her nose in Hannah's business and gotten her moved into honors English. While the rest of her classmates would breeze by with ditzy Mrs. Carlisle, she would be working her tail off under the evil eye of Ophelia Budge.

All the way down senior hall, Hannah tried to keep herself from pinning any hopes on Josh Hargrove's return. She hadn't had a real friend since he'd left. Just losers like Kristen.

The bell rang as Hannah slid through the class-room door. She made a dive for the nearest seat before Mrs. Budge could count her tardy. She liked to sit near the door anyway. She'd learned early in life that it was always good to have a handy escape route.

"Quiet, please." Mrs. Budge's booming voice rang out. Hannah slumped in her seat and let her hair fall forward to cover her face.

Mrs. Budge picked up a stack of small paperback books from her desk and moved down the aisles, dropping one in front of each student. They landed with a plop. The students groaned when they saw the title, except for Sissy Darlington, the class brain. She let out a long sigh of contentment.

Hannah refused to show any visible sign of interest. Instead, she studied the head of the guy sitting in front of her and wondered why she hadn't noticed him in class before. His sandy hair curled in a messy-but-cute way, and his shoulders were seriously wide. She hadn't been paying attention when she dove for her desk, and now she wished she had. The guy must be new, because even though she could only see the back of his head, she should be able to recognize him. Sweetgum High School didn't have that many freshmen.

And then the realization hit her, just at the moment when Mrs. Budge dropped the book on the desk in front of her.

Romeo and Juliet.

Josh Hargrove.

The two facts exploded in her brain simultaneously.

Apparently God had taken notice of her behavior last year before she'd quit hanging out at the cemetery with Kristen and her slacker friends. Apparently God hadn't forgotten, because He was punishing her.

"William Shakespeare." Mrs. Budge pronounced the name with reverence.

She droned on about his major contributions to the English language, but Hannah tuned her out as she clutched the book and willed Josh Hargrove to keep facing the front of the room. To his right, Courtney McGavin, in her freshman pompom-girl sweater and short skirt, shot him little flirty smiles, but Josh was oblivious. Good. That was a good sign, Hannah told herself. If he could ignore a bombshell like Courtney, his intelligence must not have evaporated the moment his mother drove him over the state line to Alabama.

But if he was in freshman honors English, he couldn't be a complete idiot. Or lacking in memory.

"I'm going to put you in teams of three," Mrs. Budge said, "and I want you to read, starting on page seventy-eight, to get a feel for the language."

Hannah's stomach knotted. She knew what was coming. She was Hannah Simmons after all, and while she'd gotten a few breaks recently, her luck was about to go south, just as it always did.

Mrs. Budge looked in Hannah's direction. "The three of you are a group." She gestured at the little triangle of desks that included Hannah, Courtney, and Josh. Then she moved on. "You three there. And the three in the back." She kept going, but Hannah didn't care. Her fate was sealed. If she had to face Josh Hargrove, why couldn't plain and plump Sissy Darlington be the buffer instead of Courtney?

"Hi!" Courtney swung her desk around to face Josh.

"Hey." He half stood and pivoted his desk as well, and then there he was, looking at her. And smiling.

Dimples? He had dimples?

"I'm Courtney." She stuck out her hand, professionally manicured of course, and Josh took it. "Welcome to Sweetgum."

"Thanks." His smile changed—still there but not as genuine. "I appreciate it."

Hannah took a deep breath and decided she might as well get it over with. "Hey, Josh."

The real smile returned, the one that reached all the way to his brown eyes. "Hey, Hannah."

Confusion etched Courtney's MAC-heavy face. "You two know each other?"

Hannah looked at Josh, and he winked at her. She suddenly felt ten pounds lighter. "Josh used to live in Sweetgum, Courtney. He went to elementary school with us."

Her eyes widened. "Really?"

Josh leaned back in his desk, and his long legs sprawled out. "Really."

Courtney chewed her lip. You could tell she was thinking hard, searching her memory but coming up empty. Josh took pity on her.

"I was about half the size I am now, big glasses, and in need of an orthodontist." He flashed a now-perfect smile.

Courtney blushed, but her discomfort lasted only a nano-second. She quickly regained her pompom-girl poise. "Well, welcome back." She glanced back at Hannah. "Were you all friends or something? Before he moved?"

61

Josh nodded. "Or something." Two cryptic words that sent a shiver up Hannah's spine.

"Welcome home," she said, because she couldn't think of anything else to say. Now that he wasn't focused on Courtney, he was looking at her instead. Seeing every flaw no doubt. Realizing that while he had turned into a major hottie, she hadn't. That knot re-formed in her stomach.

"Thanks." His gaze fell from hers, and he looked down at the book on his desk. "I guess we'd better read this, huh?"

"I'll be Juliet," Courtney said, regaining control of the conversation. "Hannah, you be . . . well, whoever else there is." She was like a general directing her troops. "And Josh, of course, is Romeo."

Hannah had to admire how neatly Courtney arranged things so that she and Josh played the lovers and Hannah was left to be some kind of health-care worker.

Only, as she learned a few moments later, the Nurse wasn't a health-care worker at all, but Juliet's old nanny and the butt of all the jokes.

Fitting.

The seed of hope in her chest withered and died by the time they'd finished reading the scene. Nothing ever changed in Sweetgum. She was a fool to think it ever would, Josh Hargrove or not.

Merry relished the peace in the middle of the school day, when the older kids were out of the house, Jeff was still at work, and she was at home with the baby. Most mornings she spent a couple hours at Jeff's office, helping out with secretarial duties while Hunter napped in his carrier. Jeff's paralegal, Mitzi, had more than enough to do without answering the phone and filing, so Merry happily pitched in, especially since Jeff had been forced to file bankruptcy a few months before. He had done yeoman work, reorganizing the practice and getting it going again, and Merry's involvement helped her feel like she was supporting her husband in a very material way. But by eleven o'clock or so, she and the baby headed home for some lunch and togetherness.

Hunter was six months old now, the perfect age when it came to babies. He was well past the fussiness of a newborn but hadn't yet started to crawl or be afraid of strangers. He had a sunny disposition and liked everyone, but most of all he adored Merry.

"What should I have for lunch, Hunter? Hmm?" She perused the contents of the refrigerator while the baby babbled away from his bouncy seat in the middle of the kitchen floor. Every so often, Candy, the family mutt, wandered by and sniffed the baby's ears. The dog's obsession with Hunter's ears was the source of much amusement in the McGavin household.

Merry grabbed salad fixings from the fridge and piled them on the counter. She had just pulled out the cutting board and a knife when she heard the whir of the garage door.

"Your daddy must have decided to come home for lunch," she told Hunter. "I'd better double the salad." She was busily chopping vegetables by the time Jeff entered the kitchen. "Hey, hon. I wasn't expecting you." She offered her cheek for him to kiss. He did so and patted her rear end affectionately for good measure.

"I had something I wanted to talk to you about, and I thought this might be a good time, with the kids at school."

Their daughter Courtney had just started high school. Jake, their second child, was a fifth grader. And Sarah, who had been the baby until Hunter's arrival, was a proud kindergarten student.

"Sure." She turned back to her chopping. "What's up?"

He leaned against the kitchen counter and crossed his arms, never a good sign in Merry's experience.

She laid down the knife. "Is it the practice still? I thought you were doing better."

Jeff frowned. "Well, yes and no."

"Meaning?"

"I'm pulling in more business, which is great. More billable hours means more income. But it also means more work."

Merry nodded, frowning as Jeff was. "I know. And you're working so hard already."

Jeff uncrossed his arms and put his hands in his

pockets. "Merry, it's all-hands-on-deck time if the practice is going to be profitable again."

"I understand. I don't mind you working late. I can handle the kids."

"It's not that."

"Oh?"

"Merry, I know this is going to be hard for you to hear, but . . . I need you full time at the office."

A long pause ensued as she digested his words. "Full time?" Her fingers reached for the edge of the counter, grabbed hold.

"A lot of the work I need help with right now is secretarial, and Mitzi could delegate some of the paralegal stuff to you with supervision. I guess what I'm saying is that I need you eight hours a day, not two or three."

"Why don't you hire a full-time secretary?"

He shook his head. "Too expensive. I hate to sound crass, but you're the perfect solution because I don't have to pay you a salary."

Merry released her grip on the edge of the counter. "What about Hunter?"

Jeff's shoulders slumped. "I know how much you're enjoying your time with him." He paused. "I called the day care at the church, and they have an opening in the baby room."

"Day care?" Merry felt tears spring to her eyes. "Oh, Jeff—"

"Lots of kids go to day care. Just because none of ours have so far—"

"But—"

"Merry, you know I wouldn't ask if there was any other way."

She didn't know what to say. She felt nauseated. And she couldn't look down at Hunter or she would burst into tears for sure. "Jeff—"

"There's no other solution, Mer. Believe me, if there was, I'd have thought of it."

She knew he hadn't been sleeping well lately but had figured it was the practice that kept him up.

"I'll work longer in the mornings. Hunter will be fine with me. And he doesn't bother Mitzi."

Jeff shook his head. "That's not fair to Hunter, Merry. And the day care is excellent. You know that. He'll be in good hands."

But he wouldn't be in her hands. Merry looked at Jeff, then Hunter, then at her husband once more. How could Jeff ask her to choose between them? But he wasn't asking. He was practically ordering. Resentment welled up inside her.

"You could have discussed this with me." She picked up the knife and whacked at the lettuce on the cutting board. "I thought we were a team."

"We are." He ran a hand over his face, rubbed his chin. "I promise you, Merry, if there was any other way—"

His shoulders dropped even further, his head dipped low. The movement snapped her out of her self-pity. Jeff had always taken his responsibility for their family seriously. He wasn't a man to make frivolous requests. The bankruptcy had taken a toll on his confidence, on his belief in himself as a provider.

She scraped the lettuce off the cutting board into a waiting bowl. Tears stung her eyes. Jeff was right. She didn't actually have a choice. They both had to do what was necessary to provide for their family. She reached for a tomato.

"Just give me some time to get used to the idea."

Jeff's head lifted, and his shoulders straightened just a notch. "You sure?"

Merry smiled through the tears that formed in her eyes. "No." She laughed in spite of herself. "But I know you wouldn't ask for something that you didn't truly need."

Jeff's eyes were misty too. He reached for her, drew her close. "I'm so sorry," he whispered in a choked voice.

"No." She kissed his cheek, his mouth. "Don't you even start."

"It's not forever."

Eugenie had asked them last Friday what love was, and Merry had said she found it overwhelming. But that was only part of the truth. Because for her, love meant setting her own wants and needs aside for the sake of her family's welfare. Even when it caused her as much distress as leaving Hunter was going to do.

"We'll figure it out," she assured Jeff. In the bouncy chair at their feet, Hunter gurgled happily and slapped at the toys suspended on a bar over his head. Merry looked down at him, an almost physical pain slicing through her.

How in the world was she going to find the strength to leave her baby that first day? Or any day after, for that matter?

She had no idea. She only knew that she didn't really have a choice.

"Hannah! Wait up."

Josh's voice carried the length of the senior hallway. Hannah dropped her chin and shoulders and kept walking as if she hadn't heard him, although Josh's baritone might as well have been a bullhorn.

"Hey." A hand grabbed her sleeve and slowed her flight. "C'mon, Hannah Banana. I run enough wind sprints at practice."

She flinched at the old nickname but recovered by shaking his hand off her arm. "I'm late for class, Josh."

She'd managed to avoid him after honors English by bolting for the door the second the bell rang. She'd eaten lunch on the steps behind the school so she wouldn't run into him in the cafeteria. But now, on the way to her last class of the day, her luck had run out.

At her brusque reply, Josh's fingers fell from her sleeve. She risked a glance at him and then wished she hadn't. The confusion in his eyes made her chest ache. Better to amputate now, she reminded herself, curling her right hand into a fist. She'd heard the gossip in the girls' rest room earlier, the information Kristen had held back in an attempt to humiliate Hannah.

"From geek to god in just a few short years," a freshman girl had said behind Hannah while she was washing her hands. "Evidently he was the star quarterback at his middle school in Birmingham. They say he may be the first freshman to start as quarterback here in, like . . . forever."

Hannah had dried her hands, thrown away the paper towel, and refused to cry. Josh would figure out the score soon enough, now that he was a jock. She should save herself the pain of having him be the one to pass her in the hallway without speaking.

"If I'm tardy again, I get detention." She stepped backward, trying to escape the compulsion to move closer to him. "Later."

"Hannah." He caught up with her in two steps. His legs were a lot longer than they used to be. "Stop."

Several seniors looked their way. She couldn't let him make a scene. Not here.

"Okay, okay." She turned to face him. "What do you want?"

He frowned. "I thought I wanted to talk to my friend. What's your problem?"

She swallowed. How could Josh have possibly

become a jock? But he was. And he was apparently determined to treat her as if he'd never left. As if they still caught crawdads together or traded licks of their Popsicles.

She swallowed again. "I don't have a problem."

His shoulders relaxed. She hadn't realized how tense he was until that moment.

"You do a pretty good impression of it." He smiled. "So what's up with Old Lady Budge, anyway? Is she always so harsh?"

Hannah couldn't help smiling. His dimples really were incredible.

"At least we don't have to finish that stupid play by tomorrow," she said. "She's being pretty generous giving us a whole week to read the book. I heard her class last year had to read *1984* in, like, three days."

He shifted his books from one arm to the other, and Hannah's eyes were drawn to his arms. Muscles. Josh with muscles. The dimples might be cute, but muscles were—

"What do you have last period?" he asked.

"American history." She nodded at the pile of books in her arms. Mr. Barnes, her teacher, believed in lots of supplemental reading. Lots and lots of supplemental reading.

"Those look heavy. I'll take 'em." Josh reached out for her books and stacked them on top of his.

Her knees quivered, and Hannah locked them with determination. "You don't have to—" But he had already started off down the hall, and she had no choice but to follow him.

"Am I going the right way?" He turned back to look at her. She hurried to catch up.

"Um, yeah." She could feel other kids looking at them and saw them start to whisper. By the end of the day, it would be all over school. The new jock had been spotted carrying loser Hannah Simmons's books. "You really don't need to do that, Josh. Besides, don't you have CA this period?" All the jocks signed up for competitive athletics as the last class of the day so they could get an early start on their workouts or practices or whatever they called them. "The gym is the other direction."

He shrugged. "They won't care if I'm a little late."

Hannah paled. Of course *they* wouldn't. The other players, even the coaches, would bow down to a star athlete like Josh. If she'd had any doubt before about how far apart they were now, it was definitely, totally gone.

"Josh, just give me my books back." The words came out harsher than she'd intended.

"Were you always so hard to be nice to?" He frowned and dumped her books back in her arms. "Here. Sorry for trying to help."

"Josh—" But it was too late. He was already moving away from her. Ten yards down the hall, he ran into some other football players headed toward the gym. They fell into step, and all Hannah could do was watch them walk away. Broad shoulders and confidence. Girls watching them as they passed.

It was better this way, she told herself. Safer. She couldn't afford to hope for what she couldn't have. And that thought hurt more than the sight of Josh and his crew stopping at Courtney's locker to flirt with her and her pompom girlfriends.

Six

Camille settled into a pew halfway back in the sanctuary of the Sweetgum Christian Church and set her faux Kate Spade handbag on the cushion next to her. She tugged the hem of her skirt. Somehow it felt wrong for her knees to show in church. Soft music emanated from the old pipe organ, and she took a deep breath and blew it out slowly. Maybe here, in a holy place, she could find the peace that had eluded her in the days since her mother's death. And then she looked a few pews ahead and saw the most unexpected sight. A familiar dark head and a knee-weakening set of masculine shoulders covered by an expensive suit.

The last place she had expected to see Dante Brown for the first time after all these years was in the sanctuary of Sweetgum Christian Church.

Her first impulse was to flee, but Rev. Carson

stepped into the pulpit for the morning announcements. Too late.

"We especially want to welcome our visitors today," the minister said, "so I invite our members to take a moment to greet one another and our guests."

As usual, this invitation was the congregation's cue to stand up and mingle, saying hello to people they knew, as well as to anyone they didn't. As in most congregations, some church members were better at this than others. Camille always tried to smile and be gracious, to introduce herself to anyone around her she didn't know, but she had never been comfortable with this part of the service. Sometimes she lingered out in the vestibule until it was over so she wouldn't have to participate. This morning, though, since she'd gone ahead and taken her seat, she was trapped.

"Good morning, Camille." Eleanor Krebbs, possibly the oldest living member of the church, clasped Camille's hand in her gnarled one and gave her a pat. "You've been in my prayers. I know you're missing your mother."

Tears stung Camille's eyes, but she blinked them back. "Thank you, Mrs. Krebbs." No wonder she'd dreaded coming to church. Other people's sympathy was like salt in a fresh wound, dissolving any little progress Camille might have made toward healing. How long would it be before she could come to church without anyone looking at her with pity in their eyes?

She shook several other people's hands, endured their condolences, and kept her gaze carefully averted from the spot three rows in front of her where Dante was being fawned over like a conquering hero.

Rev. Carson was calling them back to order when Dante turned and caught her looking at him. Her gaze locked with his, and she felt it once more—that undeniable mixture of fear and excitement and hope he always stirred in her. She couldn't read his guarded expression, which only increased the unwanted tension that coursed through her. Should she smile? Nod in recognition? If only she could act casual, greet him briefly, and then forget about him. Preferably for the rest of her life.

He opened his mouth, as if he were about to say something to her across the space that divided them, and then another church member caught his sleeve and he turned away.

Camille sank back onto the pew and refused to acknowledge the disappointment that swamped her. Anticlimactic. That's what Eugenie would have called the moment. And now she had to sit for the next hour with Dante firmly in her sights. Not that she was much good at concentrating on the sermon under the best of circumstances, but she would never get anything out of the service now.

"Mind if I sit with you?" a voice at her elbow said.

Camille turned to see Eugenie standing in the aisle. Surprised, she nodded and scooted over so the librarian could sit down.

"Aren't you supposed to sit on the front row?" Camille whispered to Eugenie as the organist began the prelude. The soft opening music was meant to provide a time for quiet reflection, but that was the last thing Camille was capable of at the moment.

Eugenie pursed her lips. "I prefer to sit farther back, with someone I know, rather than alone on the front row."

Camille smothered a smile. Eugenie's adjustment to the role of preacher's wife couldn't be easy. At least that's what Camille's mother had told her.

The thought of her mother washed away the smile that played at the edge of her mouth. Camille's own church attendance had been spotty at best during her mother's lengthy illness, especially once her mother couldn't leave the house. To tell the truth, she didn't know why she'd come today, except that she hadn't been able to think of anything else to do. Not that long ago she'd been sitting at her mother's bedside, reading to her while she was awake, knitting while she slept. The medical supply company had yet to come and retrieve the large hospital bed that had occupied the living room for so long, and Camille couldn't bring herself to sit in the room alone all day staring at it. So she'd come to church, looking for—what?

Comfort? Escape? Certainly not Dante Brown. If Eugenie hadn't sat next to her, she could have slipped out of the service early.

The next hour passed with unbearable slowness. The moment the organist struck the first notes of the recessional, Camille was up and out of the pew, squeezing around Eugenie. She made a beeline for the door, leaving the bewildered librarian in her wake.

"Camille, wait," a masculine voice called.

She descended the steps outside the sanctuary and pretended she hadn't heard him. Her well-worn pumps clattered as she went. Quick as she was, though, she was no match for Dante, even with his bum knee.

"Camille!"

Other parishioners turned toward him, watching with great interest. It was too late to escape. She stopped and pivoted slowly, as if her interest in the person hailing her was so vague she couldn't put much energy into the movement of her body.

"Camille." He said her name again as he moved toward her, stopping less than two feet in front of her. She had to look up to meet his gaze and could only pray that her face was as expressionless as she could make it.

"Oh, Dante. Hello. I thought that was you." *Knew it was you. Felt it was you.* She clutched the strap of her purse below where it rested on her shoulder. "It's good to see you."

"You too." He looked around, as if assessing how many eager ears were in the immediate vicinity. Plenty, Camille could have told him, and every one anxiously awaiting their next words. "Can I walk you to your car?" he asked.

"I didn't drive," she said and then stopped. She knew at once she'd made a tactical error.

"Neither did I," he said. "Why don't I walk you home?"

Such a simple question on the surface, but the murky emotional waters below threatened to drag her down.

"Um—" How could she refuse? He was nothing more than a former classmate, an old friend who had come back to town. But they both knew that his request went far beyond a desire to catch up or reminisce. Every member of the Sweetgum Christian Church still congregated on the steps would watch them leave together. By midafternoon, their actions would be common knowledge.

"All right," she finally said, if only as a means of escaping the scrutiny of her fellow church members. She cringed at how ungracious she sounded, but she couldn't afford to encourage him. One inch equaled one mile to Dante Brown, and there were a lot of inches between the church and her house.

They headed north on Spring Street, away from the center of town. *It's only a ten-minute walk,* Camille told herself. *You can make meaningless conversation for that long.* But forming words proved difficult with Dante beside her. The width of his shoulders seemed to take up more than his half of the sidewalk, and she would have sworn there was less oxygen in the air around him. He had to duck the low-hanging branches, and he motioned her ahead of him when the concrete roughened into jagged crumbles where tree roots had displaced the path.

"I'm surprised you're still here," he said after several long moments of silence. "You were so set on leaving."

So he didn't know. She shrugged her shoulders. "Things don't always work out like you plan." The understatement of the year. The decade.

He stumbled, his foot catching on a crack in the sidewalk, and when he straightened, she saw him wince in pain.

"Are you okay?"

He scowled, frustrated to be caught showing any sign of weakness, she knew. Dante certainly hadn't changed in that regard.

"I'm fine. My knee . . ." He didn't finish the sentence.

"I saw it. The hit you took. I saw it on television."

"The only people who didn't live at the South Pole." His scowl deepened. With his face looking like a thundercloud, he was more unsettling than ever.

"It still bothers you?"

He smiled then, that wide, infectious grin that

had charmed Sweetgum women of all ages. "Only when I'm chasing after a beautiful girl."

Camille flushed and hated herself for doing it. Dante's charm was never subtle, but it was nonetheless effective.

"Dante—"

He raised a hand to interrupt her. "Sorry, Cammie. I didn't mean any disrespect. To your mother, I mean." He paused as if searching for the right words. "I guess I'm supposed to say that I'm sorry she's gone, but sometimes it's a blessing to let people go. Especially when they've been in pain for so long."

Camille looked up at him, startled by his unexpected words. So he did know after all. "Yes," she whispered. "Yes, sometimes it's a blessing." A cruel, bitter blessing, but a blessing nonetheless.

"How are you doing?" he asked as they resumed walking. They were on her street now, only a few houses from her front door. If she could just get through the next few minutes, she would be okay. Their first meeting would be over, and she could put him out of her head and go about the rest of her day.

"I'm fine."

"Hmm." He didn't sound convinced.

"Really." The breeze blew a strand of hair in her eyes, and she pushed it back behind her ear. "I don't know why people look like they don't believe me when I say that."

"Maybe people don't believe you because you don't look fine. You look terrible."

Well, he'd definitely turned off the charm. "Thanks for the heads-up."

His hand caught her arm. They stopped at the walk that led to her front door. "That doesn't mean I don't still think you're the prettiest girl in town." His smile was softer now, less charming but more sincere.

"Dante—"

"I'm just saying." He let go of her arm, and she missed the warmth of his hand against her skin. "What are you doing Friday night?" he asked.

"Friday night?"

"The football game. I need all the fans I can get."

"I haven't been to a football game in years." She'd spent Friday nights, like almost every other night, at her mother's bedside. Except for the one night a month she went to the Knit Lit Society.

"You should come. It's gonna be a good game. Rivertown's our second-best rival."

The first was Chapel Grove from the next county over. Their senior year, Dante had scored five touchdowns against them and cemented his status as a football legend.

"Maybe." She shrugged. "I'm not sure about my plans yet."

"Plans? In Sweetgum?" Dante chuckled. "Come to the game, and then I'll take you out for dinner after. Tallulah's is staying open late."

"The café always closes by nine."

Dante shook his head. "Not anymore. I convinced Tallulah that if she kept the café open later on Friday night, I'd fill it with customers for her."

"The Dante Brown charm already at work," Camille said, smiling in spite of herself. "You'll have this whole town rearranged by the end of the month."

"Nah. Won't take me that long."

The teasing light in his eyes, the ease of his stance, and the gleam of his perfect teeth against his dark skin drew Camille to him. Not just physically, but emotionally as well. Like a sad, pitiful moth to a flame. Only she knew, as everyone did, that the moth always got the worst end of that deal.

"So you'll come to the game?"

"Maybe."

Her response wasn't exactly gracious, but it lit a spark of triumph in Dante's eyes. "It'll be like old times. You cheering me on. Maybe you could wear that little cheerleader skirt—"

"Jerk." But she was laughing. She pushed him in the chest, just below his shoulder, like a high school girl flirting with her boyfriend. And she realized she suddenly felt young again. Not so weighed down. As if the weekend were a time to look forward to, not dread.

"I can't pick you up because I'll be with the team. But if you can get a ride, I'll bring you home after dinner."

She was making a date with Dante Brown, Camille realized with a start. He hadn't been back in her life half a day, and already she was doing exactly what she'd sworn not to.

"Maybe it would be better—"

Before she could finish her sentence, he laid a finger against her lips. A minimum of contact with maximum effect on her nervous system.

"I can't think of anything that would be better than having dinner with you after the game." He stepped away. "And I'm leaving right now, before you change your mind." He looked at her for a long moment, and Camille felt the power of his gaze from her head to her toes. She was playing with fire, but oh, how wonderful to feel warm again after all these years.

"See you later, Cammie."

"Good-bye, Dante."

He shook his head. "Not good-bye. Good-byes are for endings." He winked. "We're just getting started."

He turned and walked down the street, whistling. Camille stood rooted to the spot. What had she done? She would regret it later. Of course she would. And if she thought the town rumor mill was cranking now, wait until she showed up with him on Friday night at Tallulah's.

But as unpleasant as being the subject of local gossip might be, she couldn't regret agreeing to see him. She'd wondered for a long time what might have happened if she hadn't been so afraid of him in high school. She'd wondered if her whole life might have turned out differently. Maybe he would have taken her with him—to college and on to the pros. Or maybe he would have dumped her before graduation, broken her heart, and left her in Sweetgum, even lonelier than she was now.

At the last meeting of the Knit Lit Society, Eugenie had wanted to know their definition of love. And she'd said quickly enough that to her love meant doing things for other people. But she hadn't told the complete truth. Because secretly, in her heart of hearts, she knew that love meant opening up her entire being to another person, a person who, like her father, could walk away and destroy her all over again. Or like her mother, who wouldn't want to leave, but wouldn't have any choice in the matter.

Standing on the sidewalk in front of her house, Camille wondered if she would ever have the courage or the faith to love someone that way again.

Seven

Maria had almost refused to attend the covered dish dinner that Sunday evening at the church, but her older sister, Daphne, had persuaded her to relent.

"If you don't go, I'll be forced to run interference between Mama and Mrs. Emerson by myself. And I'd really like to enjoy the evening a little."

Daphne rarely resorted to guilt, and the overbearing Mrs. Emerson was sure to antagonize their mother, so Maria couldn't help but give in. Daphne had no idea just how effective her strategy was. In the almost two weeks since Maria had signed the papers to begin the sale of the farm, she'd continued to put off telling her mother and sisters the truth. Better to let them continue in ignorant bliss for as long as possible. But Daphne's gentle guilting—

Maria didn't stand a chance against that. So just before six o'clock she found herself climbing from the backseat of her mother's yacht of a Cadillac. She leaned back in the car and retrieved the casserole dish with its thermal cover. The strong smell of tuna and cream of mushroom soup clashed with the pine scent of the car's air freshener. Thankfully, the ride to the church was a short one.

"Maria. You came after all." Annabeth Logan, Maria's closest friend, hurried across the small parking lot toward her. She, too, carried a casserole dish. "I'm glad you changed your mind."

"Daphne worked her mojo on me."

"I wish I had her touch." Annabeth was as petite as Maria was tall. Her plump figure showed her love of children—she had three—as well as her fondness for baked goods. Annabeth and her family ran the bakery on the town square next door to the five-and-dime. "We'd better get moving or we'll be late."

Maria nodded in agreement, but her feet felt like lead as they approached the rear of the church and the double glass doors that led to the fellowship hall. Daphne and her mother disappeared inside the building, surrounded by a gaggle of other church ladies.

Church suppers invariably followed the same pattern. The older ladies clucked like hens, shifting dishes on the three tables laid end to end until the twenty-four feet of food resembled the messianic banquet. Fifteen minutes after the meal was supposed to begin, the preacher would finally get everyone to quiet down so he could say the blessing. And then the older men, who had been lining up for the last half hour, would descend on the casseroles and side dishes and salads like locusts on a field of grain. The women and children would make do with conversation and whatever the men left behind.

After handing off her casserole to a pair of eager hands, Maria scanned the fellowship hall for her mother and sister. Annabeth, her hands also free now, joined her.

"Look. There's an empty table in the back. Let's save some seats."

Maria nodded in agreement, and they threaded their way across the room.

"Where are your kids?" Maria asked as they turned sideways in the narrow aisle to allow Henry Hale to pass. The church organist was almost as broad as he was tall, so they had to squeeze up against the folks already seated at one of the numerous round tables.

"The older two are helping Bob at the bakery, and Amy's with my mom."

"So you're on your own?"

Annabeth nodded and grinned. "I hardly know what to do with myself."

They achieved their goal and sank into chairs at the empty table. Only when they had settled in did they notice that several chairs on the other side of the table had already been tilted up and forward, the traditional church signal for reserved seats.

Maria glanced around to see who might be coming their way. She heard a buzz near the doorway, a sure sign that a person or persons of interest had arrived, but she couldn't see who it was. And then, like the Red Sea before the Israelites, the crowd parted, and Maria saw two familiar male figures accompanied by an unknown woman.

"Who in the world are they?" Annabeth asked.

Rev. Carson moved to greet the newcomers. The taller man looked every bit as arrogant as he had when he'd entered the five-and-dime demanding a fountain pen. Maria sighed. He hadn't exactly demanded the pen in so many words, but everything from his facial expression to the way he set his shoulders demonstrated that he was accustomed to getting his way. Maria watched as he shook hands with the minister, his expression guarded. His friend's face, though, appeared as open and eager as it had in the store that day. The stylishly dressed woman bore a marked resemblance to the cheerier of the men—his sister, no doubt—but her facial expression mirrored the taller man's arrogance.

"That's James Delevan," Annabeth said unexpectedly. Maria turned her head in surprise to look at her friend.

"How do you know that?"

"They were in the bakery last week, at least the two men were."

Maria made a wry face. "They came in the five-and-dime too. I'm surprised they're still here." More surprised than Annabeth could know. Maria thought the pair wouldn't be back in Sweetgum for a good while. They were as interested in keeping the sale of the Munden farm secret as Maria was.

"Look. Rev. Carson is introducing them to your sister," Annabeth said.

Daphne stood at the minister's side, smiling and extending her hand. The blond man shook it vigorously, grinning from ear to ear. The arrogant one said something and shook her hand as well. The woman, though, simply nodded and grimaced, though to give her the benefit of the doubt, she might have been trying to smile, Maria thought. She chuckled. The stranger's obvious snobbery was not going to get her very far in Sweetgum.

"The line for the food has gone down. Let's go get our plates," Annabeth suggested.

They stood and tipped their chairs up too before heading back across the room. It took several long minutes since both women stopped to chat with their friends and acquaintances. Maria supposed she was glad she'd decided to come after all. Since her father's death, she'd spent every evening at home, sitting on the porch swing with a book or puttering in her greenhouse. She needed to socialize more.

They had almost made it to the food line when Rev. Carson intercepted them, James Delevan in tow. Maria went to grab Annabeth's sleeve, but her friend slipped away.

"I think Mr. Hale's waving me over," Annabeth said as she disappeared. Maria groaned in frustration, then squared her shoulders.

"Good evening, Maria. Glad to see you." Rev. Carson patted her shoulder. "James, may I introduce you to Maria Munden? Her family owns the five-and-dime on the square."

"Miss Munden." He nodded, almost deep enough to be a slight bow, as arrogant now as he'd been when he came into the store. He made no mention of their previous meeting, however, and she determined not to do so either.

"I'll leave you two to get acquainted," Rev. Carson said, his attention caught by something on the other side of the fellowship hall.

He stepped away from them, and Maria fought back a sudden wave of panic. She was no naive girl overawed by a wealthy stranger from out of town, she reminded herself sternly. Over the years she had learned how to deal with all kinds of people. There was no reason she couldn't deal with James Delevan.

"How are you enjoying your time in Sweetgum?" She fixed a polite, if somewhat disinterested, expression on her face and waited for his answer.

"It's been pleasant."

Pleasant? Who in the world talked like that anymore? He was so stiff he might as well have gone straight to the funeral home instead of stopping at the church dinner.

A flush of shame hit her as she realized what she'd been thinking and how disrespectful it was, not only to her father but also to Nancy St. Clair and Frank Jackson.

"I'm surprised to see you here," she said. "We don't normally have many visitors at these potlucks."

"Evan and I met Rev. Carson in town today. He invited us."

"Will you be in Sweetgum much longer?" she asked him, and then she realized her question might be taken two ways. "I mean—"

"We'll be here at least another week."

Why? Maria wanted to ask, but she couldn't. Secrecy had been a condition of the sale. She could only hope that nothing had happened to thwart their plans or derail their purchase of the Munden farm.

"And your lady friend?"

"Evan's sister. She's going back to Memphis in the morning."

There was a lengthy silence while she waited for him to introduce another topic of conversation, but he merely stared around the room. She wanted to ask him why he hadn't simply introduced himself that first day at the store. Surely he had connected Munden's Five-and-Dime with the purchase of the Munden farm.

"Where are you staying while you're here?" she finally asked.

He arched an eyebrow at her, as if to suggest she was prying. "At the bed-and-breakfast on the edge of town. Sugar Mill, I think it's called."

"Sugar Hill." She couldn't resist correcting him. "A lovely place."

"It's fine." But she could hear the implied criticism.

"It's not a five-star hotel."

"Definitely not."

Maria took a deep breath, sucked in her cheeks, and contemplated biting her tongue. The man was colossally arrogant. Honestly, it was a wonder there was room for anyone else in the fellowship hall given the size of his ego.

She nodded toward the buffet. "You should help yourself before all the good stuff is gone." Her polite suggestion was the nicest way she knew to get rid of him.

From his superior height, he looked at the long tables pulled end to end and covered with casserole dishes, bowls, and platters. "There's enough cholesterol here to—"

"I suppose you're right," she said in her blandest tone. "Excuse me, but I think my mother needs me." With a short nod—as close a concession to good manners as she could make at the moment—she melted away, leaving Mr. James Delevan to contemplate the deficiencies of a church covered-dish supper. And herself to wonder why an arrogant stranger should bother her quite so much.

Later, after everyone had eaten and Rev. Carson had given a short devotional, Maria stood behind one of the large round posts that dotted the fellowship hall at regular intervals. The posts, however awkwardly placed, served the utilitarian purpose of holding up the second and third floors of the education wing. Almost two feet in diameter, they were large enough to conceal a grown woman. She was hiding from Henry Hale, the organist, who looked determined to ask her out yet again. She'd been avoiding his attentions for the better part of ten years, but Henry was not easily discouraged. The fact that he lived with his mother and wasn't in any hurry to move out gave him the leisure to be persistent.

"Come on, James. Surely you can find someone here to talk to." The voice came from the other side of the pole. She recognized it as belonging to James Delevan's friend, Evan. Maria froze. She looked around for means of escape, but if she moved now, the two men would surely see her.

"I think you have found—and monopolized— the only decent conversationalist in the room," James replied. His friend had been talking to Daphne whenever Maria happened to look their way. She couldn't see James Delevan's expression, but she heard the censure in his tone.

"James, someday your arrogance is going to backfire on you."

"I'm not arrogant."

His friend chuckled. "I can't wait to see you get caught in your own net."

"Well, it's not likely to happen in a sleepy back-water like this."

"What about Daphne's sister? She's nice. Seems intelligent."

"A little old for me. I'd rather spend the rest of the evening in my room at that excuse for a bed-and-breakfast doing Sudoku. Or watching reality television."

Maria felt the flush of embarrassment rise from her midsection until it suffused her throat and then her face. *A little old.* Well, that was what she got for eavesdropping. What had she expected him to say? That he'd been fascinated by her?

Maria did not have a false sense of pride. She had long ago accepted that her looks were average and her possibilities for marriage nonexistent, Henry Hale excepted. But she hadn't expected others, particularly strangers, to discuss those facts quite so openly. And certainly not at a covered dish supper.

She turned to walk away before either of the two men became aware of her presence, but as she did, she bumped into Annabeth, whose eyes were dancing with laughter. Maria suppressed a groan. She hadn't been the only one to overhear the conversation.

Annabeth grabbed her arm and pulled her away from the pole, back toward the table where they'd eaten. She pushed Maria into a chair and flopped down beside her.

"Well, I never," she said between giggles. "Of all the nerve . . ."

Maria felt hard-pressed to figure out what Annabeth found so funny about the conversation. But after a moment, her sense of humor got the best of her, and she felt the corners of her mouth curve upward into a smile.

"My mother always told me not to listen at keyholes." She thought of the old-fashioned doors in the family home and how she had spent a good deal of time as a child with her ear pressed to the openings. That warm remembrance, though, brought with it a dash of icy reality. Soon that home would no longer be hers.

"Well, you certainly don't have to worry about acquiring an unwanted admirer," Annabeth teased. "Mr. Delevan is dead set against you, Maria."

"The feeling is mutual."

Someone loomed at her elbow, and with a start Maria looked up to see the very man they were discussing.

"Sorry to interrupt. Would you mind if I joined you?" he asked in his stiffly formal manner.

"Actually, we were just about to go help clean up," Maria said, leaping to her feet and dragging Annabeth with her. "But feel free to sit here."

Annabeth cast her an admonishing look, but Maria refused to acknowledge it. Yes, she was being rude, but James Delevan didn't deserve to receive any better than he dished out.

"Of course. I'm sure you're needed."

She thought she saw discomfort in his dark eyes but decided she was imagining things. He would be relieved to have her disappear into the kitchen. *A little old for me.* She wouldn't want to contaminate him with her ancientness. Which probably wasn't even a word, but Maria didn't care. She yanked Annabeth's arm and headed for the kitchen at breakneck speed.

Bad enough that the man was helping Evan Baxter take away the farm she'd loved so much. She wouldn't allow him to take her dignity too.

Eight

Esther entered her bedroom that evening and slipped off her shoes. Her feet ached from spending the day in three-inch heels, but she'd had little choice. Church in the morning. A tea for the garden club at Maisie Shifley's in the afternoon. She'd had to retrieve the dog from the animal hospital, since his wounds were finally healed enough for them to release him. Then the covered dish supper at the church. And when she'd finally arrived home, she'd found that the dog had dug up every one of her azalea beds.

Her first instinct had been to find a rolled-up newspaper and discipline the beast, but when she looked at him and saw the bare places where the vet had shaved him so his wounds could be treated, she couldn't bring herself to do it. Instead, she fed him his dinner and then left him to his own devices in the kitchen after securely latching the baby gate that would keep him in that room for the night.

She really ought to read for the next Knit Lit Society meeting. Never a fan of Shakespeare, she'd procrastinated since their meeting the week before. Of course, she could just choose not to read *Romeo and Juliet* and be done with it, but she'd made a vow to herself to try to do better this year, at least when it came to the reading assignments. The knitting, well . . .

She carefully hung her silk suit on a padded hanger and stowed her pumps in their appropriate cubby. Her nightgown and robe were in the lingerie drawer, neatly folded and waiting for her. Her bedtime routine—removing her makeup, washing her face, and slathering on regenerating cream—took less than ten minutes since she had it down to a science.

She settled into bed, adjusting the pile of pillows behind her, and reached for the book on her nightstand.

Romeo and Juliet. She'd read it in high school and remembered thinking it was awfully dramatic. To Esther, romantic love was not only overrated but something to be avoided. Marriage was—and always had been for her—about forming the right alliance. Building a life together. Working as a team. Not this nonsense about dying of love for someone.

Esther picked up the book, thumbed past the overview and the introduction, and proceeded straight to act 1, scene 1, where the servants of the Capulets and Montagues were insulting one another. Romeo had just entered when she heard the phone ring.

Esther looked around. Usually she kept the portable handset nearby, but it wasn't on the bed or the nightstand.

"Where is that thing?" She climbed out of bed and went in search of the receiver, found it, and then paused when she didn't recognize the number on the caller ID. *Wireless Caller,* the display said.

She pressed the button to answer. "Hello?"

"Mrs. Jackson?" The deep male voice sounded familiar, but she couldn't quite place it.

"Yes."

The caller cleared his throat. "This is Brody McCullough. We met week before last out on the lake road. I helped you with the dog. The vet's office gave me your name and number."

"Oh, yes. I remember." For no discernible reason, she felt her heartbeat accelerate. "What can I do for you?"

"How's the dog doing? Was Doc Everton able to help him?"

"Yes, yes. He's going to be fine. His hip was displaced, but the vet took care of that."

"Is the dog still at the animal hospital?"

"Actually, no. He's here with me."

There was a long pause. "With you?"

Esther bristled at the hint of disbelief in the man's tone. "I can assure you, Mr.—I'm sorry, what did you say your name was again?"

"Brody McCullough."

"I can assure you, Mr. McCullough, that the dog is in good hands."

"I didn't mean—"

"I'm sure you didn't." But her tone let him know that she knew exactly what he'd meant. "Is there anything else, Mr. McCullough?"

"I'm sorry if I offended you. You just didn't seem to be a dog kind of person, and if he was still at Doc Everton's, I was going to offer to take him off their hands."

"You want the dog?"

"Want? No. But I've got room enough at my place, and I thought I'd at least offer until I could find him a good home."

That took a bit of the wind out of her sails. "Oh. Well, it was nice of you to follow up." She paused, unsure what else to say.

"The thing is . . ." His voice trailed off.

"Yes?"

"Look, I don't mean to be rude, Mrs. Jackson, but are you sure you want to deal with that dog?"

Anger sparked in her chest. "Mr. McCullough, are you implying that I would neglect or hurt that animal? As I recall, I'm the one who rescued him."

"You were also the one who hit him."

"Well, I never—"

"I'm sorry. That didn't come out right."

"No. It didn't." She clamped her mouth shut and bit back the words that wanted to spew forth.

Esther refused to admit that perhaps a bit of the sting came from her own conscience. She didn't really want the dog, had only agreed to bring it home so that she wouldn't look heartless in the eyes of Dr. Everton and his assistants. But now, after Mr. McCullough's comments . . .

Did she really appear so unfeeling to the world?

The thought hit her hard, extinguishing the little flames of anger. The veterinarian had only reluctantly turned the dog over to her. And now a complete stranger was questioning her fitness to care for the animal.

"Mrs. Jackson—"

"Please call me Esther." While the words invited informality, her chilly tone did not.

The man sighed. "I've offended you, and I apologize. I shouldn't have judged you—"

"But you did." She didn't want to continue this conversation. "I can assure you that the dog is safe. Good night, Mr. McCullough." She moved her finger to the Off button.

"Wait—"

Something in his tone kept her from disconnecting the call. "Yes?"

"I'm not usually such a cretin."

"Cretin?" An impressive vocabulary for a farmer, she thought, and then cringed when she realized how snobbish the thought was.

"I owe you an apology. More than an apology." Brody McCullough paused. "I don't expect you'll

99

agree to this, but I'd like to buy you dinner to make up for my insult."

Esther swallowed back the sharp retort that rose to her lips. Men's minds were so difficult to understand. Why would he think that spending more time in his company would make her feel better about his misjudgment of her?

"I don't think so."

"But—"

"Good night, Mr. McCullough."

There was another pause. "Good night, Mrs. Jackson. Again, I apologize."

She didn't answer. Just hit the Off button and stared at the receiver.

What a strange conversation. She picked up the book again and tried to concentrate.

Juliet was an idiot, Esther decided. No man was worth giving up everything for, especially not one's life. Love was an illusion. If Juliet had ever made it past the age of fourteen, she would have figured that out.

Much later, Esther laid aside the book and reached over to turn off the lamp but hesitated before turning the switch. Since Frank's death, she'd slept with the light on, which was absurd since they hadn't shared a bedroom in years. He'd involuntarily taken up residence in the guest room when his snoring became too much of a disturbance.

Tonight, though, she was determined to return to

her normal way of doing things. Despite Frank's absence. Despite the ache of loneliness that pooled in her stomach. And despite the muffled whines and yelps she could hear from the kitchen downstairs. The dog would learn to sleep alone, just as she had. It was simply a matter of forming the habit.

Esther shut off the light with a snap of her wrist. She fluffed the pillows and pulled the covers up to her chin. The darkness wasn't absolute. Moonlight came in through the windows where she'd forgotten to draw the curtains.

No, the darkness wasn't absolute, but it was oppressive. Her chest tightened, and suddenly she couldn't breathe. She was suffocating.

With a cry, she threw back the covers and bolted out of the bed. The fool dog needed her, she told herself as she jammed her feet into her slippers and hurried down the stairs. That's all it was—anxiety about the animal. After all, the poor thing was helpless, alone, and had nowhere to go.

Just like her.

No, no. She couldn't think like that.

She flipped light switches as she passed, bathing the house in a warm glow. The dog must have heard her coming, because he stopped whining. At the entrance to the kitchen, where she'd put up the baby gate, she stopped and reached inside the doorway to turn on the light.

The dog waited just on the other side of the gate,

his nose pressed to the plastic mesh. He whined low in his throat and let out two short, sharp barks. Esther stared down at him, torn between resentment and compassion. If she gave in this time . . . Well, she'd learned that lesson long ago with Frank. And with her son, Alex. Once you gave in to a male, he never stopped pushing. Other people thought she was too rigid, but she wasn't. She was realistic. People went as far as you let them, so if they hurt you, you had no one to blame but yourself.

"You can't come upstairs," she said to the dog. "You might as well accept it."

He stared back at her, uncomprehending, and let out another sharp bark.

"Good night," Esther said. She reached inside the door frame and turned the light off. The kitchen wasn't pitch-black either. A soft glow from the outside lights came through the windows above the sink.

She wasn't ten steps away when the dog began to cry, an agonizing whimper of fear. Esther stopped. Turned. Told herself she shouldn't do what she was about to do.

"All right. Come on."

She reached down and lifted the handle on the baby gate, dislodging it from the door frame. The dog bounded through like a prisoner making a dash for freedom. He headed for the stairs and raced up them until he was out of sight.

Esther followed at a slower pace. By the time she reached her bedroom, the dog had already made himself at home, curled up on her pillow.

"I don't think so. Off." She barked the last word. Might as well speak to him in his own language.

The dog looked at her, cocked his head, and remained right where he was.

"I said off." She snapped her fingers and pointed toward the floor. She should have brought up the old blanket she'd put in the kitchen for him. "Now."

The dog stood, and Esther felt pleased. She would show the animal she was in charge. "That's a good—No. You may not sleep on that pillow either."

The dog appeared unperturbed by her scolding. He circled around three times and then settled into a little ball on what would have been, once upon a time, Frank's pillow.

"I said—" Esther stopped herself. Did it really matter all that much? She knew she should make the dog move, at least to the foot of the bed. But the darkness was still there, and she was tired of being alone.

"Just for tonight," she said as she got back into bed. The dog looked at her with those big, sad brown eyes. A lot like Frank's eyes, to tell the truth. "I mean it. Tomorrow night it's back to the kitchen. I'll get you a hot water bottle or a ticking clock or something."

The dog closed his eyes, heaved a deep sigh, and promptly went to sleep.

For Esther, the peace of sleep proved more elusive. She turned so that her back was to the dog and her eyes were fixed on the large green numbers of her alarm clock. She watched as the minutes ticked by, waiting for her eyelids to grow heavy and for sleep to overtake her.

Eventually it did, but not before she'd spent a good, long time listening to the dog snore almost as loudly as Frank.

Nine

By the end of the first week in October, Hannah had figured out how to get from one class to another without running into Josh. And if she got to honors English early enough, she could sit in the back of the room. He was always one of the last ones through the door—the popular kids hung out in the hallway until the very last minute—so he and Courtney usually sat side by side in the front row.

Fortunately, Josh didn't ride her bus since he had football practice until five o'clock every day. On Fridays, though, she didn't take the bus. Instead she walked to the library to meet Eugenie. Rev. Carson would take them out for dinner, and sometimes they went to a movie at the theater on the square.

The whole nuclear family thing felt surreal to Hannah, who had grown up on the outskirts of town in a run-down trailer. Her mom had always worked as a cocktail waitress on Friday nights. Hannah had long ago learned to fix a box of macaroni and cheese and set the television antennas so that she could pick up one of the Nashville channels.

On Friday after the last bell rang, Hannah was headed down the front steps of the high school when she heard Josh call her name.

"Wait up."

She turned to watch him jogging toward her and wished the sight of him didn't make her knees so shaky.

"Hey," he said as he got nearer. "Where you headed?"

Hannah shrugged. "The library. I have to meet Mrs. Carson."

"I'll walk with you." He didn't ask, just fell into step beside her as she started moving down the sidewalk. She was surprised he was talking to her after the way their last conversation had ended almost two weeks ago.

"What's up, Josh?" She couldn't keep the edge out of her voice. He had to know the score by now. Had to know what a loser she was in the eyes of most of her classmates.

He smiled. "I figured something out."

"What's that?"

"I figured out why you were so rude to me."

A part of her froze even as she continued to keep moving. "Yeah?"

Josh nudged her shoulder with his. "You were always like that when we were kids. When you got all frosty on me, it meant you didn't feel safe."

Hannah felt her jaw drop and closed it with a snap. "Who are you? Sweetgum's answer to Dr. Phil?"

"I'm just saying." He shifted his backpack from one shoulder to the other.

"Shouldn't you be at football practice?"

"No practice. Big game tonight. I don't have to be in the locker room until five."

"Then shouldn't you be hanging out with cheer-leaders or something?"

Josh shrugged. "Nah. I'd rather hang out with you."

"Josh—"

"Yeah?"

But what could she say without emphasizing her loser status?

"Nothing." She started walking again. The sooner she got to the library, the sooner she could ditch him.

"You thirsty?"

It was Hannah's turn to shrug.

"We could stop at the Dairy Dip."

Yeah, right. If the football players weren't at practice, they would all be piled into the booths at the Dairy Dip, eating their weight in cheeseburgers while the popular girls drank Diet Coke.

"I don't think so."

"But you *are* thirsty."

"I didn't say that."

"You didn't have to. I can tell."

"Are you always this persistent?"

But he was, she remembered. Once Josh got an idea in his head, he worried it to death. She remembered the time he'd decided to jump Sweetgum Creek at the narrow place about halfway between their trailer park and town. He'd made the attempt day after day, landing in the water over and over until he was soaked to the skin. Then, finally, one day he did it, sailed from one bank to the other like a flying squirrel. Josh had grinned like he'd just won a gold medal. He clearly hadn't minded the hundreds of attempts it had taken for him to reach his goal.

"I don't like to give up," he said. "So where you headed again?"

"The library."

"Studying?"

"No. I'm meeting Mrs. Carson."

"Who's she?"

"Mrs. Carson's the librarian. She used to be Miss Pierce until she got married a few months ago."

"The old lady librarian?"

"She's not that old." Hannah bristled.

Josh held up both hands in front of him. "Whoa. Sorry. No offense."

Hannah kept her gaze on her shoes as they walked. "She's sort of my guardian now."

There it was—the truth she hadn't wanted to tell him. Shame suffused her entire body. Since everyone in town knew that her mother had run off and left her, she didn't usually have to tell anyone about it. But Josh hadn't been here, didn't know that even her own mother didn't think she was worth sticking around for.

"What about—"

"My mom? She took off."

His eyes widened in astonishment. "Are you kidding me?"

"C'mon, Josh. You remember what she was like. You were there all the times she showed up drunk for school stuff." She might as well jog his memory, get the truth out in the open.

He nodded. "Yeah, well, at least she showed up. Mine never thought I was worth taking off work for."

Hannah was quiet for a moment. She'd forgotten that. Josh's mom had been pretty and always smiled at Hannah, but she never came to school functions or any of Josh's Little League games.

"Will your mom come to the game tonight?" The question was spontaneous, but the moment she asked it, she blushed. What if his mom still didn't show up to support him?

He nodded. "Yeah. She'll be there. I wasn't good enough at baseball for her to bother, but football . . ." He paused. "Anyway, she comes to football games."

"Someone told me you were the star of your middle school team back in Alabama."

"I did okay."

They turned the corner onto Spring Street. The library was only a few blocks away now.

"I heard you got starting quarterback. No freshman at Sweetgum High has ever started at quarterback."

"It's no big deal." But he looked pleased that she knew about it. "Look, if you don't want to go the Dairy Dip, why don't you come to the game tonight?" His face had gone all serious, which caused a different kind of anxiety to bloom in Hannah's middle.

"I have plans already." She didn't want to tell him about dinner and a movie with the Carsons. She was enough of a nerd already.

"C'mon. Show some school spirit."

Hannah couldn't look at him. "I don't want to ask the Carsons to come and get me that late," she prevaricated. "Old people don't like to drive at night."

"I can walk you home."

Now the feelings in her stomach rose up to fill her chest, a mixture of pleasure and apprehension. "Josh—"

He stopped in the middle of the sidewalk, and despite her intention to ditch him, Hannah did the same.

"It's just a football game," she said. "Why are you making such a big deal about it?"

Josh rubbed the bridge of his nose. "Were you always this much trouble?"

Hannah had to smile at that. "Definitely."

He smiled back. "Yeah. I thought so."

How could she resist that delicious grin? Or the allure of finding an old friend who also happened to have turned into a hottie? "Okay. I'll go to the game, if you'll quit bugging me."

"Cool." He turned and started walking again, and Hannah had to scramble to catch up. For the next few blocks she allowed herself to enjoy the sensation of just being with him, talking to him, and letting his sunny smile wash over her. Might as well indulge while she could. He'd return to Courtney and her kind soon enough.

As Camille rode with Merry to the football game that Friday night, she was regretting her decision to have dinner with Dante.

Not that long ago, Friday nights at the high school stadium had been the center of her world. She'd felt powerful there, alive, with the crowd and the lights and the attention. Her father had always been there in the stands, cheering her on just as she cheered the team on. Her mother had

110

been there too, looking happy and proud to be sitting beside her handsome husband. Until, suddenly, neither of them had been there.

"Courtney refused to ride with me," Merry said as she pulled her minivan onto the grassy field at the far end of the stadium that served as an overflow parking lot. "I'm glad you decided to come."

Camille was glad, too, for Merry's company. She hadn't been to a football game in several years because she hadn't wanted to leave her mother alone. But she'd always loved the excitement of Friday night—the warm fall evening, the smell of popcorn in the air, the fizz of an ice-cold Coke on her tongue, the sounds of the marching band drifting over the stands. Once a week, the entire town of Sweetgum could put aside its differences and come together to cheer for the team.

She hadn't told Merry about Dante, although she assumed the other woman had likely heard something through the rumor mill. As Camille had expected, their walk home from church had not gone unnoticed.

The two women made their way to the gate, paid the admission fee, and visited the concession stand. Merry stopped every few feet to talk with someone, and Camille stayed with her, smiling but not falling into conversation with anyone in particular. She was steeling herself for the moment when they would climb the stairs into the stands and she would see Dante down on the field.

"Sorry," Merry apologized when they finally made their way to their seats.

They sat in one of the higher sections with the other adults, leaving the lower part to the students and the marching band. Camille could see Merry's daughter Courtney sitting with the pep squad, a group of freshman girls who carried pompoms and served as the incubator for next year's cheer-leaders. On the far side of the student section, she caught sight of Hannah, sitting by herself, her elbows on her knees and her chin in her hands. She looked like she was attending her own execution rather than a sporting event.

Finally, when Camille had thoroughly inspected the stands, she allowed her gaze to move to the sideline. The edge of the field closest to them was lined with Sweetgum's players, their white uniforms still pristine. That would change in just a few minutes.

And then there was Dante in a white oxford shirt, tie, and dress slacks. Just the sight of him made Camille's mouth water more than the smell of pop-corn ever had.

"Close your mouth, Camille." Merry's amused voice penetrated the fog that had come over her at the sight of Dante. She jerked around to find Merry laughing at her, but there was kindness and good humor in her eyes. "He is a very attractive man."

Camille glanced around to see if anyone had

heard Merry's comment and then ducked her head, feeling sheepish. "I don't know—"

"What I'm talking about?" Merry scooped a handful of popcorn from the bucket they were sharing and lifted it to her mouth. "Nice try, honey." She munched thoughtfully for a long moment while Camille tried to figure out how to dig herself out of the hole she'd created, but Merry spoke again before Camille could think of anything to say.

"I know you just lost your mom, but she'd be the first one to tell you that life goes on." Merry's smile dimmed, her face growing serious. "And she would want you to find some semblance of normality, Camille. That includes men and dating and, I hope at some point, someone worthy of you for the long haul."

Camille waved her hand. "I'm not interested in that."

"Then you're the first woman I've ever met who wasn't."

At that exact moment, Dante turned away from the field, and she could see him scanning the crowd. He stopped when he caught sight of her. The effect was just as potent from a distance as when he'd been standing in front of her on the sidewalk at her house. He smiled, and the effect of that was just as intoxicating, too.

"Somebody's happy you're here," Merry said in a teasing tone as she gave Camille a nudge.

"We're just friends." That was all she could think to say.

"Sure you are, honey. Sure you are." Merry didn't sound any more convinced than Camille was. And in a few hours, after everyone in Sweetgum saw them together at Tallulah's, no one in the world would believe that this connection between them was purely platonic.

And Camille wouldn't be able to pretend it was anymore either.

Hannah wiggled in her seat, the hard wooden bleacher offering no comfort whatsoever. She couldn't believe she'd agreed to come to the game, much less let Josh walk her home. If she had still lived in the trailer park with her mom, she never would have told him yes. For one thing, it would have been too far to walk. And for another, she couldn't have stood to have Josh see how much worse the trailer looked than it had when he'd moved away.

Tonight, though, she could take him to the parsonage and not be ashamed or embarrassed. Her mother wouldn't be lying on the couch in nothing but a T-shirt, smoking a cigarette and finishing off a six-pack. Eugenie and Rev. Carson would be sitting in the wingback chairs in the living room, reading or listening to music. They'd probably offer Josh milk and cookies. It would all be normal and safe and . . . temporary. Security never lasted.

Hannah knew that. But she had it for now, so she might as well take advantage of it.

"I didn't know you liked football."

Hannah twisted on the bleacher to find Camille St. Clair sliding into place next to her. She was too surprised to respond for a moment. Heat flooded her cheeks, and she felt that familiar sense of shame wash over her.

"I don't really." She couldn't think of anything else to say.

"Well, that would explain why you're here." Camille's gaze went to the sidelines. "Who is he?"

"Who is who?" Hannah snapped, but the flame in her cheeks didn't subside. How did Camille know?

"Most girls only attend football games to watch the boys," Camille said with a conspiratorial smile. "If not the ones on the field, then the ones in the stands. Which are you? Field or stands?"

Hannah thought about denying it, but what other reason could she invent to explain her presence at the game?

"Field," she said miserably, propping her elbows on her knees and resting her chin in her hands. "Because I'm a complete idiot."

Camille laughed. "No, honey, you're not an idiot. Just a girl."

At that moment, a roar went up from the crowd. Hannah jumped to her feet to see what was happening, as did Camille. All she could see was a Sweetgum player streaking up the field, everyone else in pursuit.

"What's happening?" she asked Camille.

"Quarterback draw. Dante's been setting them up for it for the last two series."

"Huh?" Camille might as well have been speaking Latin for all Hannah understood.

"It was the new quarterback," Camille said. "He just scored a touchdown."

Hannah's flush of shame was replaced by one of pride and pleasure. "Really?"

Camille shot her a look out of the corner of the eye. "Oh no, Hannah. Not the quarterback."

Hannah's silence betrayed her. Camille reached over and put an arm around her, squeezed her shoulders.

"You have my sympathy. Quarterbacks are the worst. After fullbacks, of course." She smiled in a way that Hannah didn't understand, but she thought it had something to do with what Mrs. Budge was always calling irony.

"Don't tell anyone," Hannah said in a low voice. Despite the wild cheering around them, Camille nodded to show she'd heard.

"It'll be our secret."

Camille smiled funny when she said it, which made Hannah wonder. She followed Camille's gaze to the field, to the sight of Coach Brown stalking the sidelines, yelling at one of the players.

And then Hannah cast a sidelong look at Camille and realized why she understood Hannah's predicament so well.

After the game, Hannah loitered outside the entrance to the locker room, trying not to make eye contact with any of the cheerleaders or pompom girls waiting on their dates. Camille's warning kept replaying in her mind, and she could feel the other girls' gazes from time to time—some curious, some disdainful.

Finally, Josh emerged along with the other players. His wet hair clung to his head in tight, dark curls. When they were kids, he'd had a buzz cut, soft and bristly at the same time. He used to let her rub the top of his head for luck. That memory sent a strange sensation through her midsection. Or maybe it was the thought of touching Josh now, feeling those curls beneath her fingers, that made her feel like she'd just gotten off the Tilt-A-Whirl.

"Hey." He walked up to her as if she didn't embarrass him at all. Other kids called invitations to join them at a party in somebody's cow pasture or at their parents' lake house, but he just smiled and waved. "Maybe next time." He turned back to Hannah. "You ready?"

She heard a few of the cheerleaders making comments, grumbling about Josh's defection, but he seemed oblivious. "Sure," she answered.

"You hungry yet?" He slung his sports bag over his shoulder. "We could stop at the Dairy Dip and get a burger. You still like Coke floats?"

She shrugged, suddenly shy. "I guess."

When had she ever been so aware of a boy walking next to her? And when had he gotten so tall? She practically had to crane her neck to look him in the eye. Probably came in handy for seeing over all those players on the field.

"Good game, by the way," she said, even though she barely knew the difference between a first down and a touchdown. The team had won, and everyone seemed happy.

He shook his head. "I'll be lucky if I don't lose my starting spot. Don't know what was wrong with me tonight. I couldn't throw it in the ocean." She could feel him looking at her.

"What?" she said, suddenly afraid. Maybe she should have taken Camille's warning more to heart.

Josh stopped in the middle of the sidewalk. Cars whipped by on the street, kids honking and yelling in celebration of the victory. "I think *you* were what was wrong with me tonight."

Her breath froze in her chest. The dim glow of the streetlight lit the firm angle of his jaw. "What did I do?" She hated the breathless sound of her voice.

He laughed. "You showed up."

"Josh—"

"I'm glad you did."

"Even if I messed you up?" She couldn't resist saying it.

He shrugged the sports bag off his shoulder and let it fall to the ground. "I should have been expecting it."

"Expecting what?"

"You always mess me up."

"Josh, what are you talking about?" He moved closer, and she could hear a strange buzzing in her ears.

"This."

And then right there on the sidewalk, with cars driving by and in full view of everyone in Sweetgum, he kissed her.

And Hannah Simmons, for the first time in her life, decided to believe that dreams really might come true after all.

Ten

Later that evening, inside Tallulah's Café, Camille stood at the hostess stand and surveyed the crowd of people. She tried to look nonchalant, but every nerve stood on end with heightened awareness. The high school kids were no doubt crowded into the Dairy Dip, but all the adults in town were here at the café—parents, teachers, old coots who themselves had once battled for glory on the gridiron.

More than a few heads turned to look at her standing there by the entrance.

"Evening, Camille." Tallulah appeared beside her. Her bright blue eyes contrasted with the deep wrinkles in her tan face. No one knew the older woman's age with any certainty, but she had to be more than seventy, given how long the café had been in operation.

"How are you, Tallulah?"

"Fine as frog's hair." She picked up a menu. "Is it just you?"

"Actually, I'm meeting someone."

Camille had to give the older woman credit for showing no surprise. "Two then." Tallulah grabbed another menu. "Table or booth?"

Camille hesitated. A table meant their conversation would be overheard by half of the restaurant, but a booth would look like she and Dante were on a date.

"Booth please," she finally said, deciding that as long as she knew it was just a meal shared by two old friends, that was all that mattered.

"This way." Tallulah motioned for Camille to follow her. "I'll put you back here in the corner."

Before Camille could request a less secluded spot, Tallulah headed off and Camille had no choice but to follow. She was just slipping into the vinyl seat when she heard a commotion at the doorway. She looked up to see Dante coming into the café. As if on cue, everyone broke into applause.

"Way to go, coach," a man called from the other side of the room.

"On to state!" another one hollered.

Dante smiled and nodded, raised a hand in acknowledgment. "Thank you, folks. But we've still got a long way to go. Just keep cheering for us."

He looked around then, searching for her. Camille lifted her hand—not high in the air, just enough for him to see her. His smiled grew wider, and he headed toward her, stopping here and there to accept more congratulations along the way. When he finally made it to the booth, to her surprise he slid in next to her rather than taking the seat opposite.

"Thanks for waiting," he said, settling in, his shoulder rubbing against hers.

She was already scrunched over as far as she could go, so she couldn't avoid the contact. The sensation, though, wasn't unpleasant. Oh, who was she kidding? It was all she could do not to lean her head over and rest it on his shoulder.

"No problem. I've only been here a couple minutes. Merry wanted to drop her daughter off at a party before she brought me."

He picked up one of the menus Tallulah had left behind and flipped it open. "So you haven't ordered yet?"

"No." She grabbed the other menu and did the same. At least it gave her something to do until the waitress came to take their order.

"I could eat everything on here," he said with his usual good humor.

"I'm sure Tallulah would be glad to let you."

"I'm always too nervous to eat before a game."

"Still? I would think that wouldn't be so bad now that you're a coach and not a player."

"Yeah, you'd think so, but it's worse."

"That doesn't seem fair." She hadn't thought about the pressure he would be under. She'd been too busy worrying about the stress his presence placed on her.

He shrugged. "Goes with the job."

"I'm surprised you came back."

He set the menu down and turned to look at her. "Why does that surprise you?"

"Because you could go anywhere, do anything. Be anything." She tried not to let her envy show.

He shrugged. "I don't think the rest of the world shares your opinion."

"You were a college football star and played in the NFL. I would've thought the offers came pouring in."

He shook his head. "Washed-up pro football players are a dime a dozen, Camille."

"But coaching opportunities—"

"Aren't as plentiful for men of color," he said in a dry tone. "Even with a college degree. There's a lot of competition, and I'm young. I was lucky to get this job. I know guys I used to play with who are driving cabs and tending bar."

"I wondered why you were available after the start of the season."

"Coach Stults called me when he decided to retire. I'd given up on finding a coaching job this year."

Camille sipped the ice water the waitress had brought, unsure what to say. Here she'd been assuming that he had just kept right on living a charmed life, even after his injury. Surely he'd made enough as a pro player that he didn't need to worry about money. At least not for a while.

"You did a great job tonight," she said. "Coach Stults made a good decision asking you to take over."

He didn't smile, but she could see from the light in his eyes how much her compliment pleased him. "I have to do a better job of getting them ready next week. My quarterback was so distracted tonight, I thought he might start running for the wrong end zone."

Camille smiled. "I think what was bothering him might have been sitting in the stands."

"Or cheering on the sideline?" He winked at her. "I remember how distracted I used to get. Guess I'll have to cut him some slack."

Camille blushed and then was glad she'd taken a booth in the back where the lighting was a bit dimmer. "Do you know who the distraction girl is?" Hannah might have a crush on the quarterback, but Camille wondered whether the star athlete returned her feelings.

Dante laughed. "I hope it's the one I saw him kissing on the sidewalk on my way over here."

Camille was intrigued. "What did she look like? Maybe I can tell you who it is."

"Some blond freshman."

"Probably a pompom girl." Poor Hannah.

He shook his head. "No. This was definitely not a pom squad girl. Dirty blond, not those fake streaks. Didn't seem like the groupie type."

Could it have been Hannah? "I think I may know who your mystery girl is."

"And is she going to ruin my season?"

Camille smiled. "Not on purpose. I doubt she cares much about football." She paused. "I'm just . . . surprised a quarterback would look at her twice."

Their food arrived, and the waitress slid the plates in front of them.

"Thank you," Dante said to the young woman. He looked at Camille. "Maybe you should tell me her name. So I'll know who to be on the lookout for."

"Hannah Simmons. Actually, I know her pretty well. She's in the Knit Lit Society with me."

"The what?"

"My book club. We're all knitters."

"Camille St. Clair in a book club." He took a bite of his steak. "My, my. Will wonders never cease."

"Hey." She shoved him, just a little. "I have a brain. Just because you never noticed anything but my cheerleading uniform . . ."

"Is there going to be a pop quiz when I take you home?" he teased. "I might need to study." He leaned toward her. "And I might need a tutor."

He was smiling, but the intensity of his gaze meant he was completely serious too. At least he was completely serious about Camille.

She felt overwhelmed, as if the paneled walls of the café were pressing in on her. She reached for her water and took a sip. *He's just flirting,* she admonished herself. *Don't blow it out of proportion.*

But panic rose in her throat. Her body was sending her a message. *Be wary. Be cautious. Don't put yourself in a position to get hurt.* She knew, in that moment, that Dante Brown still had the potential to destroy her if she let him get too close.

Somehow she got through the rest of the meal. She prayed he wouldn't notice the change in her, and he didn't seem to catch on. When they'd finished eating, he paid the check. So many people wanted to talk to him that it took them several minutes to make their way to the door of the café. Camille ignored the speculative glances. They were good-natured and inquisitive rather than judgmental.

Outside, he offered to drive her home, but Camille declined. She pretended not to see the disappointment in his eyes. "I'll walk."

He shook his head. "It's too late for you to walk home alone. I'll go with you."

She looked at him, thought about his knee, and changed her mind. "On second thought, maybe you should just drop me off."

He started to say something, and then he seemed to change his mind too. "Come on, Cinderella. I'm not getting any younger."

She hadn't given much thought to the end of the evening until now, but all of a sudden the image of Dante standing beside her on the front porch loomed in her imagination. What if he tried to kiss her? Or, worse, what if he didn't?

They made the short trip in silence, Camille apprehensive and Dante apparently lost in thought. When he pulled into the driveway, she barely waited for him to stop the car before she opened the door and jumped out.

"You don't have to get out," she said, waving and backing away from the car. "Thanks again for dinner."

She practically ran up the front steps and, spotting the book she'd left on the porch swing earlier, grabbed it before reaching in her purse for her keys. Thank heavens he hadn't come up on the porch and seen her copy of *Romeo and Juliet*. He did sit in the driveway, though, until she'd unlocked the door and let herself safely inside. Only when she'd switched on the lamp by the door and turned off the porch light did she hear him drive away.

Camille looked down at the book in her hands.

Shakespeare knew all about doomed lovers. Camille tucked the book under her arm as she turned and mounted the stairs. She'd finish reading the play tonight, to remind herself of what she already knew.

Her feelings for Dante Brown had to be squashed before they seduced her into doing something incredibly foolish.

Eugenie resisted the urge to wait up for Hannah in the parsonage living room. Instead, she sat at the kitchen table, nursing a cup of herbal tea and working on her project for the next meeting of the Knit Lit Society. Her fingers maneuvered the yarn and needles automatically, her attention not really on her task. She was listening for the sound of footsteps on the porch, the slide of a key in the lock of the front door. She knew Hannah was safe enough with Josh Hargrove. Eugenie remembered him from when he was younger, before he had moved away. The boy had a good head on his shoulders, and she doubted that had changed.

"Still awake?" Paul's voice interrupted her thoughts. She looked up to see him standing in the kitchen doorway. He wore striped pajamas, and his hair was tousled from sleep.

"I want to make sure Hannah gets in okay."

Paul smiled. "I remember how Martha and I used to wait up for the kids. I don't know who has a tougher time during adolescence—parents or children." Paul's children with his late wife were now grown and had families of their own. "Want me to sit with you?"

Eugenie envied him his sangfroid. She knew she should probably go on to bed and quit worrying, but even though she was sixty-five years old, parenting was new to her, and she felt as green as a blade of spring grass.

"You go on back to bed." She smiled at her new husband. "Hannah should be home any time now."

He crossed the room and leaned over to plant a kiss on her cheek. "Wake me up if you need me." He tapped the end of her nose. "And don't worry. Hannah's just fine."

He headed back to bed, and Eugenie's attention returned to her knitting. A quarter of an hour later, she finally heard the sounds she'd been hoping for—the soft click of the deadbolt on the front door and footsteps in the foyer. Hannah was home.

"Eugenie?" The girl appeared in the kitchen doorway where Paul had stood a few minutes before. "I didn't know you were going to wait up." Hannah looked both pleased and skittish. The girl glanced at her watch. "It's not quite eleven yet."

"I wasn't worried about you missing your curfew." Eugenie folded her knitting and tucked it into the bag that sat at her feet. She smiled at Hannah, hoping to relieve the girl's worry. "I was just trying to finish up my project for the meeting." She nodded toward the chair next to her. "Are you hungry? Sit down and I'll fix you something."

Eugenie knew that her approach was hardly subtle, but she hoped Hannah would want to talk about her evening. Eugenie didn't know everything a parent was supposed to do, but she thought listening to a teenage girl talk about her date fell in the motherly concern category.

"I'm not hungry," Hannah said, but she did sit down. "Josh took me to the Dairy Dip for a hamburger after the game."

"Was it crowded?"

Hannah shrugged. "Sort of. A lot of kids went to parties instead."

Eugenie knew about the parties Sweetgum teenagers had been throwing for the last forty years. They usually involved a remote location, one or more kegs of beer, and some eventual consequences—usually legal or reproductive.

"Would you rather have gone to a party?" Eugenie felt compelled to ask.

Hannah shook her head. "Those kids aren't my crowd."

Eugenie wondered if Hannah even had a crowd. In the months since Hannah's mother had taken off and Eugenie had been appointed the girl's foster parent, she'd never heard Hannah mention a particular friend. Nor had the phone ever rung for her. It was as if the girl existed in a vacuum.

"How was the game?"

Hannah shrugged. "We won, but Josh didn't

seem very happy about it." And then the girl did the strangest thing. She blushed, bright as a poppy. Eugenie wanted to find out why but made herself bite her tongue. She thought of Shakespeare's Juliet, about the same age as the girl sitting beside her. The old bard had been wise enough to know that even the youngest heart could harbor deep feelings.

Eugenie glanced at the clock on the wall. "I think it's time for me to get some rest." She looked at Hannah once more. "Are you sure you don't need anything?"

The girl paused. "Thank you for waiting up." She looked away, not meeting Eugenie's eyes. "It's nice to . . . ," she faltered, ". . . well, to have someone who cares if I make it home okay."

Hannah's words knifed through Eugenie, but she forced herself to smile. "You'd better get to bed soon. Aren't you helping Camille at the dress shop tomorrow?"

Hannah wasn't an actual paid employee at Maxine's, but Camille had agreed a few months before to let the girl help out around the store in exchange for some clothes to supplement her meager wardrobe. And even though Eugenie and Paul could more than afford to buy Hannah whatever she needed, she thought it was good for the girl to have the satisfaction of working for a reward.

"I won't stay up much longer," Hannah replied.

"All right then. Good night." Eugenie wondered if she should pat the child or show some sort of affection, but she'd never been particularly demonstrative. She settled for smiling at her. "I'll see you in the morning."

Eugenie left the kitchen and headed for her bedroom. Perhaps she wasn't the most natural parent God had ever made, but surely she was an improvement over Hannah's mother, whose neglect would have an impact on the girl for years to come.

"Finally," Paul mumbled when Eugenie slipped into bed beside him. He drew her close to his side, and with a snort, settled back into slumber. Eugenie put her head on his shoulder, rested her hand on his chest, and exhaled pure happiness.

Given time, Hannah would find her way. Given time, anything was possible, even winning over the Hazel Emersons of the world. She knew it as surely as she could feel Paul's arms around her.

Eleven

Maria reached for the vase on the mantelpiece and carried it to Daphne, who sat on the sofa, carefully wrapping breakables in newspaper before placing them in the box at her feet. Their mother had retreated to her bedroom to sob in private, and the house had regained its Sunday afternoon peace.

Fall sunshine streamed through the living room windows as Maria and Daphne continued to cull through, pack, and grieve the family keepsakes.

"Couldn't we rent even a small storage space?" Daphne asked, her voice low.

Maria shook her head. Her resolve had to be firm or else she would crumble entirely. "We can't afford it."

"It can't be more than a hundred dollars a month," Daphne said, but her feeble protest wasn't meant to sway Maria so much as express her grief.

"I'm sorry—"

"It's not your fault." Daphne sighed and let the vase rest in her lap. "Why didn't Daddy tell us the truth?"

Maria shook her head. "I don't know."

She'd broken the news of the farm's sale at dinner the night before. Daphne had sat quietly, tears sliding down her cheeks. Daphne had managed the farm all these years under their father's direction. Their mother shrieked in hysterics until they convinced her to take a Xanax. Stephanie wanted to know if it meant she would have to share a room with one of her sisters when they moved to the small living quarters above the five-and-dime. Maria had soothed, reassured, and gritted her teeth. And then she'd told them that packing would begin the next morning. They had less than a week to vacate the house and turn over the keys.

The sound of tires crunching on the gravel drive outside caught both sisters' attention.

"Who is it?" Daphne asked. She was hemmed in on the couch by piles of books, pictures, and their mother's bric-a-brac.

Maria crossed to the window and peeked out. An unfamiliar black Mercedes had pulled up in front of the house. "I have no idea." Two men emerged from the car, and Maria's stomach knotted. "It's them."

"*Who* them?" Daphne moved objects aside so she could escape the couch and join her sister at the window.

"James Delevan and Evan Baxter."

"The men from the potluck?"

Maria turned to look at Daphne. "The new owner. And his henchman."

"Which is which?" Despite her distress, Daphne managed a small teasing smile.

"James is the henchman. Or lawyer, whichever you prefer."

Daphne reached out and rubbed her sister's shoulder. "You can't hold it against them, you know. It's business."

Maria twisted her mouth in a way that resembled a smile without actually being one. "You're entirely too nice."

"Well, one of us has to be." Daphne's teasing laugh soothed Maria's irritation.

"Then you should answer the door," Maria said.

"See what they want. They can't chuck us out until the end of the week."

"Maria—" The firm knock on the door interrupted whatever Daphne was about to say. "Never mind. I'll get it."

Maria looked around for something to be doing when the men entered the room. She grabbed a feather duster and applied it vigorously to the empty built-in shelves on one side of the fireplace. That was certainly something she knew how to do after all those years trapped in the five-and-dime.

Male voices rumbled in the foyer, and then Daphne entered the room with James and Evan in tow.

"Hello, Maria," Evan said in his usual good-natured manner. "I was apologizing to your sister for the intrusion." If he'd had a hat with him, it would have been in his hands. His gentle smile and self-deprecating manner were meant to ease the awkwardness of the situation. "James and I need to walk the property again, if it wouldn't be a problem."

Maria knew the real estate agent had shown them around more than once, along with a bevy of surveyors, but she hadn't been there to see them striding over every inch of her beloved farm, plotting to put up high-end lake cottages and a new marina and retail space. She'd made certain her mother and sister had been away from home during those times too. Now, though, there was no more need for secrecy. The deed was done.

"Of course. We're just packing," she added inanely, but it was all James Delevan's fault. Much as she tried to hide it, his presence discomposed her.

"Are you still staying at Sugar Hill?" Daphne asked with more politeness than Maria could muster.

"Off and on," Evan answered with a smile. "We're back and forth between here and Memphis."

James glanced at his watch. "We won't keep you—"

"Maria! Daphne! You didn't tell me we had guests."

Althea Munden swept into the room on a cloud of White Linen, and Maria suppressed a groan. "I thought you were resting, Mom."

"Not any longer." She smiled, but her fading southern charm, like her lipstick, was fuzzy around the edges. "Maria, aren't you going to introduce me?"

"Of course." She took a deep breath. "Mom, this is James Delevan and Evan Baxter. Evan is the new owner of the farm." Per her promise, she hadn't told her mother and sisters about the plans for development. The loss of their home was enough grief to deal with right now. As was the sudden darkening of her mother's face.

"Are you here to throw us out?" she snapped at the unsuspecting Evan. "Maria told me we had until the end of the week to pack."

Evan's expression clouded. "No ma'am. I mean, yes, you have until the end of the week, of course, and we would never dream of hurrying you."

Maria winced. That was exactly the wrong thing to say to her mother. She would wrangle every extra moment she could before surrendering possession of the house.

"They need to look the land over again," Maria said to cut the conversation short. She turned back to the men. "We won't keep you, of course."

But even as she said the words, she saw how Evan was looking at Daphne, as if he'd just hit the state lottery jackpot *and* been presented with a platter of prime rib. Maria hesitated, which turned out to be a mistake. Her mother had seen the expression on Evan's face as clearly as Maria had.

"Daphne? Why don't you show Evan whatever he needs to see?" Her mother turned to James. "And I'm sure Maria would be happy to escort you around. Have you seen her greenhouse? It's her pride and joy."

Maria couldn't fight the flush that rose in her cheeks. "Mom—"

"That would be great," Evan said before Maria could finish her protest. He turned to Daphne. "Do you have time?"

One look at her sister, her face shining as

brightly as Evan's, and Maria knew she would have to tough it out and endure a half hour of James Delevan's company.

"Maria?" Daphne asked, looking to her for agreement.

"Yes, we have time." She bit the inside of her cheek to keep from sighing in resignation before she turned to James. "If you want to follow me—"

She couldn't even finish the sentence, instead moving past him to the front door. She half expected him to refuse to go with her, but he surprised her by following close on her heels.

Although it was only mid-October, the leaves had already turned to brilliant orange and yellow. A bright blue sky, dotted with puffy white clouds, completed the perfect autumn picture. Maria almost resented the beautiful weather, its contrast to her turmoil was so great. Thunderstorms and lightning would have suited her mood much better.

She led James around the side of the house and past the kitchen garden to the greenhouse, happy for Daphne to bask in the glow of Evan's admiration but frustrated at being forced into James's company. And seriously put out about having to show him something as precious to her as the greenhouse.

"The agent didn't have the key when we were here before," James said as they approached the low-slung glass building.

"I must have forgotten to give it to her," Maria

said, although that wasn't exactly the truth. The agent hadn't asked for it, and Maria hadn't reminded her.

She produced a set of keys from her pocket, opened the door, and gestured for James to precede her. "Be my guest."

He quirked an eyebrow and then did as she indicated. Maria hesitated in the doorway. She didn't want to watch his reaction. Or, more honestly, she didn't want to be disappointed in his response to what he saw. After a deep breath, she followed him inside. He stood halfway down one of the two narrow aisles, carefully studying the rows and rows of herbs and aromatic plants.

"Who helps you with this?" he said, turning his head to look at her.

"Daphne, when she can."

He gave a long, low whistle. "Impressive. Not what I was expecting."

His response wasn't what she had been expecting either. She'd thought he would murmur a few platitudes and then dismiss her work as almost everyone else had done.

"Do you sell these to local nurseries?" he asked, his brown eyes serious. He wasn't simply humoring her but showing actual interest.

She shook her head. "I have a workroom in the barn for drying and mixing."

He reached for a roll of labels she'd left sitting on an open space between the rows of lavender and lemon verbena. "Three Sisters Botanicals?" he asked. "You make your own soaps and sell them?"

Maria flushed. "I ordered those on a whim. I'm not really in business or anything." She had asked her father several years ago if he would consider stocking her soaps, scrubs, and lotions in the five-and-dime. He'd all but patted her head and assured her that while her products were a nice hobby, good for Christmas presents and family use, she shouldn't consider it a serious endeavor. Better to learn the business and follow in his footsteps at the five-and-dime.

"What will you do with all of this when you move?" James asked. Concern showed in the lines around his eyes, and Maria turned away. The last thing she wanted—or could handle—was pity from James Delevan.

"I'm not doing anything with it. I guess it will be carted off like everything else before the development starts."

An uncomfortable silence hung in the air between them. She wished she hadn't shown him her grief, and he looked as uneasy as she felt. What was done was done, and for the right reason. No sense looking back or regretting.

"Where will you live?" he asked, not quite meeting her gaze.

"Above the five-and-dime."

"There's enough room?"

"Not really." She didn't say anything more.

"Can I see your workroom?"

She looked at him, surprised. "Yes." Not what she'd been expecting at all. "It's this way."

He followed her from the greenhouse, and she could feel his gaze boring into the back of her head. Well, at least she'd thrown him a curve ball. It felt good to return the favor.

He caught up to her as they walked toward the barn, his long stride outpacing her shorter one. He held the door for her as they entered the ramshackle building. She nodded her thanks and reached for the light switch.

"It's through here. Watch your step."

The room was just inside, to the right. A corner of the barn had been partitioned off to provide her with a work area. Long planks propped on sawhorses served as workbenches. The shelves above were lined with the product of her labor, an endless stream of soap wrapped in paper, scrubs in their small jars, and pump dispensers filled with lotion.

"You've got enough stock here to open your own store."

That had been the idea, of course, but she refused to tell James about it. "Maybe."

"You've never thought of selling these at the five-and-dime?"

"No." No need to elaborate. Just lie.

"What about here at the lake? In the retail space we're developing? Resort clientele would be ideal—"

He was trying to be nice, but he might as well have driven a stake through her heart.

"It will be all I can do to keep the five-and-dime afloat," she said and then wished she hadn't.

He shrugged. "Just a suggestion."

Maria bit her lip. She didn't need to explain herself to him, of all people, but she felt a strange compulsion to tell him the truth. That her life had never been her own and it never would be. That along with the farm, his friend Evan was buying what hope she'd had left in her dreams.

"What did you really want to see?" she asked. Her question sounded harsher than she'd intended, but she didn't try to soften it.

James gave her a long look. "The shoreline, if you don't mind walking down there with me."

Maria nodded. "No problem."

But it was a problem. Any time spent in the company of James Delevan was excruciating. Like this tour of the greenhouse and the workroom, he made her long for what she could never have.

"This way," she said and hurried out of the room.

Twelve

Merry arrived at the October meeting of the Sweetgum Knit Lit Society encumbered only by her purse and her knitting book. Jeff had offered to keep Hunter at home. Out of guilt, Merry suspected. She'd left a casserole in the oven and Courtney in charge of getting dinner on the table. With any luck, Jeff would have the younger ones in bed by the time she got home.

Eugenie, as always, was already in the classroom when Merry arrived.

"Good evening, Eugenie. How are you?"

"Well, thank you." Eugenie looked past Merry, as if expecting someone to appear in the doorway behind her. "Where's the baby?"

"Jeff's giving me the night off."

"That's nice of him."

Merry half smiled, half grimaced. "It's the least he can do right now."

"Everything all right?" Genuine concern showed in Eugenie's eyes. Merry had confided a little about their financial straits to Eugenie without going into too much detail.

"Jeff wants me to work full time at the law office."

"I thought you were already helping out."

"Just mornings."

"What will you do with Hunter?"

Merry felt tears spring to her eyes.

Eugenie frowned in sympathy. "I see. Big changes, hmm?"

"I wish I could do both. Help Jeff out as much as he needs and be with Hunter."

"You couldn't take the baby with you to Jeff's office all day?"

Merry shook her head. "Not for much longer.

He'll start crawling soon. That wouldn't be fair to Jeff or Hunter."

"Or you," Eugenie observed.

Merry let out a small laugh. "I'm not sure I even factor into this equation."

Eugenie shook her head. "But you do. You're the equal sign, trying to make both sides of the equation balance."

Now Merry laughed for real. "That's exactly how I feel. As if I have to somehow find the perfect formula to make it all work."

More members of the Knit Lit Society appeared in the doorway, interrupting the conversation.

"Good evening, Maria. Camille." Merry greeted the others. Esther followed close behind them.

"We're just waiting on Hannah," Eugenie said. She glanced at her watch.

Merry hid a smile. Poor Eugenie, who'd never had children, taking on a teenager out of the blue. It had to be a shock to the system.

"She's probably with Josh Hargrove," Camille said, her face alight with mischief. "They've been hanging out a lot lately. Dante says Josh has the potential to play professional ball."

"He's a good kid," Merry assured Eugenie, even as she hid her curiosity about Camille and the new football coach. The word around town was that they'd had dinner at Tallulah's after the football game two weeks ago, but she hadn't heard much since.

As if on cue, Hannah came running into the room. "Sorry," she said to Eugenie, gasping for breath as she collapsed into her chair. Eugenie looked as if she might scold her but then thought better of it.

"Perhaps we should get started," Eugenie said. "I know you all have a lot to say about *Romeo and Juliet*."

Merry thought the librarian was being pretty optimistic. Rather than read the play, she'd rented a performance on DVD. Shakespeare's language never made sense to her on the page, but when an actor spoke the lines, giving them the proper inflection, she could almost get the gist of it.

"So," Eugenie said. "What struck you most about the play?"

Everyone was quiet, intently focused as they unpacked their needles and yarn and began to knit.

"Did you all read it?" Eugenie asked with quiet patience and only the slightest hint of exasperation.

"Of course," Esther said, "but I have to be honest, Eugenie. I've always thought this Romeo and Juliet business was a bunch of nonsense. Star-crossed love is a sentimental indulgence." Esther's face had a pinched look to it, which was hardly unexpected under the circumstances. Merry had heard through the grapevine that Frank Jackson had not left his widow in good financial shape. People in Sweetgum were polite enough not to mention it to Esther's face but not good enough to refrain from gossiping about it.

Eugenie nodded, not in agreement but in acknowledgment of Esther's opinion. "What about the rest of you? Do you think Romeo and Juliet were self-indulgent?"

Camille set her knitting on the table. "I think you can't let your feelings run away with you. Even if you'd like to let them. You have to keep things in perspective. Keep your goals in mind."

Hannah flipped her copy of the book onto the table in front of her. "Shakespeare had it right. It had to end badly."

"Why is that?" Eugenie asked.

"Two people from different groups trying to get together. Cliques are there for a reason."

Maria shook her head. "There's no such thing as true social division. Not really. I mean, I know some people think they're better than others, but we're all the same at heart." She stopped and then flushed, obviously embarrassed at her own vehemence, and returned her attention to her yarn and needles.

"Other people's interference doomed them in the end," Merry said to divert attention from Maria. "All those people carrying messages that didn't get there in time. If Romeo and Juliet had just been left alone, they probably would've gotten married, had some kids, and turned into a boring old couple who finished each other's sentences." She laughed. "That doesn't sound nearly as romantic, does it?"

"Romance is highly overrated," Camille said, and Esther nodded in agreement. Their emphatic dismissal saddened Merry. She wanted everyone to find their happily-ever-after as she had with Jeff, even if there were sometimes big bumps in the road, like the day care issue. Though if she were honest with herself, some of her reluctance to work full time came from what she knew other people would say about Hunter being in day care. The group of moms who had been her mainstay since Courtney was a baby would look at her like she was Abraham about to sacrifice Isaac on the stone altar.

These women e-mailed one another articles about the evils of warehousing children in day care. Many of them had their children in the Mother's Day Out program at the church, but in their minds, nine o'clock until two in the afternoon didn't count as day care, not when it was only two or three days a week. It gave them enough time to play some tennis at the country club, do their shopping, and maybe have lunch with friends without feeling as if they were depriving their children. But the moms who used the extended care hours were a different breed entirely, and Merry was about to cross that great divide. A traitor to the sanctity of motherhood, a—

Okay, it wasn't that bad. Most of her friends would understand. Only a very few would be as judgmental as she feared, and they weren't people whose opinions she valued. Still, she dreaded the whispers and the sidelong looks. Or maybe her concern about other people's opinions was just a smoke screen to keep her from focusing on the real issue—how incredibly difficult it would be to drop Hunter off at the church each morning and know she wouldn't see him again until dinnertime.

"So what projects did you come up with?" Eugenie asked, breaking into Merry's reverie and deftly turning the disagreement to a more productive vein. "I thought that limiting ourselves to garter stitch might stimulate us creatively."

"I'm afraid I wasn't very original," Merry said, opting to go first. "Just a shawl." She reached into her bag and retrieved the dark blue garment, laid it out on the table in front of her. "I thought it might suit the Nurse character. Sturdy. No-nonsense, kind of like her."

Eugenie nodded her approval, which always made Merry feel like she'd accomplished something. "Other projects?" the librarian asked. "Camille?"

"I did a little cap. For Juliet." The sparkly pink yarn didn't look particularly Shakespearean, but Merry could see Camille wearing the small hat come wintertime.

"Very nice." Again, Eugenie nodded in approval. "Esther?"

Esther shook her head. "I'm sorry, Eugenie. I wasn't able to finish mine."

147

Merry hated seeing Esther look so pinched and pale. She hoped Eugenie would go easy on the new widow.

"I know you've had a lot on your plate," Eugenie said, and Merry relaxed a little. The librarian's recent marriage had definitely softened her a bit. "Maria?" Eugenie asked, diverting everyone's attention to the newest member of the group.

"I made a pillow, scented with lavender. For Romeo, I guess. To give him sweet dreams about Juliet."

Hannah snorted, but Eugenie silenced her with a look. Merry watched with interest as Maria blushed like a schoolgirl. Who would have known that beneath the guise of a thirtysomething spinster beat the heart of a romantic?

The pillow was pale blue. Merry reached out to run her fingers over the soft wool. "It's lovely, Maria. Very impressive."

"Thank you." She shot Merry a grateful look.

"Hannah, why don't you show yours?" Eugenie prompted. Merry watched with interest as the girl pulled a bundle of deep red wool out of her bag.

"It's no big deal," the girl began, but Eugenie interrupted her.

"I think it's quite accomplished. You should put it on, to give the full effect."

Hannah looked like she'd rather eat dirt, but she complied with Eugenie's request. She whipped the garment about her shoulders. It was a little elbow-length capelet, at once charming and sensuous. Much like Juliet herself, Merry thought. The color suited Hannah very well.

"You worked very hard on it," Eugenie said. "And your effort paid off. I'm very proud of you."

The girl blushed to the roots of her hair, but Merry could tell she was pleased by the librarian's approval.

"What about you, Eugenie?" Merry asked. "What's your project?" No doubt the librarian had read the play forward, backward, and sideways. She was sure to have found the perfect project for *Romeo and Juliet*.

"Actually . . ." Eugenie paused and cleared her throat. "Actually, I'm not quite finished with mine."

A dead silence fell on the group. Merry suppressed a chuckle. In all the time the Knit Lit Society had been meeting, she'd never known Eugenie not to be fully prepared. Sometimes she even had more than one project ready to display.

"Time seems to have gotten away from me this month," the librarian said, not quite looking any of them in the eye. Merry looked around the group and realized she wasn't the only one holding back a smile.

"After all the times the rest of us haven't finished by the meeting," Merry said, hoping to relieve Eugenie's embarrassment, "I'm sure you're due a free pass."

Eugenie flashed Merry a grateful look. "Now, for next month, I thought I'd be a bit more specific about the project." She laid both hands on the table in front of her. "For the Song of Solomon, I thought we'd use the purl stitch to make something for someone we love." She paused. "Not necessarily love in a romantic way, of course."

Merry heard more than one sigh of relief. While she and Eugenie, as the married ladies in the group, should theoretically have their love lives sorted out, the rest of the group was definitely in flux.

"Is that agreeable?" Eugenie asked, but Merry knew that none of the others would take exception to her assignment. "Good, then. Very well done, everyone."

As they gathered up their things and made their way out of the church, Merry paused by the hallway that led to the children's education wing where the Mother's Day Out program was housed. She stared down the darkened hallway, worry and fear fighting for equal share of her attention.

Hunter was so small and defenseless. But this was their church, and if she was going to trust anyone to care for him, it would be the people that gathered here.

With a small sigh, Merry hoisted her tote bag higher on her shoulder and headed out into the night.

Thirteen

Early in November, Eugenie opened the Bible that lay on the counter in front of her. From her position behind the high-fronted checkout desk, she could keep an eye on the entire library. At the moment, the only patrons were the ever-present Hornbuckles, an elderly couple who were deaf as posts. Taking advantage of the rare moment of inactivity, Eugenie flipped through the Bible's pages until she found what she was looking for. The Song of Solomon.

The selection had seemed obvious when she'd been making her book list for the year. It was perhaps the oldest love story in Western literature. And although in the Christian tradition the book had mostly been interpreted as an allegory for the relationship of Christ to the church, Eugenie took the older perspective and viewed it as a celebration of God's gift of romantic love. At least, she did since Paul had come back into her life.

Eugenie skimmed the lines of ancient poetry she hadn't read in years, but as she progressed through the book, her cheeks began to suffuse with color.

Let him kiss me with the kisses of his mouth!
For your love is better than wine.

Had Song of Solomon always been this sensuous? She shifted uncomfortably on the stool and then glanced up and over each shoulder. Those authors of bodice-ripping romance novels had nothing on King Solomon.

Ah, you are beautiful, my beloved,
    truly lovely.
Our couch is green.

As she continued to read, embarrassment gave way to bemusement and then, quite suddenly, she was mesmerized. What she felt for Paul was nothing new. The relationship between a man and a woman was a wonderful, amazing thing, celebrated throughout the centuries. But to see that sensual, almost mystical connection here, between the covers of her Bible, was unexpected. And disturbing. And exhilarating.

She was so lost in her reading that she barely registered the *whoosh* of the library's front door opening to admit a patron. She looked up to see Hazel Emerson marching toward her. Eugenie forced a smile.

"Good morning, Hazel." Whatever Hazel wanted, it had nothing to do with broadening her mind. Sharpening her claws, more like. Eugenie had spent the past six weeks bending over backward to please Hazel and her ilk. Standing beside Paul in the receiving line after church. Visiting shut-ins. Even volunteering to serve on the board of the Mother's Day Out program. The requests for her participation, though, rather than slacking off, had actually picked up. The more she did, the more people found for her to do.

"Eugenie. I was hoping I'd find you here," Hazel said. She wore a fur jacket that was too heavy for the mild November day.

Eugenie swallowed the urge to make a sarcastic reply. Instead, she spread her hands to indicate her surroundings. "My natural habitat. What can I do for you, Hazel? Did you need to use the reference section?" She couldn't resist the last remark.

"Oh, goodness no. I wanted to talk to you about the women's auxiliary again. We still haven't seen you at a meeting."

"I know." Eugenie steeled herself to be patient for Paul's sake. She had to remember why she was volunteering for all these church activities. "But as I said before, I really can't get away during the day."

Hazel pursed her lips. "As the pastor's wife, you're expected to take a leadership role in the auxiliary."

Eugenie knew there was no point in arguing, but she wasn't going to agree to Hazel's request either.

"I'm afraid that's not possible," Eugenie said.

Hazel pursed her lips more firmly. "I would reconsider if I were you."

Eugenie shook her head. "I'm sorry, Hazel." She

didn't offer any further explanation, just let silence fall, which was easy to do in a library. Paul had warned her that she was like a popular college freshman during sorority rush. "Everyone will want you to get involved with their pet project," he had said. "As far as I'm concerned, you can pick and choose. The church is paying me, not you."

Which was kind of him, Eugenie thought, but also not completely realistic. The tradition of the highly involved pastor's wife was too deeply ingrained in southern culture to discount quite so easily. But she hadn't expected to find herself in over her head so quickly.

Hazel crossed her arms over her chest, her pocketbook dangling from one elbow. "I would think you'd want to support your new husband as much as possible." She cast a dismissive glance around the library. "I hardly think your little job here is worth the sacrifice of your husband's ministry."

Eugenie felt her cheeks redden. "Paul understands the importance of my work."

The other woman's eyes flashed. "So you won't even consider coming to the meeting?"

"I don't really have a choice, Hazel. It's no reflection on what is, I'm sure, a very fine group of Christian women." She resisted the urge to cross her fingers behind the height of the checkout counter.

"The steering committee won't be happy about this."

"I'm sorry to hear that. Please do give them my regrets." Eugenie picked up a stack of books from the counter in front of her. "Now, if you'll excuse me, I need to catalog these new arrivals." As a dismissal it wasn't very subtle, but it was the only thing she could think of.

Hazel glanced at her watch. "I need to be going anyway. I have an appointment at the beauty salon."

"Have a lovely day," Eugenie said in her friendliest voice, but inwardly she seethed. What right did someone like Hazel Emerson think she had to come in and start telling Eugenie how to manage her life? Was this just a glimpse of her future as a minister's wife? The thought depressed her.

"Good-bye, Eugenie," Hazel snapped before stomping out the door.

After she'd gone, Eugenie did catalog the new books, but she also started to worry. People like Hazel could make life miserable for Paul if Eugenie didn't do as they expected. She'd been forced to humor and placate the city council for the last thirty years in order to achieve her goals for the library. The pressure on Paul, as a minister, to keep people happy must be even greater than what she had experienced. How to strike the right balance though? That was the question—one she spent the rest of the day pondering.

Camille sat on the stool behind the counter at the dress shop. Through the large plate-glass windows, she watched shoppers passing up and down the street. Most of them she recognized, although there were a few unfamiliar faces—lake people or folks from around the county who came into Sweetgum to shop. Of the people she knew, very few stopped in to see her.

Although she was only twenty-four, Camille had been running her mother's shop since she was nineteen. She was savvy enough about the business to know that slow sales in early November did not bode well for the holiday season. She doodled on the pad of paper next to the register, trying to come up with an idea for a spectacular advertising campaign in the local newspaper that would turn the sales slump around. She'd pit her management skills against anyone, but marketing was not her strength.

Underneath the pad of paper was the course catalog for Middle Tennessee State that had arrived in the mail that morning. She should call and tell them to take her off the mailing list; she was only tormenting herself. She'd thought that once her mother was gone, she would finally be free to leave Sweetgum and pursue the future she'd always dreamed of. That dream had been the one thing that kept her head above water during the upheavals of the last five years, but her plan had depended on finding someone to buy the dress shop, and given its current financial state, who would throw their money away like that?

Camille slid the pad to the side and flipped open the catalog. If she could go to college, what kind of classes would she take first? She enjoyed fashion and looked forward to her modest buying trips to Atlanta twice a year. But maybe she'd rather try something new—computers or engineering or fine arts. Anything, really, if it got her out of Sweetgum.

After a long, silent morning, the bell above the door rang.

She looked up, thankful for the first customer of the day, and saw Dante. He wore a shirt and tie and looked far more enticing than he had a right to. She felt a strange fluttering in the region of her heart and tightly curled the fingers of one hand in protest. She was determined not to let him get to her.

"Afternoon, Dante." She came around the counter and stopped beside one of the clothing stands. She put a hand on a rack in a nonchalant pose, but really it was to steady herself.

"I thought I'd drop in and renew my invitation. I'll make reservations at the Watermark."

She shook her head. "I can't."

"Can't or won't?"

"Dante—"

"C'mon, Camille." He stepped closer, and she gripped the rack more firmly. He was like a magnet, always drawing her closer even as she fought against it. "We'd have a great time," he said, tempting her. "And you need to get out of Sweetgum, at least for a little while."

Truer words had rarely been spoken, she thought glumly. But was an evening's liberation worth the risk of his company?

Her hesitation encouraged him. "We could drive up early in the afternoon. See a movie first. I'll even take you to a chick flick."

She smiled in spite of herself. "My choice?"

His face tightened in a pained expression. "Yeah. Your choice."

She was sorely tempted. "I don't know."

He looked so delighted at her hesitation that she would have thought she'd already agreed. "I'll take that for a yes."

"Dante, you can't just—"

"Camille, I learned a long time ago that with you no means no. But hesitation means you can be persuaded." He smiled and her willpower softened in proportion to its charm.

"When did you learn I was so persuadable?"

His expression grew serious. "When you almost agreed to go to the prom with me."

"When did I do that?" But the moment she asked the question, the memory came tumbling back.

He'd cornered her coming out of the girls' bathroom a week before the senior prom and asked her, probably for the tenth time, to be his date. She'd wanted to agree so badly, and she'd had such a horrible day. At that moment, she'd have liked nothing more than to grab him, tell him to put his arms around her, and bury her head against his broad shoulder. He seemed to promise security and comfort. But then Natalie and Cody had walked by and called out some teasing remark about how Dante was finally going to get lucky, and she'd withdrawn, packing her emotions back into their deep freeze, and turned his invitation down flat.

She looked at him now, a little older, definitely a man and not a boy, and she had the same urge to cling to him for strength and support.

"I'm not asking for anything big, Camille. Just an evening of your company."

"Okay." What? Had she lost her mind?

"Okay?" His smile was as wide as his chest. He pounded one hand with the other. "All right. I'll pick you up at one o'clock on Saturday."

"Not this Saturday, Dante."

"Then the next one."

She shook her head. "I can't."

"Then the one after."

Camille nodded, the adrenaline rushing through her veins at odds with her outward calm. "The one after," she agreed.

He turned and hustled for the door.

"Dante? Where are you going?" Camille felt a knot form in her stomach. She didn't want him to leave.

He looked back, laughter in his eyes. "I'm getting out of here before you can change your mind."

And then he was gone, and Camille was laughing too. It felt good, though she was out of practice. Maybe it was okay to hope. To trust Dante just a little and take a risk. Even if she did feel as if she'd agreed to jump out of a plane without a parachute.

Maybe things might work out for her after all. Even if she was still stuck in Sweetgum.

Fourteen

Maria and Daphne clambered down the stairs from their rooms above the five-and-dime, as eager and excited as schoolgirls. They rarely left their mother home alone, especially since their move. Stephanie hardly ever spent an evening under their own roof, which meant the two older sisters had very little social life.

Tonight, though, was a rare exception. Stephanie had caught a cold and was at home for once, being pampered by their mother. The irony of Althea doting on the daughter who ignored her was not lost on Maria, but rather than hold on to resentment, she chose to relish the unexpected night of freedom.

She and Daphne planned to eat dinner at Tallulah's Café and then catch a romantic comedy at the movie theater. The sisters laughed as they made their way down the street to the café, clutching their well-worn coats around them against the sharp November wind.

"Well, if it isn't the Munden girls." Tallulah greeted them with a bright smile and a glint in her eye. "You all look as lovely as ever."

Maria laughed. "Tallulah, no wonder this place is always packed, the way you sweet-talk everyone."

The older woman winked at her. "Whatever works."

The three women were still laughing as Tallulah led Maria and Daphne to their table. "You all enjoy," the café owner said before moving away.

For the first time since her father's death, Maria's heart felt like it might one day lighten again. Until she looked to her right and saw the two men seated at the table next to them.

James Delevan and Evan Baxter.

"Ladies. Good evening." Evan greeted them with enough enthusiasm to make Daphne's cheeks pink. James looked perturbed, as if they'd come to the café for the purpose of annoying him.

Daphne, though quiet, spoke to Evan with charm and warmth while Maria sat and tried not to look as if she were sulking. James eventually nodded to her, and she replied with a strained smile.

"You should join us," Evan said as he motioned to the two empty chairs at their four-top table.

Daphne looked as if she'd just been offered a winning lottery ticket. "If you're sure . . ."

"Certainly." James stood and motioned for them to move over. "We haven't ordered yet."

Maria moved stiffly as she bemoaned her bad luck. One night to enjoy herself. That was all she'd hoped for.

"Do you ladies have big plans tonight?" Evan motioned for their waitress.

"Not really," Daphne demurred. "Just dinner here and a movie across the street. That's about as exciting as Sweetgum gets, I'm afraid."

"Sounds good to me," Evan said. "I needed a break from the city."

"Is that why you bought our farm?" Daphne asked.

Maria bit her lip and looked away. Per their agreement, she still hadn't said a word to anyone about the plans for the lakeside development.

"Partially," Evan said. His face clouded a bit, and Maria could tell he was trying to answer Daphne's question as honestly as he could. "I wanted a retreat from Memphis, and I was looking for a good investment."

Fortunately, the waitress arrived with their dinner salads, and the conversation fell into a lull. The salads were the typical southern concession to the genre—some iceberg lettuce topped with a cherry tomato, a slice of cucumber, and a few sprinkles of heavily processed American cheese. Evan dug in to his salad with the same enthusiasm he seemed to have for everything in life. Daphne delicately approached hers. Maria watched as James eyed the bowl in front of him. Dubious. His expression was definitely dubious.

"That's the closest you'll get to health food at Tallulah's," Maria said with a straight face.

"I figured that," James said. "Especially when I saw macaroni and cheese listed as a vegetable on the menu."

Maria chuckled, but she covered up her amusement by stabbing a large piece of lettuce with her fork and munching on it.

"Would you like to join us at the movie?" Daphne asked Evan and James out of the blue.

Maria wanted to kick her under the table, but she refrained. From where they sat, they could see out the window and directly across the street to the theater's marquee. The only movie showing was clearly a girlie one. Maria knew the men would decline.

"That would be great," Evan said, smiling like an idiot at Daphne.

Maria and James exchanged a mutual look of disappointment, and then realizing what they'd just done, shared a guilty smile. At that unexpected moment of camaraderie, Maria's stomach tightened, not leaving much room for the iceberg lettuce that resided there.

"Daphne, they may have other plans," she chided her sister, hoping to reverse the disastrous course her sister was setting them on. While Evan Baxter was a laid-back, unaffected guy, she doubted he saw Daphne as anything other than a pleasant diversion for the evening. She worried his attention might get her sister's hopes up. Almost as much as she dreaded spending the rest of the evening as James's pseudodate.

A few moments later, their entrées arrived. Between eating and Evan's easy management of the conversation, Maria found the experience of dining with the two men far less trying than she would have imagined. James Delevan even turned out to have a sense of humor, telling a couple of amusing stories about his life in Memphis and his travels abroad.

The movie proved a little more awkward. The men had insisted on paying for dinner, but when the four of them stepped up to the box office, Maria was determined that she and Daphne would pay their own way. Here, though, James's arrogance once again asserted itself. He thrust his credit card through the opening in the box office window, and Maria could do nothing but stand on the sidewalk and seethe. What was worse, she refused popcorn and candy at the concession stand, two of her favorite indulgences, rather than be further indebted to him.

"Sure you don't want something?" James asked as they moved away from the concession counter and toward the doors into the theater. He popped a couple of Milk Duds into his mouth,

164

and Maria could feel her own mouth starting to water.

"No. I'm fine." Maybe she could sneak out in the middle of the movie and snag some candy. And pay for it with her own money.

He shrugged. "Suit yourself."

They were two steps from the door when James stopped abruptly and grabbed his jaw.

"You okay?" Evan asked.

James shook his head. He turned away, and at that moment Maria realized what had happened.

"Did you lose a tooth?"

James shook his head, more to ward off her questions than in response. "I'm fine." The words came out garbled.

"You're going to need a dentist." Despite how much he annoyed her, she felt sorry for him. He continued to hold his jaw and wince.

"Is it broken?"

He shook his head. "I just lost a crown."

He faced her now, and the look of misery in his eyes overrode her common sense. "I can call Dr. Baker and see if he'll meet us at his office."

James looked horrified, and she could only guess that his expression came from the thought of letting a country dentist get hold of him.

"Really, that's not—" He stopped, winced in pain, and grabbed his jaw again.

"I think it's completely necessary." Maria dug in her purse for her cell phone.

Evan nodded his agreement. "But I can take him, Maria. You don't want to miss the movie." Even as he made the offer, though, Maria could see his disappointment. He cast a longing glance at Daphne, and then his ears turned pink when he saw that Maria had caught his look.

Maria knew what she had to do. The happiness of her sister was worth putting up with James Delevan. "You don't know where Dr. Baker's office is," she said to Evan. "If you wouldn't mind keeping Daphne company for the movie, I'll take James."

James scowled. "I can make it to the dentist on my own."

Maria decided there was no point arguing with him. She flipped through the contact numbers on her phone until she found Dr. Baker's home number and pressed the green button to dial it. In a few short minutes, she'd arranged for an emergency office visit.

"You two go on to the movie," she said to Daphne and Evan. "If you'll see Daphne home, Evan, I'll bring James back to Sugar Hill when we're done."

She didn't wait for anyone to agree. Instead, she put her hand on James's arm and gently led him away. The pain must have increased, because he didn't protest.

Evan and Daphne called their good nights, and Daphne shot Maria a quick, happy smile of thanks. Maria wanted to smile herself, but she refrained.

She didn't want James to say anything to spoil Daphne's enjoyment of the evening. Better to play it cool. Draw his attention away from Daphne and Evan.

"My car's behind the five-and-dime," she said as they exited the movie theater. They always parked behind the store, in the small gravel lot. "It would almost be quicker to walk to Doc Baker's office, but we'll need the car afterward to get you home."

"Fine," he mumbled, and despite herself, Maria felt some sympathy for the man. He was clearly in a lot of pain.

In less than ten minutes, they had walked to the car and then driven to the dentist's office. The small brick building sat a few blocks north of the town square, not far from the tiny hospital. The lights were on, which meant Dr. Baker had already arrived.

The dentist greeted them at the door and immediately ushered James into a treatment room. Maria plopped into a chair in the waiting room, picked up a magazine, and idly leafed through the pages. She could hear Doc Baker talking to James, who could only grunt and moan in reply.

"You'll just feel a pinch," the dentist said, and she envisioned the silver-haired doctor holding the syringe with its long needle behind his back. He was very good at never letting you see what he was about to stick you with, one of the things Maria appreciated most about him.

The anesthetic must have worked, because she didn't hear James groan anymore after that. Instead she heard a one-sided conversation that made her blush clear to the roots of her hair.

"Maria Munden's a nice girl," the doctor said, his words interspersed with the whine of a drill. "Couldn't do better. Except for Daphne, of course."

James grunted a wordless reply, which could have meant anything from "I agree" to "You're an interfering busybody."

"Shame about Tom Munden. And losing their home. But maybe it will be good for them. Time for a fresh start."

James's unintelligible grunt this time was clearly a question.

"You didn't know about their father? No one saw that coming. Maria will take care of them though. She's got too much of her father in her to let her family down."

Now Maria flushed with both embarrassment and pride. She'd forgotten what a gossip Dr. Baker was, but she was also flattered to be compared to her father.

"Don't know why the young men around here didn't snap up those Munden girls long ago." Okay, definitely embarrassment again. Maria leafed through the magazine in vain in an attempt to distract herself. "Some folks say they're too particular. I say they just haven't found the right fellows."

Maria wanted to throw down the magazine, run into the treatment room, and drag James Delevan away from Dr. Baker, but all she could do was sit, listen, and hope he would change the subject. Fortunately, he soon did. The rest of the time he worked on James, the dentist kept up a running commentary on the town's excitement at having Dante Brown back to coach the high school football team. Finally, Dr. Baker finished and the two men emerged into the waiting room.

"All done," Doc Baker said, slapping James on the back hard enough to make him wince. "Told him he's too old for Milk Duds. Better stick to Junior Mints after this." He handed Maria a small square of paper. "Here's a prescription for some pain medicine. I can call Hank to come open the pharmacy if you'd like."

James raised a hand. "Not necessary. I'll be fine."

The dentist shrugged. "Suit yourself."

"Thank you, Dr. Baker. We appreciate it." Maria hesitated. "Should James call the office in the morning about settling the bill?"

Dr. Baker winked at her. "This one's on me. Just call me Dr. Cupid."

Maria wished that the floor would open up and swallow her, and James looked like he was thinking the same thing. He reached for his back pocket and drew out his wallet, but Dr. Baker waved his hand.

"No sir, young man. No need." He nodded toward Maria. "Save your money to spend on this young lady."

Could she be any more humiliated? Probably. Which meant she'd be better served by hustling James out of the waiting room and back to Sugar Hill rather than standing and arguing with Dr. Baker about payment. Thankfully, James seemed to be of the same mind. They said their good nights to the doctor and headed for her car.

They were on their way out of Sweetgum toward Sugar Hill before either of them spoke. Maria hated the awkward silence, but she had no idea what to say to James Delevan that wouldn't further demean her in his eyes.

"Thank you," he said as she turned off the highway onto the long driveway that led to the Sugar Hill Bed-and-Breakfast. "You didn't have to do that." He slurred his words a bit, which made him seem more human.

"It was no problem."

"I'm sorry you missed your movie."

She shrugged. "There'll be others." When, she had no idea, but she wasn't going to let her disappointment show. Her happiness for her sister would make up for it. "I'm sorry about Dr. Baker," she replied. "I forgot to warn you he's a bit of a gossip."

"A bit?" James answered, but he was smiling. "He's better than the *National Enquirer.*"

Maria had to chuckle. "You're right. But he's a good man. And a good dentist." She paused. "Are you sure you'll be all right, painwise? I can still get your prescription filled if you've changed your mind." She steered the car onto the broad sweep of gravel in front of the B&B. From its position at the top of the hill, she could see the distant lights of the marina and, farther to the east, lights from the town.

"Thanks, but I'll be fine." He hesitated, his hand on the car door latch. Then he turned toward her, his expression serious. "You surprised me."

"I was just being a good neighbor. Or a good host, I guess you'd say, since you're just visiting Sweetgum."

He shook his head. "You could have left me on my own, and I'd have been okay." He paused. "But you didn't. Thanks."

What could she possibly say in reply? Any time? Frankly, she hoped this was the last time she'd ever have to be in his company. He was too arrogant, too handsome, and too comp—

She broke off the thought, because what she'd been about to acknowledge, even if it was just to herself, was that he was the most compelling man she'd ever met.

"I'm glad your tooth's all right," she said, unable to think of anything else.

"Maria—" He leaned toward her, and against her better judgment, she felt herself sway his direction in response. His dark eyes had gone even darker, and he looked like a man about to—

She caught herself just in time. She jerked back, straightened her spine, and placed both hands firmly on the steering wheel.

"I'd better get back to town." Her interruption was deliberate and born of sheer panic. "Before my mom gets worried."

His head snapped back, and he opened the car door abruptly. "You seem a little old for a curfew."

She could see he was angry. No doubt James Delevan didn't get shot down very often. Not that she had shot him down exactly, but he had been about to—

Before she could complete the thought, he unfolded his long-limbed body from the car and leaned down to deliver his parting salvo. "Good night, Maria." The words were coldly formal.

"Good night." She might be on the wrong side of thirty, but she sounded like a breathless teenager.

He turned and strode away, and she sat for a moment, watching him, until she realized with a start that he would know she was watching him. She reached for the key and turned the ignition. With hands trembling far too much for her liking, she set the car in motion and drove away.

She would not, could not, absolutely refused to be attracted to James Delevan. Thank heavens he would be gone from Sweetgum again soon, although no doubt he'd be back from time to time as the lakefront development moved forward.

She drove home in the darkness, acutely aware of how alone she was and deeply troubled by how much it bothered her.

Fifteen

On the second Monday in November, Merry pulled her minivan into a parking space at the back of the church.

"Here we are, Hunter," she said to the baby strapped into his seat in the rear. She kept her voice cheery, but her heart was as heavy as Hunter's overstuffed diaper bag. She'd been able to postpone this day for a few weeks, but now the time had come. Merry climbed out of the van and opened the rear door. Hunter smiled up at her and waved his fists in the air before putting one in his mouth to chew on.

"That tooth will be through soon," she assured her son, knowing that her tone would soothe him even if he didn't understand a word of what she said. She'd given him some baby pain reliever before they'd left the house because she didn't want his first day at child care to be associated with teething discomfort.

"Merry!" a voice called. She unbuckled Hunter and pulled him out of his seat before turning to see who it was. Thankfully, the woman coming toward her was friend and not foe. Merry wondered, though, what Eugenie was doing at the church at this hour of the morning.

"Eugenie. How are you?"

"Very well, thank you. Is this Hunter's first day?" The other woman shot Merry an unexpected smile of understanding.

"I think he's excited. Or he will be. I'm the one who's traumatized."

Eugenie nodded. "He'll be fine. And you will be too. Just give it time."

Merry blinked back tears. "Thanks. I knew it would be difficult, but—"

"You'd rather be boiled in oil?"

"Yes." Merry had to laugh a little at Eugenie's words.

"I'm sure your reluctance is normal. Keep that in mind."

Eugenie's support meant the world to Merry. The two women walked into the church together through the preschool entrance. At this early hour, all of the children and parents were the full-day ones. Although Merry recognized a lot of them, it wasn't her usual crowd.

"I'm surprised to see you at the church this early," Merry said.

"A meeting of the altar flower committee."

Merry made a sympathetic noise. "Roped you into that, too, did they?" She'd been surprised by how quickly Eugenie had gotten involved in so many church activities. It was the last thing Merry would have expected of the reserved librarian.

"Yes, well . . ." Eugenie shrugged. "I want to support Paul."

Merry opened her mouth to offer the older woman some advice, but just as quickly shut it again. Right now she was the last person in the world who needed to be giving out advice to people about how to manage their lives.

"I hope it goes well." Merry nodded toward the corridor that led off to the right. "We're headed this way."

"I'm sure Hunter will be fine," Eugenie repeated before lifting a hand in farewell and continuing on her way.

Merry knew the way to the Mother's Day Out baby room well enough since the space doubled as the church nursery on Sunday mornings. Sandra, the lead teacher, stood in the doorway watching for them.

"I've been waiting for this little man."

Since Sandra also worked for the church as a nursery attendant on Sunday mornings, she was well known to both Merry and Hunter. That familiarity had been the saving grace in the situation. No spending the day wondering about the person caring for her baby.

"Here we are." Merry fought to keep the tremor out of her voice.

"We've got everything ready for him." Sandra led the way into the room. "Here's his cubby." She pointed to a row of cubed shelving on the wall. "And this will be his crib." She gestured toward the one closest to the window. At least Hunter would have a view.

"Great," Merry answered, wishing she could mean it. The room was bright, cheery, and clean, with every toy Hunter could possibly need on the low shelves. Why didn't that make her feel any better?

"We take a walk in the stroller each morning," Sandra said. "And we have time on the infant playground twice a day, weather permitting."

Merry thought of the cute double-decker strollers that allowed the caregivers to push four children at a time and the shaded play area designed especially for the littlest students. Clearly Hunter was going to be a busy boy. And most likely a perfectly happy one. The knowledge did nothing to alleviate the knot in her stomach.

"Why don't I take him," Sandra suggested as she reached for Hunter, "and you can put his things in the cubby?"

Merry recognized Sandra's suggestion for the distraction ploy it was, but she agreed to it anyway. She let the other woman take Hunter from her arms and then turned away to hide the expression on her face. She busied herself stowing Hunter's belongings.

A few moments later, she had regained her composure and could turn back to the room. Her son sat happily on a large mat on the floor, Sandra at his side. Hunter picked up a plastic ring and flung it happily into the air.

"Bye, honey." Merry knelt down to kiss the top of his head. "Mommy's got to go to work."

Hunter smiled at her and blew some spit bubbles, then turned his attention back to Sandra, who had retrieved the ring so he could throw it again.

"Have a good day," Sandra said from her position on the floor. "Hunter will be fine."

Why did everyone keep saying that?

Because it's true, a voice in Merry's head said, and for the first time she felt like maybe day care wouldn't be the nightmare she'd feared.

"All right. I'm off." She wiggled her fingers at Hunter, stood, and moved toward the door. She made herself walk through it, thinking that the first day hadn't been as bad as she'd feared.

At least not until she was three steps down the hallway and she heard her baby burst into tears.

Don't go back. Don't go back. If she did, she might never be able to walk away again.

Please, God. Give me the strength to do this. She sent up the silent, heartfelt prayer. And somehow, with help from a power greater than her own, her feet kept moving, all the way to the car. Only then did she let go and let the tears wash down her cheeks.

• • •

Esther braved the crisp November morning to sit on the back veranda and drink her coffee. It was a ritual she'd followed for years, as sacred in some ways as church, and since Frank's death she'd found herself clinging to the familiar more and more, even as she knew it to be slipping away. After hours of meetings and sifting through financial statements and visits from real estate agents and appraisers, she had submitted to the inevitable.

Although November was the worst time possible to enter the real estate market, the For Sale sign would go up in the yard today. Soon her home would belong to someone else. She gripped her coffee cup more tightly. No point in giving in to the grief that squeezed her heart. Things were going to change. They had to change. Frank's death had taken that choice out of her hands.

The dog, which her grandson had named Ranger, had come outside with her and disappeared into the backyard. She glanced at her watch. It had been ten minutes since she'd seen or heard him. The mutt had fully recovered from his injuries and was now eating her out of house and home, not to mention still sleeping on the pillow next to her. If she were honest, Esther had done little to discipline the dog. It was easier to give in to his demands—feed him the extra treats, let him gnaw on her Cole Haan sandals. Residual guilt and the miasma of despair had done their damage on her once indomitable will. Now even a stray mutt could get the better of her.

Wearily, Esther stood and went in search of the wayward animal—and found him around the corner of the house, digging up one of her prize rosebushes.

"Ranger!" She raced forward, ignoring the hot coffee that sloshed over her hand. "Get out of there." Her robe flapped behind her, her progress slowed by her slip-on house shoes.

Ranger ignored her and kept his nose in the hole, the dirt flying up behind him in an arc. When Esther reached him, she leaned down to grab his collar. He turned and growled at her, deep in his throat. She snatched her hand back.

"Stop it." She glanced around and spied the garden hose coiled on its rack on the side of the house. She reached over, yanked off a length of the hose, and turned on the spigot. Spray erupted, and she turned it on him.

The dog leaped into the air with a yowl. He landed with a thump and then cowered, his head buried between his front paws.

"That's it. I've had it." Her pulse pounded in her ears.

She was fond of the dog—despite her best intentions, she'd let herself get attached. She could put up with him scratching his private parts and begging for food, and she could even deal with him relieving himself in the upstairs hallway. But her roses were her passion. This time, he'd gone too far.

Esther grabbed Ranger by the collar and dragged him back to the house. He whimpered and cast longing looks toward the half-mutilated rosebush. She shoved him inside the back door and shut it firmly behind them.

Since she had no idea where else to turn, Esther picked up the phone and made another appointment with Dr. Everton. Clearly it was time for some professional help, and the elderly vet would know what to do.

Thirty minutes later, she was showered, dressed, and headed out the door. The fact that she'd hit Ranger with her car had done nothing to dim his enjoyment of hopping in the passenger seat and going for a spin. Esther rolled down the window so he could hang his head out. More than one bemused resident of Sweetgum stopped and swiveled to watch them go by, but Esther found she didn't care about their curious stares. Ranger was having fun, and even though she was put out with him over the rosebushes, she shared his pleasure.

Their mutual enjoyment didn't last long, however. They arrived at their destination, and Esther had to square her shoulders and prepare to face facts. Ranger was out of control, and she needed help to regain the upper hand.

The animal hospital occupied an old bungalow on Spring Street, a block or so north of the church.

The former living room served as a reception area, with the bedrooms converted to treatment areas and the kitchen kept for the staff to use as a break room and general work area. Old Dr. Everton had let the place go in the last few years, so peeling paint and chipped linoleum were the order of the day.

Fortunately, no one else was waiting. Esther breathed a sigh of relief. She wasn't sure how a healthy, agitated Ranger would behave around other dogs. He'd already shown a lethal interest in the cat next door that liked to perch on top of the fence and tease him with her just-out-of-reach purring.

"Good morning, Mrs. Jackson." Pam, who did double duty as receptionist and veterinary assistant, greeted them with her usual cheer. She had a pleasant face and an easy smile. Esther knew the woman enough to say hello in the grocery store, but that was all. Now she found herself wanting to hurry around the desk, deposit Ranger in her lap, and beg for mercy.

"Hello, Pam. Thank you for getting us in so quickly."

"It's pretty quiet around here today."

On the counter next to her, a large fluffy cat had draped itself across the in box. From the back of the building, Esther could hear the barks and meows of animals being boarded. Pam's definition of quiet, Esther decided, was a loose one.

"I'm just at the end of my rope with him," Esther confided, desperation driving her to lower her guard and admit that she didn't have everything under control. "This morning he dug up one of my rosebushes."

Pam came around the desk and knelt beside Ranger. She rubbed him vigorously behind the ears, and in a split second the dog had flipped on his back and offered up his belly for Pam's further ministrations.

"Oh, you're a pushover." She rubbed his stomach vigorously and looked up at Esther. "Where does he sleep at night?"

"In the kitchen," Esther lied without batting an eyelash. There was no way she was going to confess that Ranger slept on Frank's pillow. It was too . . . revealing. Like walking down Spring Street in her peignoir set.

Pam straightened, leaving a disappointed-looking Ranger to roll off the floor and give himself a good shake. "Well, I'm sure the doc can help you. He's good with animal behavior."

Esther nodded as she made a face. "I'm here to take my medicine."

Pam looked surprised, then chuckled. "You'll certainly be his most interesting appointment of the day." She nodded toward the chairs under the window. "Have a seat, and he'll be with you in just a minute."

Esther disliked waiting, but she supposed she

had no choice. Dr. Everton was the only veterinarian in town.

As promised, her wait wasn't lengthy. Ranger had stretched out on the linoleum and was snoozing contentedly when Pam's voice interrupted her thoughts.

"Esther? You can take Ranger on back."

Esther tugged on the leash, but Ranger wouldn't budge. "C'mon, dog." She pulled harder, and the dog slid across the linoleum. *Fine,* Esther thought. *Whatever works.* She towed him, like a reindeer pulling Santa's sleigh, past the reception desk and into the hallway.

"First door on the left," Pam called out after them, laughter in her voice.

Esther marched determinedly toward her goal. Ranger began to resist, but his paws couldn't gain any purchase on the slick floor. Triumphant, Esther pulled him around the corner and into the exam room. Only when Ranger slid to a stop at her feet did she hear the male laughter from a few feet away.

"Beauty conquers the beast." More laughter. "Hello, Esther."

Esther's head shot up, and there, standing in the middle of the exam room, was Brody McCullough.

"You!"

"Me." He wore wire-rimmed glasses, which he hadn't had that day on the road. "You seem surprised."

"Where's Dr. Everton?"

"You haven't heard?" His smile softened. "He retired two weeks ago. I bought his practice from him." He paused, then chuckled. "I've been told the Sweetgum grapevine is usually pretty efficient."

"But you're a . . ." Words failed her.

"A veterinarian. Yep."

He wore a white coat over a professional shirt and tie. His khakis had probably seen better days, but they were neatly pressed. His lace-up shoes were designed for a man who spent most of the day on his feet. Esther certainly couldn't fault his appearance.

"What seems to be the problem today?" He lifted Ranger onto the small stainless steel top of the examining table. The dog, his nerves in high gear, was visibly shedding.

Esther bit the inside of her cheek. As desperate as she'd been only an hour ago, she now found herself reluctant to lay out the facts.

"That day, by the road, you didn't tell me who you were." She couldn't keep the accusing tone from her voice.

"I hadn't taken over the practice then, and I knew Ranger wasn't in serious danger." He stopped, and a flush rose to his cheeks. That intrigued Esther. The good doctor—or veterinarian, as it were—wasn't completely imperturbable. "I'm afraid I was in a bit of a hurry." He stroked Ranger behind the ears. "I never would've sent you on your way if I thought this guy was in serious jeopardy."

"Oh." Esther wondered what his hurry had been, then just as quickly reminded herself that the new veterinarian's private life was none of her concern.

"So what are his symptoms?" the vet tried again. The gold flecks in his red hair shimmered under the bright lights in the exam room.

"He keeps digging up my flower beds," Esther managed to say at last. "And he urinates in the house." She held up a hand when the vet started to speak. "I take him out frequently during the day and at bedtime. It's not like he doesn't get the chance to do his . . . business in the yard."

Brody smothered a smile. "Well, he has been through a fair bit of trauma. He may need time to adjust. Those kinds of behaviors are usually triggered by anxiety."

"What in the world would he have to be anxious about?" Esther had been cooking chicken for his dinner, for heaven's sake.

"Do you allow him on the furniture?"

Esther shook her head.

"What about the bed?"

She hesitated for just a split second too long before answering. Brody McCullough gave her a knowing look.

"I couldn't leave him in the kitchen all alone," Esther protested. "He was miserable."

"Your mistake was letting him get the best of

you." Brody continued to rub Ranger behind the ears. "Dogs are pack animals. You have to show them that you're in charge."

Esther fully grasped the irony of the vet's admonishment. She, Esther Jackson, had been in charge of almost everything in Sweetgum for years. She couldn't remember when she hadn't chaired the spring social at the country club. The garden club had bowed to her will for decades. And even the women's auxiliary at the church consulted her before making any important decisions. So why was she having such difficulty keeping one medium-size dog in check?

"So what do I do now?" Even though the dratted animal had peed on her best oriental carpet and scratched up her kitchen cabinets demanding a treat, she wasn't ready to part with him. Truth be told, he provided just the kind of companionship she enjoyed—constant, watchful, and unable to talk back.

"I'd suggest you try some obedience classes."

"Obedience classes?"

"There's a man who lives outside of town who offers them on a regular basis. Pam told me about him. I can give you his card."

Esther had always achieved whatever goal she set for herself through sheer strength of will and determination. She couldn't imagine she would need anyone's help to resolve her issues with Ranger.

"Maybe you could just recommend a book?" She was not averse to reading up on the subject. When she had a spare moment.

The vet nodded, but the movement was reluctant. "I can, but I'd really advise you to sign up for the classes."

"I'll think about it." She had no intention of letting anyone else witness her inability to control Ranger. She reached over to reattach his leash.

"Esther?" Brody laid a hand on hers where she held Ranger's collar. The simple human touch weakened her knees. Not in a romantic way. She was long past that. But other than the occasional hug from her grandson, Esther's human contact was limited to politely shaking hands while passing the peace at church.

"Yes?" She refused to jerk her hand away, kept it still. But she gripped Ranger's collar far too tightly.

"I do apologize for my phone call that night. I didn't mean to disparage your ability to take care of Ranger. It's clear you're fond of him."

Esther nodded. "I overreacted. Don't give it another thought."

They stood there for a moment. Brody opened his mouth as if to say something, then closed it again. Finally, Esther resumed her task, clipping the leash onto Ranger's collar, and Brody dropped his hand.

"If you need anything else, please don't hesitate to call."

"Thank you, Dr. McCullough." Calling him by his title, the formality of it, helped her cope with the strange moment. Esther was not someone who reached out to others or who did well with others reaching out to her. But at that moment, she wanted to stay in the exam room. She wanted to sink into the chair behind her, take refuge from the mess of her life, and let Brody McCullough be in charge. But she couldn't.

"We'll see Ranger for his checkup in a few months," Brody said. "Pam will call you to schedule it."

"Thank you." She nodded. "I appreciate it."

She scooped Ranger up from the exam table and set him on the floor. Ranger was delighted to leave. He raced ahead, straining against the leash and pulling Esther down the hallway and out the door. In her high-heeled Donald J. Pliner pumps, she labored to keep up with him. He stopped when he came to her Jaguar and waited beside the passenger door, tail wagging, for her to let him in.

Esther was supposed to put him in his crate when he rode in the car, but she just couldn't bring herself to do it. He enjoyed hanging his head out the window so much. With a sigh and a furtive look over her shoulder, she opened the passenger door and Ranger bounded in.

"Tomorrow," she warned the dog in dark tones. "Tomorrow we turn over a new leaf."

Ranger looked blithely unconcerned as he settled in for the ride home. And Esther wondered if she had the wherewithal to manage all the leaves in her life that needed rotation.

Sixteen

The November meeting of the Sweetgum Knit Lit Society fell on the Friday before Thanksgiving. Eugenie half worried, half hoped that several members would phone her in advance to say they couldn't make it. If that happened, she could cancel the meeting altogether and they'd never have to discuss the Song of Solomon.

Sadly, though, no one did any such thing, and so twenty minutes before the appointed hour, she was wiping off the table in the Pairs and Spares Sunday school class.

The tabletop was sticky with spilled coffee and doughnut sugar, which meant that Napoleon, the church custodian, must be on vacation. She vaguely remembered Paul mentioning it to her. She often listened with only half an ear when Paul talked about church business. She was so overwhelmed with all her own new church activities that she just didn't have the energy.

Eugenie was depositing the wad of paper towels into the brimming trash can near the door when she heard her husband calling her.

"Eugenie? You here?"

She stepped into the hallway, and the smile that spread across her face when she saw him was as inevitable as it was pure. "I'm here."

He gave her a quick kiss and squeezed her shoulders. "I wasn't sure I'd have a minute to come up between meetings."

Although most of Sweetgum was at the homecoming football game, Paul and a handful of the church leadership had scheduled a stewardship meeting. The annual pledge campaign, where they asked people to turn in an estimate of their giving for the next year, was not going as well as he'd hoped. The thought caused her stomach to twist. She had never mentioned her conversations with Hazel to Paul, and he seemed to take her sudden immersion in church life at face value.

"Have you had any great insights into the mysteries of church giving?" she asked with sympathy. When it came to managing the library, at least she had compulsory tax money—instead of voluntary philanthropy—to count on.

"I don't think that mystery will ever be unraveled," Paul replied, teasing, but then his expression sobered. "I think it's far more likely we'll be faced with some budget cuts for next year."

From what Eugenie could tell, the yearly budget of Sweetgum Christian Church had as much fat as an anorexic. "I'm sure people have just forgotten to turn in their pledge cards." Guilt, undeserved as it was, pinked her cheeks.

"I hope you're right." He exhaled. "Anything else you need for this evening?"

"No. We're fine. Looks like Napoleon's gone this week."

"That noticeable?"

"It's nothing." She was sorry she'd brought it up. He tended to worry about the endless details of running a church, and she hadn't meant to contribute to his stress. It was also why she'd never told him about Hazel's insinuations about the validity of her faith. Thankfully, the gossip hadn't reached his ears.

"I may need to come in tomorrow and make sure everything's in shape for Sunday," he said with a frown.

Esther bit back the protest that sprang to her lips. For a minister, working evenings and weekends was as much a part of the job as money worries and busybody parishioners. Frankly, she still couldn't comprehend how he could find so much satisfaction in it. To her the church seemed like a black hole of human need. Unlike the library, where her boundaries were clear and where her role as librarian was put aside when she locked the doors in the evening. Unless, of course, she chose to extend those boundaries, as she had done with Hannah.

"I'd better get back." Paul kissed her again, soft

and lingering, and Eugenie was once more reminded of the Song of Solomon. However embarrassed she might be about its sensual nature, she could certainly appreciate it now that she was married to Paul, and she intended to do everything within her power not to lose him again.

Later, after all the members of the Knit Lit Society had assembled and the discussion was underway, Eugenie decided to confront her own embarrassment and bring up the very issue that had been worrying her.

"So," she said to the group assembled around the tables. Unaccustomed color rose in her cheeks. "I realize that this particular selection might have come as rather a . . . surprise to some of you."

She was sorry Ruthie wasn't there. With her breezy good humor, she would have laughed kindly at Eugenie's discomfort and helped dispel the tense undercurrent in the room. To Eugenie's surprise, assistance came from a quite unexpected source.

Esther nodded toward the Bible open on the table before her and laughed. "If your husband preached from Song of Solomon on a regular basis, I think we might double our membership." Esther seemed in good spirits. Eugenie wondered what the source of her cheer might be, especially given her rumored financial difficulties. Even when Eugenie didn't want to listen, she couldn't totally ignore local gossip.

Everyone laughed at Esther's observation, and Eugenie saw more than one pair of shoulders relax.

"What did you think about what Solomon had to say about love?" she asked. "What would you say was his definition?"

Merry shook her head. "I'd say he must have had a lot of nannies to take care of the children he had with all those wives. I mean, Jeff is my beloved and everything, but at this point, with four kids, I'd rather he did dishes than tell me my hair is like a flock of goats flowing down the mountainside."

Esther nodded in agreement. "I only had one child, and I felt the same way."

Camille's thin smile told Eugenie that she probably had a different take on the matter. Everyone in town knew that Dante Brown was determinedly courting her. Eugenie wished him luck. Camille had closed down her emotions long ago, had been forced to so she could deal with her father's defection and her mother's long illness.

"Romantic love's just something women made up to rationalize clinging to a man," Camille said. "I don't know why Solomon had to drag God into it."

"I disagree." Maria spoke with firmness. "I've seen that kind of love between two people. We all have. I think it's what we all secretly long for."

Eugenie nodded her head. "I guess it's no secret that I would agree with you, Maria."

This comment elicited a chuckle from the other

women—all except Hannah. She bit her lip, and Eugenie realized with a start that the girl was about to cry.

"Of course, love can be complicated," she said hastily.

Although Hannah hadn't confided in her, Eugenie had heard the gossip about Hannah and that young man, Josh Hargrove. She knew they'd been friends when they were younger. She remembered them coming into the library in the summers. Now, though, their relationship appeared to be rising to a new level, an adult level. Eugenie wasn't so old that she couldn't remember what that had been like when it had happened to her. She could easily recall the excitement, the terror, the uncertainty, and the occasional devastation.

"I don't think Solomon accounts much for the outside world," Camille said with disdain. "Sure, it can be great if it's just you and the other person. But love doesn't occur in a vacuum. In real life, it's not that simple."

Ah, Eugenie thought. So Camille wasn't completely indifferent to Dante.

"Especially if you fall for the wrong person," Maria interjected.

Eugenie's head shot up at this. What in the world was going on with Maria? "So is Solomon's description of love just a fantasy? Can two people ever really achieve that kind of intimacy?" Eugenie asked.

Merry blushed. "They can." And then she smiled. "At least, Jeff and I have. Not every day and not every hour. But most of the time. Or at least enough to make life a really wonderful thing."

Eugenie had to nod her assent at Merry's assertion. "I think so too."

Camille shook her head. "I think it's cruel to put that kind of unobtainable ideal out there and then lead people to think they can have it." She stopped, nodded at Merry and Eugenie for politeness' sake. "Although maybe there are exceptions," she offered by way of apology.

"Why put this book in the Bible then?" Eugenie asked, interested to see what the women would say.

"It's simple. Love comes from God," Merry said. "All forms of love."

"And none of them are easy," Maria pointed out. "But this book"—she waved at the Bible on the table in front of her—"when something like that is in there, it says that God wants us to have the gift of romantic love."

"Are you sure it's not just to show us what we're missing?" Camille replied. "Or another example of what we can never achieve as human beings?"

"What keeps us from having that kind of love?" Eugenie wanted to push them on this question. "Why is it so difficult to establish that level of intimacy?"

"Because men are stupid," Hannah answered flatly. Her eyes were suspiciously damp, Eugenie noticed. Something had definitely gone wrong with the Hargrove boy. Tonight was the first time Hannah had missed a football game.

"Because most of them can't see what's right under their noses," Maria said, adding her two cents to the condemnation of the opposite sex.

"Intimacy doesn't work because you can't depend on a man," Camille said. "They never turn out to be worth your trust."

Merry laid a gentle hand on Camille's arm. "Not all of them are that way, honey. Just some."

Camille pulled her arm away from Merry's touch. "I've yet to meet the ones who aren't."

"Are women any better, though?" Eugenie said. "We don't always make it easy on the men." She knew that from personal experience. When Paul had reappeared in her life, she'd pushed him away and continued to hold him at arm's length until she'd finally come to her senses and decided that holding on to past resentments wasn't nearly as fulfilling as moving forward with the man she'd always loved.

"Loving someone that much is always risky," Merry said. "There are no guarantees. Even after you get married."

"You can't love without making yourself too vulnerable." Clearly Camille felt strongly on the subject.

"Love isn't worth it." Hannah didn't look up from her knitting.

Eugenie suppressed a smile. She wasn't so old that she couldn't remember how painful a first love could be, and it appeared that Hannah was discovering that for the first time.

"Well, I suppose we all have to form our own opinions about whether it's worthwhile to fall in love," Eugenie said. "Now, I'm eager to see your projects. What do you have tonight?"

"I hope it didn't have to be all purling," Merry said. "I made Jeff a checkerboard scarf. I thought it looked more like something a man would wear." She showed the maroon piece, on which she'd alternated groups of knit and purl stitches to create the desired effect.

"I made Paul a scarf too," Eugenie said. She'd chosen a warm shade of blue to match Paul's eyes.

Maria produced a round piece of lavender wool from her bag. "I made a hat for Daphne." She shook her head, but a small smile played at the corner of her lips. "I don't know what I would have done without her these last few weeks."

Eugenie nodded, wanting to console Maria somehow, but now was not the time. Perhaps simply having a place to talk about her difficulties, even with as little as she had said during the meeting, would be of some help.

"I made something for myself," Camille said, her chin lifted a little, as if daring anyone to question her on her choice. "It's a shell. I can wear it under one of those new denim jackets I have in the store." She spread the lipstick pink garment on the table, and they all oohed and ahhed over it.

"Anyone else?" Eugenie asked. Esther and Hannah still hadn't shared their projects, but she didn't want to push either of them.

"Not tonight." Esther swept her customary tangle of yarn back into her designer bag.

"Me either." Hannah didn't look at Eugenie when she answered. Eugenie knew that the girl had started on a sweater—her first—and from the amount of yarn the girl had asked for, it must have been intended for Josh Hargrove. If Eugenie had known for sure, she would have told Hannah about the old knitting superstition—never knit a sweater for a boyfriend or you'll break up. Sweaters were reserved for husbands, fathers, and brothers.

"All right. Thank you, everyone." She looked down at the reading list on the table in front of her. "Next month's assignment is *Gone with the Wind* and the seed stitch. You can use single or double, whichever you prefer." She paused, smiling. "Just don't everyone knit Scarlett O'Hara a petticoat."

The others laughed, and the meeting ended on a positive note. But as Eugenie and Hannah turned out the lights and left the church, she couldn't help worrying. The holidays were just around the corner—Thanksgiving next week and Christmas coming faster than any of them probably would have liked. It was a stressful time of year. She hoped they could all weather the strain.

"Good night, Eugenie. Good night, Hannah," Merry called as she disappeared into her minivan. Camille had already left, and Esther was unlocking her car. She could see Maria's disappearing figure as she headed toward the square. Change was in the air. Eugenie could sense it. She hoped that whatever obstacles and transitions lay ahead, the members of the Knit Lit Society could see one another through them.

Seventeen

Even though the air held a distinct chill, Camille was on the front porch waiting for Dante when he arrived on Saturday. Better not to let him past the front door. She leaned back into the tattered cushions on the porch swing and stared at the open book in her hands without comprehending it.

Gone with the Wind. Camille couldn't relate to the single-minded Scarlett, who pursued her own desires at the expense of everyone around her. Well, then again, maybe she could—at least in theory. She'd certainly fantasized enough about what she would do with her life if she didn't have to care about anyone other than herself. Or, more to the point, if she could bring herself not to care.

Camille turned the pages, trying to concentrate, but every time she heard a car engine her head bounced up even though it was a good twenty minutes until Dante was due to arrive. She resisted the urge to go back in the house and change her outfit. It had taken her an hour to decide on this ensemble—black low-rise jeans, high-heeled boots, and a deep purple sweater. She had her black pashmina tied around the handle of her trendy black patent handbag. It would keep her warm in the movie theater or later at dinner, if the restaurant was chilly. Not that she thought she'd have trouble keeping warm with Dante around. Just looking at him—

No. She was not going to do that, not about to indulge in those feelings. She could go near the flames without throwing herself into them.

At least she hoped she could.

Another car engine broke the peaceful silence. Camille looked up to see a familiar black sports car approaching. The car turned into the driveway, and a moment later, Dante emerged.

Camille bit her lip. He looked amazing in blue jeans and a button-down, the preppy pink oxford shirt the perfect contrast to his dark skin. He wore the shirt untucked, which somehow emphasized his broad shoulders all the more. He wasn't wearing a coat. Maybe the cold didn't bother him. Maybe he was strong enough to withstand it, to withstand just about anything.

Camille swallowed. That strength might be her undoing.

"Hey." He moved toward the porch, mounted the steps, and walked toward her. "I'm a little early."

She laid the book on the swing beside her. "That's okay. I'm ready to go."

He glanced at the book. "What are you reading?"

"Just something for the Knit Lit Society." She stood, not wanting him to see *Gone with the Wind*, not sure what he'd make of that particular title. "Let me lock the front door."

While she turned to fish her key out of her purse, he reached for the book, picked it up, and flipped it over.

"I didn't know anyone actually read this anymore." He raised one eyebrow. "It's kind of—" He stopped, frowning. "Let's just say life on the plantation looks different from my point of view."

Camille blushed, aware that the racial stereotypes in the book were appalling. "I think Eugenie wants us to read it in terms of the love triangle. I'm sure she's not condoning any of the . . ." She, too, stopped, trying to find the right words. "I don't think Eugenie's advocating the social conditions of the time." She slid the strap of her handbag on her shoulder. "Besides, nobody thinks like that anymore. At least not the people I know." Dante looked at her intently. Camille shifted in her high-heeled boots. "What?"

He shrugged. "I just always thought that was the reason."

"What was the reason?"

"I always thought you wouldn't go out with me because I'm black."

Camille bristled. "Did you really think I was that shallow?"

"You wouldn't be the first girl who turned me down because of that."

She didn't know what to say next. Because no way was she going to tell him the real reason she'd kept rejecting him all through high school.

"Don't you think we'd better get going? We're going to miss our movie."

He opened his mouth as if to say something but then closed it. Instead, he nodded agreement to her suggestion and waved her down the porch steps. When he opened the car door for her, she slid in, her stomach in knots, but her anxiety didn't have anything to do with their conversation.

Being in Dante's car made every hair on the back of her neck stand on end, a distress signal that warned her to beware. The rich leather seats, the faint scent of his aftershave, and then, as he slid into the driver's seat, his very presence all put her mind—and her senses—on high alert.

"What movie did you pick?" he asked as they drove through Sweetgum en route to the state highway that would carry them to Interstate 65. Camille had been a little worried about keeping the conversation going for the ninety-minute drive to Nashville, but at least they could talk about their plans for the rest of the day.

"The new Reese Witherspoon movie. It's on at the theater in Cool Springs." The large shopping area in the southern suburbs of Nashville would be both anonymous and neutral, two reasons she'd chosen it.

Dante groaned. "You really did pick a chick flick."

Camille laughed. "You said it was ladies' choice."

He drummed his fingers against the steering wheel and shook his head. "I'll never make that mistake again."

"Well, what would you have picked? Something with three explosions per minute?"

He chuckled. "Sounds good to me."

The familiar scenery rolled past under the gray winter sky. Rolling hills covered with bare-branched trees sloped away on either side of the interstate. Wintry, but still green in places, even in November.

"Do you miss Texas?" she found herself asking.

He shook his head. "I wasn't there long enough to miss it."

"Where were you before that?"

"Atlanta. Chicago. I bounced around the league."

She cringed. She hadn't meant to bring up an

unpleasant subject. "What was your favorite place?" She couldn't imagine what it would be like to be able to explore all those cities. To go to museums and the theater. Not to mention the shopping.

He thought for a minute, fiddling with the buttons on the car stereo until a song with a smooth, silky beat issued from the speakers. "Boston was cool. Lots of history."

"Your degree's in that, isn't it?" In addition to his coaching duties, he was teaching American history. She'd learned that from Natalie a few weeks back when she came into the dress shop once again to gossip, not to buy.

"I have an education degree. History's my specialty."

"Along with coaching." She cast him a sidelong smile.

"Yeah. Along with coaching."

She could see him in the classroom, easygoing but no pushover. "Do you enjoy it?"

"Coaching?"

"No. Teaching." Or was it just a job, she wondered. Something to pay the bills. Like the dress shop was for her.

"I do. Wasn't sure I would. I majored in education because I thought it would be easy and I'd meet a lot of girls." He chuckled. "The professors let me know pretty quick that I hadn't signed up for an easy ride."

"But you stayed with it?"

"Yeah. I did."

"You said awhile back that coaching jobs were hard to find. Would you have settled for just being a teacher?"

He shook his head. "No. I belong out on the field, one way or another."

Given the football team's success, she couldn't argue. For the first time in three years, they'd won district. And even though they'd lost in the first round of the play-offs, most of the starters were underclassmen, like Josh Hargrove. The team—and Dante—was looking at several successful years in the near future.

"What about you?" he asked. "You never went away to college?"

"You haven't heard my sad story through the grapevine?" After the night they'd had dinner at Tallulah's, she would've thought there'd be no shortage of people willing to give him all the details of her life over the last five or six years.

"I've heard a lot of gossip. I'm more interested in what's fact."

"Spoken like a true historian."

"So? What's your story?"

Now it was her turn to shrug. "Not much to tell. I stayed home to take care of my mom. She lived a lot longer than her doctor ever thought she would." The mention of her mother brought tightness to her throat and tears to her eyes.

"And now?" He didn't look at her but kept his eyes on the straight line of the highway in front of them.

"Now it's too late."

She waited for him to tell her that it wasn't, that she was young and had her whole life ahead of her. That's what most people said. She'd had this same conversation over and over again at her mother's funeral visitation and afterward, at the house, where everyone had been invited back for cake and coffee.

"Sweetgum's all right," he said. "Peaceful. You know everyone. Know where you stand."

She shrugged. "Maybe. I don't have much to compare it to." And then, in case that sounded too self-pitying, she waved toward the sign on the side of the road that indicated Nashville was getting closer. "We should be coming up on our exit pretty soon."

Thankfully, she succeeded in changing the subject, something she was apparently going to have to do a lot with Dante. She didn't want anyone getting too close to her private thoughts, and she especially didn't want him to know how much she hated the idea of spending the rest of her life in Sweetgum.

The chick flick was every bit as satisfying as Camille had hoped and every bit as torturous for Dante as she'd expected. They emerged from the movie theater, laughing over their different reactions to the film.

"C'mon," Camille teased him. "Everybody loves a happy ending."

"I think you mean a sappy ending." He pushed open the glass door for her, and they stepped out into the wintry day. The clouds had thickened while they were inside the theater, and the temperature had dropped. Camille shivered, and Dante put an arm around her shoulders. He did it with all the casual smoothness she would have expected, and despite herself, she liked it, liked the way it made her feel protected.

"I have to say, you took it like a man." She could joke with him, keep it light and easy. They stepped off the curb into the parking lot and walked briskly to the car.

"Hey!" A masculine voice shouted at them from behind. "Hey, you."

Dante dropped his arm and turned around. Camille pivoted in her high-heeled boots. A tall, pale man in his forties strode toward them. He wore khakis and, like Dante, a button-down oxford shirt under a trendy anorak. Camille thought maybe she'd left something behind in the theater. She checked her purse, made sure the pashmina was still tied to one of the handles.

"Is something wrong?" she whispered to Dante. "Do you know him?"

"Let me handle this." He stepped forward so that he stood between her and the other man.

"Dante—"

"Let me handle it, Camille."

The tall man stopped a few feet in front of Dante. "You need to take that elsewhere," he said, his manner icy.

"Take what elsewhere?" Dante's tone was even, calm.

"You know what I mean." The man leaned forward on the balls of his feet, his hands loose at his side but his fingers clenching and unclenching.

"Maybe you'd better make it clear for me," Dante said. "In case I'm too stupid to understand."

The man frowned and began to look flustered. "I'm just saying . . . Some people don't like to see, well, you know. That sort of thing." He waved a hand at Camille and Dante and then took a step backward.

"You mean a guy with his arm around his girl-friend?" Dante's stance remained relaxed, his voice normal.

The man held up both hands in front of him. "Not me, dude. I'm cool. But some folks around here . . ."

Camille had heard enough. She stepped around Dante. "I think you should mind your own busi-ness," she said. If worse came to worst, her purse was heavy enough, thanks to all her makeup, that she could clock him with it if she needed to. Although she doubted he'd get that close to her with Dante at her side. "Why don't you go inside and enjoy your movie?"

The man's cheeks reddened. "You ought to choose your boyfriends more carefully." He leered at Camille, and the look made her feel like she needed a shower. "You can do better."

Camille thought steam might actually come out of her ears. Without thinking about it, she stepped forward and poked the man in the chest. "I can assure you, whoever you are, that not only could I not do any better, I'm lucky to be here with him in the first place." She gave him a last poke for good measure. "Like I said, I suggest you mind your own business."

She whirled and grabbed Dante by the hand. "Come on. The bigotry index in this parking lot is unbelievable."

Dante resisted her first tug, but then he acquiesced. She practically towed him toward the car, half afraid the stranger might decide to pursue the matter and come after them and half afraid that Dante would decide the man needed to be taught a lesson.

"You're about to pull my arm off," he said, but there was amusement in his tone. She glanced back at him, and he was actually laughing.

"I'm glad you find this funny." Her heart pounded in her chest, both from fear and exhilaration. She had bottled up her emotions for so long that it was cathartic to have an outlet for them. Even if it was an encounter with racism in the form of a man whose mother ought to have taught him better.

"I've never seen you light into somebody like that," Dante said, unlocking the car door and gesturing for her to get inside. "That was better than the movie."

Camille sank down onto the leather seat in a puddle of relief. Dante walked around the car and slid in beside her.

"I'm glad you found it entertaining," she said, waving a hand in front of her flushed face to fan herself. Energy coursed through her, leaving her agitated and breathless.

"Want to know my favorite part?"

"What?"

He leaned closer, too close, but Camille couldn't move. His face was only inches from hers, his mouth—

"My favorite part was when you told him I was your boyfriend."

"I never said that." Was that her voice, all breathy and soft?

"You implied it."

"That's not the same."

"Close enough for me."

And then he closed the gap between them and kissed her. She'd always, always wondered what it would be like to be kissed by Dante Brown. And now she knew. And it was as wonderful, as sensual, and as frightening as she'd always thought it would be. Rhett Butler had nothing on Dante Brown.

She indulged herself for one long, pleasurable moment before she pulled away. "Dante—"

"Don't say it." He put a finger to her lips and leaned back into his own seat. "Just let me have this one moment, okay?"

He removed his finger from her lips, and she swallowed. His gaze was pure velvet and filled with emotion. Tears pricked at her eyes. Why did it have to be Dante that made her feel this way? Why couldn't it be someone who wanted to get out of Sweetgum as badly as she did, not someone who wanted to stay put?

"You know this is never going to work," she said, as much to convince herself as to convince him.

"There's no reason it can't." He reached up to cup her cheek with his hand. "There never was."

"We want different things."

"How do you know?"

"Because you're happy where you are, and I'm not. I never have been." She paused, trying to find the right words, the ones that would convince him that there was no point pursuing a relationship. "As soon as I can figure out a way to get out of Sweetgum, I'm going."

"Maybe I can give you a reason to change your mind. A reason to stay."

"I don't want you to."

"Do you know what you're giving up?" His gaze held hers, wouldn't let her turn away.

"I've always known what I was giving up."

"I don't mean me. I mean your life in Sweetgum. Your home. Your roots."

"I'm trying to escape my roots. Why aren't you?" She leaned back and waved a hand toward the theater. "Don't you want to get away from that kind of thinking? That kind of prejudice?"

Dante shook his head. "That kind of stupidity is why I came back to Sweetgum. People can be ignorant there, spiteful even, but they know me. They see me as Dante, not an anonymous black man they can hate on. I've never experienced that kind of racism in Sweetgum. People being jerks? Yeah. That kind of pure, evil hate? No."

Camille didn't have an answer to this.

Dante put a hand on her shoulder and gave it a brief caress. "We better get going or we'll miss our reservation."

The thought of food, even a meal as upscale as the one they were sure to eat at the Watermark, made her feel queasy.

"Maybe we'd better—"

"No." He was abrupt but not rude. "I refuse to let someone like that ruin our date."

Camille knew he was right. The minute you let a hater affect your decisions, you were under his power, had let him influence you.

"Then we'd better get going," she said. "I looked at the menu online last night, and I already know what I want." She wiped her cheek with the back of her hand, surprised to find tears. She hadn't even known she was crying.

Dante smiled at her with approval. "That's my girl."

And for once, Camille didn't argue with his assumption.

Eighteen

Esther hadn't intended to be home when the prospective buyer showed up to look at her house the day after Thanksgiving. She'd been coached by her real estate agent on all the dos and don'ts, and the seller's presence in the home was a definite faux pas.

But the dog—Well, the dog was no more under control now than he'd been the day she dragged him into the veterinary clinic.

The doorbell rang a second time. Esther stood in the middle of the foyer, torn between going after the dog and answering the summons. "Ranger!" she bit out one last time, hoping he would respond, but no such luck. With a shake of her hair and a quick straightening of the hem of her sweater, she moved to answer the door.

The man standing on her front porch was the last person in the world she expected to see.

"Dr. McCullough!" She said his name in the same tone of voice she'd used to try to summon

Ranger. Then she collected herself, forced a smile, and responded in a far gentler tone. "Hello."

"Esther." From the way his eyes widened, she guessed he was every bit as surprised to see her as she was to see him. "I'm sorry, I must have the wrong—"

"Are you meeting a real estate agent?" He nodded, and her chest tightened. Of all the luck. "Then you're at the right place."

For some reason, her pulse was racing. She couldn't think why, except that Brody McCullough had seen too much in their last two encounters, and what he'd seen made her feel nervous. And vulnerable. And more than anything in the world, Esther disliked feeling vulnerable.

"Please come in. I wasn't supposed to be here, but I was having a little trouble—"

As if on cue, Ranger came racing through the foyer, his paws skidding on the slick surface before he crashed to a stop at Brody's feet.

"Hey, boy." The vet reached down to rub the dog's head. He looked up at Esther with an apologetic smile. "I didn't mean to intrude on your privacy."

"You're in the market for a house?"

Of course he was, she scolded herself. The man was new in town.

But Brody shook his head. "No. I'm renting a condo at the lake." He suddenly looked uncomfortable, and Esther had no idea what to make of that.

"I have a friend, a college buddy, who's moving to the area. He's the one looking for a house."

Esther glanced at her watch. "I'd better be going. Leave you all to look things over in peace." She reached down and grabbed Ranger's collar. "Just let me get him on the leash."

But Ranger didn't want to be dragged so ignominiously from Brody's presence. He hunched down, his backside practically sinking through the floor. The tile was slick, but Esther still struggled to tow the animal's dead weight across the floor.

"Wait. You're going to hurt your back." Brody reached out and curled his fingers around Esther's wrist.

The unexpected touch sent a shock through her. She released Ranger's collar and snatched her hand away.

Brody's eyes met hers, and she realized he saw her reaction in them. Color flooded her cheeks, so she turned away and marched toward the kitchen. "Treat, Ranger," she called to the dog, a shameless bribe. "Let's have a treat."

The dog followed hot on her heels, but to her dismay, so did Brody.

"That's his second favorite word," she said, trying to act nonchalant. As if she hadn't jumped a mile at his touch. As if she didn't find him—She was not going to finish that thought.

"I'm afraid to ask," Brody said as he followed her into the kitchen, "but what's his favorite word?"

"G-o," Esther said, resorting to spelling it out. If she said it, there'd be no appeasing the dog until they took at least a walk around the block.

Brody laughed. "Does it hurt?"

Esther blushed, although she didn't exactly know what he meant by his question. "Does what hurt?"

"Being so tightly wrapped around that dog's paw."

This time her flush rose clear to her hairline. "I—" She started to defend herself, but she was reaching into the treat jar and realized her actions spoke volumes more than her words. "Okay, okay. Guilty as charged."

"The only thing I'm charging you with is caring about this walking pile of trouble here." He paused. "Is he still sleeping on the pillow?"

Esther couldn't see any use in denying it. "Yes. But at least he's stopped digging up the rosebushes."

"How'd you get him to do that?"

She couldn't help smiling a little. "I let him dig up the hydrangeas instead."

Brody McCullough's laugh, Esther decided a second later, was one of the most wonderful sounds she'd ever heard. Deep, rich, like leather and mahogany and velvet all woven together. She let it wash over her, and a little of the grief and strain and worry of the last months eased.

Her gaze caught his, and an indefinable look

passed between them—part recognition, part connection. Part attraction. Esther turned away before he could see her blush again.

She was on the wrong side of fifty, and he had to be at least ten years her junior. She was a widow, and he was bound to be the most eligible bachelor in town. She'd never made herself ridiculous before, and she wasn't about to start.

Thankfully, the doorbell rang again.

"Excuse me," she murmured, and she walked away as quickly as her high heels and the hardwood floors would allow. Ranger didn't follow, having apparently decided that he'd rather stay with Brody—or at least in the vicinity of the treat jar.

Although she'd fully intended to absent herself as soon as she'd let the real estate agent and her client in the front door, Esther somehow found herself staying and giving the prospective buyer a personal tour of her home. The man, James Delevan, was tall and distinguished. Although he might have been the same age as Brody McCullough, he seemed far older. His face was a bit world-weary, Esther decided. Handsome but tired. She wondered what had brought him to Sweetgum but was too polite, too southern, to come right out and ask.

"The veranda is my favorite part of the house," she said as they neared the end of the tour. She ushered the two men and the real estate agent, a young woman in her midthirties, out the French doors that led from the kitchen to the outside. She'd saved the best for last. Even at the beginning of winter, the view of the yard, with its extensive flower beds, rivaled an English garden for beauty.

"I can see why." James Delevan nodded with approval. "You've put a great deal of work into this."

"Yes." A lump settled in her throat and prevented her from saying anything more. Her pride in the beauty she'd created melted under the despair of losing everything she'd worked for. The maple she'd planted shortly after her son, Alex, was born. The hostas that came from her mother's home. A stand of crab apple trees in the back corner near the fence that provided fruit for jelly and shade for picnics. Her greenhouse, not large but adequate for cultivating her roses. All of this would be someone else's very soon.

"You've been very kind to show us around," James said with a nod. He looked at the agent, who was new to the business and didn't seem to know quite what to do next. "I think it's time to leave Mrs. Jackson in peace." He turned back to Esther. "You should be hearing from us very soon."

Why should good news make her feel so bad? "I'll look forward to it."

She could feel Brody's eyes on her, watching

her, assessing her, and she refused to look his direction. Right now she needed every bit of strength to maintain her composure.

Her beautiful home. Her stomach knotted, and she felt the same stab of grief she did when she thought of Frank. Not that anyone could equate the two losses—a husband and a house—but they were wrapped up in each other, inseparable. If she could have the first back, she would also have the other.

Esther trailed the other three as they made their way back through the house. Brody had secured Ranger in his crate at the beginning of the tour through blatant bribery. Esther appreciated his offer to entice the dog into dreaded captivity, but now he wasn't there to nip at their heels and distract her from her unwelcome, unwarranted attraction to Brody McCullough.

"Good-bye," she called to James Delevan and the agent as they descended the front steps and headed down the walk toward a low-slung Mercedes sedan. Esther didn't know whether the car belonged to the man or the young woman, but they both looked perfectly at home in it. She paused outside the front door, waiting for Brody to say good-bye and leave as well, but he lingered, and she couldn't simply shut the door in his face, no matter how much she might want to dash into the house, fling herself on the bed, and bury her face in the pillow.

"Esther . . ." He took a deep breath, then let it out slowly. "Look, I know that was difficult for you—"

"I'm fine." The tremor in her voice belied her words.

"I don't think you are."

She lifted her chin, turned to look him square in the eye. "I don't believe you're in a position to form an opinion one way or the other, Dr. McCullough." She hadn't ruled Sweetgum society for almost three decades for nothing. "Although, of course, I appreciate your concern."

"I think I should take you out to dinner."

Esther shook her head, mostly to disguise the way his statement made her knees shake in a similar manner. "I'm not hungry."

"I'm not talking about being hungry."

She arched one eyebrow, giving him her haughtiest look. "Oh? Then what are you talking about, doctor?"

"Common decency. Concern. Being a friend."

"A friend?" He was her vet, for crying out loud. "I wasn't aware we had anything more than a professional relationship."

He shook his head, a rueful grin on his face. "Esther Jackson, you are one tough nut to crack."

"How flattering."

But he refused to be chilled by her manner, to be frozen out. "You can't fool me though. That's the thing. I know your secret."

"My secret?" Everything within her froze. Which one? She had a number to choose from.

"I've seen you with Ranger. You're not the ice queen you want people to think."

The words *ice queen* hit her hard. She was composed and in control, but that didn't mean she didn't have feelings, didn't experience pain or feel happiness as deeply as anyone else.

"What people think of me is out of my control."

"Not entirely." He took a step closer, and for a moment she feared he would reach out and touch her. Feared it and wished for it, all at the same time. "You're a lot like your house."

Her head snapped up. "What does that mean?"

"Oh, it's beautiful. Polished. Decorated like you were getting ready for a photographer from *Southern Living*. But it's all window dressing."

"Window dressing?" Hurt pinged through her chest. "Are you saying I'm a phony?"

He shook his head. "No, no. What I'm saying is that the house is a facade. It's everything you would expect it to be, but there's no warmth here. No passion."

Anger blossomed in her stomach and rose upward. "You have no right—"

"There it is. The passion. It's behind all the window dressing. Just like what you've created out there." He motioned toward the back of the house. "That view from the veranda—the yard, the garden—that's where the life is. Every part of it is a testimony to your touch. I can tell just by looking at it. Not like the house. You hired a decorator for that, didn't you?"

How could he know that? How could he see into her soul when he barely knew her?

"I have no idea what you—"

"Have dinner with me," he said again. "Please."

Their gazes met, locked. Esther had never felt like this in her life. No one had ever challenged her for control, not like this. And yet she knew he wasn't trying to manipulate or dominate her. In her experience, relationships had always been about gaining the upper hand and never leaving herself vulnerable. Especially after—

Maybe it was midlife hormones. Maybe it was reading too much *Gone with the Wind* in one sitting. Or maybe it was just the crushing loneliness and fear that had weighed on her every day since she'd knelt beside Frank's dead body on that putting green.

"All right," she said, breathless with fear and a growing feeling of excitement. "All right. I'll have dinner with you."

Her husband hadn't been dead for more than four months. People in Sweetgum would be scandalized. But at that moment, Esther didn't care about anyone else's opinion. For the first time in a very long time, she could feel the blood flowing through her veins, the breath moving in and out of her lungs. Normally, she only felt this way in her garden, but since the moment she'd met Brody McCullough on the lake road, something in her had reawakened.

"I'll pick you up at seven," he said.

"Fine."

And then he was gone.

She was a fool, but at that moment she couldn't bring herself to care. Not when the scent of pine from the windbreak on the west side of the house filled her senses almost as much as Brody McCullough.

Nineteen

December arrived on the winds of a cold front that frosted windshields in the early morning and gave the popular girls at Sweetgum High a chance to show off their Ugg boots.

Hannah, in Converse tennis shoes she'd covered with ink doodles, followed the line of pompom girls into the rest room after her first class. A six-minute passing period didn't allow for much standing around, although that's exactly what a lot of the girls were doing. Putting their hair up, taking it down, applying lip gloss and then removing it in favor of a different shade. Hannah waited her turn for a stall. Fortunately, it didn't take long. She was almost done when she heard Courtney's voice above the general din.

"It's so pathetic, the way she's chasing him. He practically has to step over her in the hall since she's always underfoot."

Hannah's spine tingled. The last couple of weeks hadn't been much fun since Josh had blurted out the truth. Almost as soon as he'd moved back to Sweetgum, Courtney had maneuvered him into asking her to the homecoming dance. And so on that important night, Hannah had slunk off to the Knit Lit Society instead of entering the gym with Josh. He'd apologized all over himself, brought her a single rose—everything he could think of to make it up to her. But it had still hurt, even if it was clear he would've preferred to spend the evening with her.

For a while, since last year, Courtney and the others had left Hannah alone. It helped that Courtney's mom was also a member of the Knit Lit Society. They'd finished middle school in a sort of truce, but once they'd walked through the doors of Sweetgum High, that had changed. Especially once Josh made his preference for Hannah clear.

"Josh is such a hottie," another girl chimed in. "I can't believe he'd look twice at a loser like Hannah Simmons."

Hannah's hand froze on the lock of the stall door.

"Well, she can crawl after him all she wants, but he took *me* to the homecoming dance." Courtney always sounded confident.

"By senior year you'll be prom king and queen." A third voice joined the conversation.

"Yeah, and Hannah'll be throwing herself at his feet while they put the crown on his head." Everyone laughed at that. Hannah swallowed hard, determined not to cry.

"C'mon, you guys, we're going to be late." The zip of purses, the sound of cell phones snapping shut. Hannah stayed put long enough to give them time to leave the rest room. She would have waited until the bell rang, but she couldn't afford another tardy. She slipped out of the stall and crossed to the sink to wash her hands. The lone remaining occupant of the rest room, a chess club geek named Gloria, smiled sympathetically. Hannah tried to return her smile, but when she looked in the mirror she saw that it came out more like a grimace.

"Pompoms are so superficial," the girl said.

"Yeah." Even though Hannah knew Courtney's comments sprang from jealousy, she also felt the bitter sting of rejection. Josh had said he couldn't back out of taking Courtney to the dance. His mom had insisted he keep his word. But a little seed of doubt had been planted in Hannah's mind and heart.

With a last glance in the mirror, and then a wish that she hadn't, Hannah hoisted her backpack strap higher on her shoulder and left the rest room.

Merry straightened the notepad on her desk blotter and laid her pen across it at a perfect forty-five-degree angle. She took a moment to admire the pristine top of the desk.

A few weeks ago, when she'd started work full time, the desktop had looked nothing like this. Then, piles of paper, stacks of legal folders, random law books and legal journals had been shoved, crammed, and piled on the desk. Mitzi, Jeff's assistant, was a very capable paralegal, but organization wasn't her strong suit, so Merry had taken over the job of office management. She'd filed until her eyes were almost crossed, shelved and cataloged the heavy books and multitude of law review magazines. She'd answered the phone, typed correspondence, made endless copies of endless documents. She'd even had time to sneak in a little reading for the Knit Lit Society. By all rights, she should be exhausted. And grumpy. After all, she'd never wanted this job in the first place and was only doing it because Jeff was so desperate.

But somewhere in the last few weeks, once she'd gotten more accustomed to the wrenching pain of leaving Hunter at day care each day, she had come to enjoy what she was doing. Family management and office management weren't such different creatures. Plus, at Jeff's law office, no one was likely to throw a sippy cup at her and scream "Juice!" at the top of his lungs.

Merry chuckled. She'd been out of the grown-up world for so long that she'd forgotten what it felt like. Satisfying work was a self-esteem boost, she had to admit. At home, she knew she was a good, if imperfect, mother, but any validation of her efforts was mostly indirect. A blissfully napping baby who'd been fed, changed, and rocked into dreamland. A teenager who muttered a thank-you as she stalked off to her room with a new outfit Merry had ordered online only to be told it was the wrong color. Her son Jake's rambunctious hugs when she made his favorite dinner of Sloppy Joes. Or Sarah's pleasure in a new box of crayons for the first day of kindergarten. At home, feedback usually came tinged with criticism or a lead-up to a request for something else. But in Jeff's office . . . Well, the phrase "night and day" sprang to mind.

"Merry?" Jeff's voice pulled her away from her admiration of her desktop.

"Yes?" She looked up and found him perched on the side of her desk.

"You were off in your own little world." He smiled. "Plotting my overthrow?" He looked around the office. "It's a good thing you don't have a law degree or I'd be out of a job."

"Thanks." Even after four kids and years of marriage, his compliment pleased her immensely because she knew Jeff's good opinion wasn't given lightly. "Did you need me for something?"

He slid several folders onto the desk. "Can you type these up for me?"

When it came to using a keyboard, Jeff had ten thumbs, so he still wrote most things by hand, sometimes printing off a template, then scratching words out and inserting others. Because she knew how his mind worked, she didn't find it difficult to make sense of his method.

"Will do."

Jeff laughed. "I think I've created a monster."

"No, just a brilliant office manager."

He paused, his smile softened, and then his expression grew more serious. "I know it's not easy. You have even more on your plate than before. Promise me you'll say something if it gets to be too much."

Merry nodded. "I will. But really, I'm okay. One of the other working moms from the church gave me a really good piece of advice."

"What's that?"

"When in doubt, lower your standards."

She laughed along with Jeff, because for years she had been the one who'd insisted that cloth napkins must be used at all times, that the ornaments on the Christmas tree had to be arranged just so, that children could never be seen wearing jeans to church. In the last few weeks, she really had lowered her standards, and to her surprise it felt pretty good. Her schedule was hectic, but in some ways she was more relaxed, as if by giving herself permission to be imperfect, she'd made it easier to do things well. A paradox she hadn't anticipated.

"I'll leave you to it," Jeff said, leaning over to give her a quick kiss. He reached down and picked up his briefcase. She hadn't noticed it earlier.

"You're headed out?"

"Court date in Columbia. I'm sorry. I thought I told you."

"Will you be home late?" Now that she had a better understanding of his world, she could be more understanding about the hours he kept. Before, all she could see was that he seemed to be choosing work over family. Now she knew that in many ways, his time was not his own. He was at the mercy of clients, judges, court reporters, and just about everyone else with whom he came into contact.

"Don't wait supper on me."

"All right. We'll see you when you get back." Thank goodness for the invention of the Crock-Pot. "I'll save you a plate."

"I'll have my cell phone, but I have to turn it off in the courtroom."

"No problem."

The morning hours passed with their usual speed. Merry finished the project Jeff had given her and helped Mitzi with some of her work. The phone rang more than usual, and she collected a dizzying array of pink message slips for Jeff. Clients called to be scheduled and rescheduled. The FedEx guy made his daily delivery, and Daniel Gonzalez, the postman, left her a large stack of mail to deal with. Most days she brought her own lunch and ate it at her desk while she sorted the mail or ordered office supplies online. She was trying to decide which catalogs to keep and which to pitch when the phone rang yet again.

"McGavin Law Office. How may I help you?"

"Merry?"

"Yes?" Something about the caller's voice made her pulse beat more quickly.

"It's Sandra, from the day care."

"Is everything okay?"

There was a pause, and then Sandra spoke again. "I'm sorry to disturb you, but I think you'd better come to the church. There's something wrong with Hunter."

Eugenie was never one to shirk her duties, but that first Monday in December, she slipped away from the library midafternoon to dash to Kendall's Department Store. She'd seen their ad in the Sunday *Sweetgum Reporter*, and the men's cashmere sweaters featured caught her attention. A perfect Christmas present for Paul. She'd been wondering what to get him. At first she thought of knitting him a sweater, combining it with her project for the Knit Lit Society, but somehow time had gotten away from her. Plus, she doubted the seed stitch was quite right for a man's sweater.

She entered Kendall's through the elegantly etched glass door. In her forty years in Sweetgum, she didn't think this particular store had ever changed. Dark wood, gleaming countertops, the marble floor polished until it glowed. Kendall's was a throwback to an earlier era, before shopping malls and the Internet. At Kendall's, you could still find attentive customer service, brass doorknobs, and beautiful gift-wrapping.

"Good morning, Eugenie." Alfred Kendall, a striking man in his midfifties, was the third-generation owner of the department store. His smile was as warm as his greeting. Over the years, Alfred had helped her pick out a myriad of wedding gifts, baby layettes, and Christmas presents. "What may I help you with today?"

"Hello, Alfred. I wanted to look at the cashmere sweaters that were in your ad yesterday."

Alfred nodded sagely. "For Rev. Carson? A good choice. We have several colors that would suit him well."

He led her to the men's department and personally assisted her with her choice. She finally settled on a medium shade of blue—cerulean, Alfred called it—as well as a cream-colored oxford shirt and a jauntily striped tie. Eugenie was afraid she might have gone overboard. She and Paul hadn't set a budget for their first Christmas together, but she was still a working woman with her own income, and she couldn't think of anything or anyone she'd rather spend her money on than her new husband.

"Will there be anything else?"

Eugenie paused. Her eyes flitted for the barest of moments past Alfred's shoulder, beyond the edges of the men's department and across the store to a section she seldom visited. Lingerie. Just

231

the name brought a blush to her cheek. So tempting and so embarrassing. She couldn't. Not after all these years of playing the town spinster. Alfred Kendall would probably have heart palpitations if she asked to look at the negligees.

"No, Alfred. I believe that's everything for now."

"Would you like to have these gift-wrapped?"

"Yes, please." The packages would look perfect under their Christmas tree, with Kendall's distinctive green foil wrap and gold bow.

"If you don't mind waiting, they won't take long."

Eugenie nodded, signing her credit card slip with a flourish, and Alfred disappeared to the back of the store. Left alone, the temptation was too great. She gravitated toward the lingerie section like the moon pulled through its orbit by the earth. She edged toward a rack of beautiful gowns, silk and lace and satin in pale, sumptuous colors, and had just reached out to finger a sleeve when a voice behind her almost made her jump out of her shoes.

"There you are."

Hazel Emerson. Eugenie swallowed a groan before she turned to greet her nemesis.

"Good afternoon, Hazel." She forced herself to mold her face into a pleasant expression.

"Well, I hope you're satisfied." The other woman's eyes narrowed with anger, and the lines around her mouth looked deep as ravines.

"I'm sorry?" Eugenie couldn't imagine what Hazel meant. She'd done what the other woman had wanted, throwing herself into church life to prove herself and her faith to the congregation.

"You're doing your best to ruin your husband, and now you've succeeded."

Eugenie paused before she spoke, a habit that had served her well over the years. "Ruin my husband?" she finally asked, deciding she'd better seek clarification before she said anything that might actually harm Paul's career.

"The pledge campaign was a disaster. Budget cuts right and left. We'll be lucky if we can pay the light bill."

Eugenie forced herself not to betray the slightest hint of surprise. She'd been aware that the budget wasn't in great shape, but Paul hadn't indicated that any imminent disaster loomed.

"Hazel, I doubt that matters are as dire—"

"He's going to go part time! How much more dire could they be?"

"Part time?" At that, she couldn't keep the surprise from showing on her face. "Where did you hear that?"

"My husband's on the finance committee. Are you telling me you didn't know?"

Eugenie gritted her teeth and shook her head. "Not about Paul cutting back on his hours."

"Oh, I doubt very much he'll cut back on his hours. Just on his pay." Hazel shot her another dark look. "But since you have your own salary, why should you worry?"

233

Thankfully, at that moment Alfred Kendall reappeared with her beautifully wrapped packages. In light of Hazel's bombshell, though, they didn't excite her as much as they had only a few moments before.

"Here you are, Eugenie. Oh, hello, Hazel." He nodded in greeting. "I didn't hear you come in."

"Thank you, Alfred." Eugenie relieved him of the packages, eager to make a beeline for the door. "I'd better get back to the library." She tossed a quick good-bye to Hazel over her shoulder and sped toward the entrance.

If Hazel Emerson had possessed this information for more than thirty minutes, then Eugenie could be sure everyone in Sweetgum already knew. Why hadn't Paul told her that the budget difficulties hadn't been resolved?

It was the first secret either of them had kept in their marriage. That scared Eugenie, almost as much as the fear that the budget troubles were her fault. She knew better than anyone the power of small-town gossip. She also knew as well as anyone that when it came to ministers, expectations were as high as they were unfair. She'd thought it would be enough, saying yes to everyone who asked for her help. What more could they want?

She hurried around the corner toward the library, wondering when Paul would tell her about his difficulty. And why he hadn't already.

Twenty

Hannah always looked forward to Saturdays, mostly because they didn't involve going to school. When she was little, school had been something she liked because it allowed her to escape from her mother for a few hours each day. When she reached middle school, though, things changed. "Peer pressure," adults liked to call it. "Social mutilation" was Hannah's name for the torture that went on each day between eighty thirty and three o'clock. Freshman year hadn't changed anything. She was still an outsider, and hanging out with Josh hadn't brought her any newfound popularity—just more scorn from Courtney and her crowd.

Josh had a different lunch period than she did, so she only saw him for a few minutes before school, when everyone congregated on the steps waiting for the bell to ring. Sometimes they talked for a few brief moments after school before he had to be in the weight room for off-season conditioning.

Saturdays, though, as precious as they'd been— an escape from the nightmare of high school— were even more precious now. Because now she spent Saturdays with Josh.

Today they were meeting at Sweetgum Creek, at the familiar place where it narrowed and Josh had spent all those hours trying to jump across it. Hannah pushed aside some underbrush as she approached the creek and prayed there wasn't any poison ivy. She slid down the steep bank and almost lost her footing in the crumbling soil before righting herself in the sandy stretch that lined the edge of the water.

It was almost like a little beach. The creek, not more than five or six feet wide here, tumbled over scattered rocks and pooled in places near the edge. Even though it was the first Saturday in December, gnats still swarmed, and here and there small fish flopped on the surface in search of food.

Hannah slid her backpack off her shoulders and opened it. She'd brought an old blanket for them to sit on and some sandwiches and Coke. She'd also brought a bottle of water because Josh was pretty health conscious and would probably refuse the soft drink.

Hannah stretched out on the blanket and let the hood of her sweatshirt act as a pillow. She looked up at the gray December sky and wondered when full-on winter would arrive. She did her best not to think about the thing bothering her, a subject that troubled her enough that she'd almost gone to Mrs. Carson to talk about it. At the last minute, she'd changed her mind. She wasn't sure Mrs. Carson knew much more about men—or in this case, boys—than she did.

The winter formal was next Friday night, and

Josh still hadn't mentioned it. He couldn't possibly be unaware of the event. The school halls were plastered with signs, and the cheerleaders had set up a table in the cafeteria to sell tickets. Josh had to know the dance was next week. And he had to know she was expecting him to ask her, especially after the homecoming incident.

"Are you asleep?"

She jumped at the sound of his voice and scrambled to a sitting position. Why hadn't she heard him coming through the underbrush? Because she'd been lost in thought, daydreaming about him, of course. On her own little Josh Hargrove planet.

"Sorry." He plopped down beside her on the blanket. "Didn't mean to scare you." He wore jeans, a long-sleeve T-shirt, and a fleece vest.

"You didn't." She smiled at him and tried not to look too eager. "I was just thinking."

"About me?" he teased, and when she blushed, he laughed and leaned over to kiss her. "Excellent."

She didn't know whether he meant the kiss was excellent or he liked the fact that she was thinking about him, but she didn't care. He was happy to see her, and that was all that mattered.

"Sorry I'm late," he said. "My mom wanted me to do some stuff for her before I left." He frowned at the mention of his mother.

Hannah shrugged. "No big deal." But she'd noticed in the last week or so that he'd started to show up just a little late for whatever they'd planned to do. *Don't be paranoid,* she told herself, but she couldn't quite silence the doubts that had taken root.

"What do you want to do today?" he asked.

Hannah nodded toward her backpack. "I brought some sandwiches. We can just hang out if you want."

She wanted to talk to him, draw him into conversation, and somehow, in a subtle way, bring up the subject of the winter formal. Or better yet, get him to bring it up. If they were going together, she needed time to talk to Mrs. Carson about a new dress. Camille had one at the shop that had almost made her drool, a dark purple silk that looked sophisticated without being too old. It was an amazing dress, and although Hannah wasn't particularly a girly-girl, she desperately wanted that dress. Even more desperately, she wanted to wear it to the winter formal as Josh's date.

"What time do you have to be home?"

Hannah glanced at her watch. It was a little after noon. "I told Camille I'd come by the dress shop in a while and help her do some stuff."

"What kind of stuff?"

"Cleaning. Pricing things. Just stuff."

"I still think it's a ripoff that she doesn't pay you."

Hannah looked away. She'd been too proud to tell Josh that she worked at the dress shop in exchange for clothes. It sounded too pathetic, too . . . trailer park. "I like helping Camille."

"Can't you blow it off, just for today? I've barely seen you this week."

His dismissive attitude irked Hannah. She didn't like being taken for granted as a girlfriend, but her real fear was that maybe he wasn't taking her for granted at all. Maybe he just liked her as a friend and she was reading too much into it. But how could you read too much into a guy's feelings when he kissed you on the sidewalk after a football game in full view of God and everybody? That had to matter more than who he took to homecoming.

"I have a life, too, Josh." She turned away to dig in her backpack for the sandwiches. Mrs. Carson had helped her make them—thick piles of turkey on fresh bread from the bakery on the town square. The librarian didn't think a sandwich was finished until you'd put some fancy mustard, lettuce, and tomato on it. For Hannah, who had lived on bologna and Wonder Bread for years, it seemed like a lot of bother. But it also seemed nice.

Josh put his hand on her shoulder, and she swiveled back around to find him looking at her sheepishly, apology in his eyes. "I'm sorry. I'm being a jerk."

She nodded. "Yes, you are." She only wished she had the guts to elaborate on that statement.

"Can I still have a sandwich?"

"Have two." She tossed a couple of Ziploc bags

at him. "Or else you'll be hungry in an hour." All that weight lifting must burn off a jillion calories, because Josh was always hungry.

"Thanks." He leaned forward and brushed another kiss across her lips. His mouth, so soft against hers, made her think of Scarlett O'Hara and Rhett Butler. Before Josh, she would never have understood the hoop-skirt-wearing main character. But now . . .

"Josh—" She stopped, unwrapped her sandwich, and stared at it as if it contained the answer to all the mysteries of the universe.

"What?" He took a bite of his sandwich large enough to choke a horse.

"I was wondering . . ." How in the world was she supposed to ask without asking?

Josh chewed, swallowed. "Wondering what?" He grinned. "Great sandwich, by the way."

"Thanks." She picked at the bread, tore off a few crumbs, and tossed them to a bird perched on a rock a few feet away.

"What were you wondering? How I got to be so awesome?"

His teasing grin made her stomach flip, which she would have enjoyed more if she hadn't just swallowed a bite of her sandwich.

"I guess I was wondering"—she took a deep breath—"I guess I was wondering if I needed a new dress for the winter formal."

She waited, her heart pounding, for his

response. For a long moment, he didn't say anything, just looked at her with an unreadable expression.

"Hannah—"

Now she really regretted that bite of sandwich. She could see the pity in his eyes. She'd been a fool, read too much into his attention. He didn't want to date her, not openly. But then why had he kissed her? Taken her to the Dairy Dip? She felt the blood rushing to her cheeks.

"Never mind." She jammed her sandwich back into the Ziploc bag, then stuffed it into her open backpack. "It's not important." She reached for the zipper, knowing that she had to get out of there. Had to run and run and keep running. She was such an idiot. In a flash she was on her feet and swinging the backpack over her shoulder. "I've got to run. Camille's expecting me."

"Hannah, wait." He was on his feet too, and he caught her arm, holding her in place. "I need to explain."

She whirled around to face him. "Who are you taking?"

One tiny sliver of hope still lodged in the vicinity of her heart. Stupid, idiotic hope. And then she looked in his eyes, and it died.

"I'm taking Courtney."

Hannah bit her lip to keep the tears from flowing. Pain was always better than weakness. She'd learned that from her mother at an early age.

"Whatever." She looked down at his hand on her arm. "Like I said, I've got to go."

"You know I'd rather take you." He released her arm but didn't move away. "But my mom—She's been a mess since the divorce. She hates it here. And it made her so happy when I took Courtney to home-coming." He frowned. "It's just a stupid dance."

"Then why go at all?" She shouldn't ask. Shouldn't stand there and let him grind her heart into the sand beneath their feet. "Tell your mother you don't want to go."

"She just wants the best for me—" He broke off when he saw her bite her lip again, almost drawing blood. "I didn't mean it like that."

"I understand." Hannah shook off his hand and stepped back. "Your mom wants you to date the perfect little pompom girl, Merry McGavin's precious daughter. Not some piece of trash like that slutty Tracy Simmons's spawn."

"Stop it." Now he was angry too. "You know that's not true."

But it was true. "Nice try, Josh."

"I just need time to get her used to the idea of you and me. After my stepfather dumped her, we didn't have much choice but to move back here. She's been really depressed. She talks about Courtney nonstop, keeps pushing me to ask her out. I wanted to tell you, but—"

"But what? You thought my feelings might be hurt?" Her laughter was short and sharp, like a

242

dog's bark. "Smart guy. No wonder you're in honors classes." Bitterness poured from every word. Why had she trusted him? She knew better. She'd always known better.

"You're not the only one who's had it tough, Hannah."

"So says the star quarterback." Why was she even standing here, listening to this? "See you around."

She took off toward the trees, half wanting Josh to follow her and half praying he didn't.

"Hannah!" he called after her.

Before she had reached the underbrush, she was crying. She pressed her lips together so she wouldn't make any telltale noises. More than anything, she did not want him to know how badly he'd hurt her.

By the time she made it back to the road and into town, it was clear he wasn't coming after her. A fine sheen of perspiration covered her forehead, and she swiped at it with the back of her hand.

Never again. He could apologize all he wanted, talk about his mom until he was blue in the face, but it wouldn't matter.

Stupid, stupid, stupid. But it wasn't Josh she was mad at. She was mad at herself for letting down her guard, for thinking that a childish connection might still lay between them.

For believing that she would ever, ever, in a million years, be good enough for someone like Josh Hargrove.

Twenty-One

Merry looked down at Hunter's sleeping form in the hospital crib. Tubes and sensors decorated his little body like some macabre Christmas tree. She reached out, stroked his cheek with her finger, and felt the guilt rise up in her throat like bile.

Kawasaki disease. Rare, but treatable with intravenous gamma globulin. Merry looked at the bag of medicine hanging from the IV stand. Ten thousand dollars a pop. Thank goodness Jeff hadn't let their health insurance lapse. They'd been at Vanderbilt Children's Hospital for five days already, and she had no idea how much longer they would keep Hunter.

"He's going to be okay, Merry." Jeff slipped his arm around her shoulders. "He just needs time for the medicine to work."

"I know."

Jeff's hand cupped her shoulder, caressing it. "I'm sorry I have to leave."

Merry turned to him and rested her head against his chest. "Daphne Munden was sweet to offer to look after the kids today."

She felt Jeff nod. "Are you sure you don't want to take a break?" he asked. "Go home, just for tonight? I'll stay with him."

Merry shook her head. "Will you explain to the kids?" She wished she could see them, hold them, for just a moment. Courtney in all her adolescent arrogance; Jake, smelling of sweaty boy; and little Sarah, who had made Hunter a get-well card out of construction paper and stickers.

"They understand, Merry. It's okay."

If only she hadn't gone back to work full time. If only she hadn't left him at day care.

"Merry." Jeff spoke softly, but his voice held a note of reproof. "You have to quit doing that."

"Doing what?" She tried to play innocent, but how could she when she only felt self-reproach?

"Hunter didn't get sick because we put him in day care."

Merry's shoulders slumped. "I know it's not rational, but that doesn't mean my feelings aren't real."

"But real and reasonable aren't always the same thing."

Merry pushed away from him. "Jeff—"

He reached for her, but she eluded him. "You'd better start home," she said. "It's already getting dark outside."

His gaze lingered on Hunter. " 'Night, pal," he said. He looked at her. "I'll try to get back up here tomorrow."

"Stay with the kids. They need one of us to be there."

"Merry?"

"What?" She wanted him to leave so she could cry in peace. She did that a lot while Hunter slept.

"If you blame yourself, then you have to blame me too. I insisted you come to work full time, that we put Hunter in day care."

"Jeff—"

"Just think about what I said. Sometimes bad things just happen." He kissed her cheek. "I love you."

Merry watched him disappear through the door, and then she slumped in the comfortable chair next to Hunter's crib. He had brought her a pile of women's magazines, courtesy of Eugenie and the library. Eugenie had included a note, assuring Merry of her prayers for Hunter and letting her know that the Knit Lit Society had decided unanimously to postpone their December meeting until Hunter felt better. Merry glanced at the copy of *Gone with the Wind* that protruded from the tote bag at her feet. She wasn't exactly in the mood to read about Scarlett and Rhett's loss of their daughter, Bonnie Blue.

Hunter sighed in his sleep, and Merry turned her attention back to him. She'd learned the evening hospital routine quickly. The on-call pediatrician had stopped by earlier to check on Hunter and reassured them he was progressing as he should. The nurse had been in to check his vitals, and dining services had delivered a nutritious, if somewhat institutional, meal for Merry. An early evening peace settled over the hospital. Exhausted, Merry relaxed into the recliner and let her eyes drift shut.

"Merry?"

A soft voice at the door woke her. Merry rubbed her eyes and shifted forward in the chair.

"Camille." She smiled, standing to greet her visitor. "I wasn't expecting you."

Camille was dressed for an evening out in black pants and a shimmering emerald green blouse. She carried a black wool coat and a cashmere scarf. "Dante and I came to Nashville for dinner, but I wanted to stop here first."

"You didn't have to do that," Merry said, her throat tightening. She was certain that the last place Camille ever wanted to be again was a hospital. The poor girl had spent more than her share of time in them already, looking after her mother.

"How's Hunter?" Camille moved farther into the room and stood beside the crib. "He doesn't look sick. If you don't count all the medical paraphernalia." She waved a hand to indicate the tubing and IV stand.

"He'll be okay, given time." Merry forced back the sob that threatened to break free. "It was touch and go for a bit."

Camille reached out, and Merry took her hand. The younger woman's grip was firm and reassuring. "I'm sorry. I know how frightening it can be."

Merry knew she did. Camille had been through worse than this with her mother. How the girl had managed, Merry had no idea.

"Thank you. You didn't have to come."

Camille paused, then gave Merry a look that told her she understood. "Yes, I did." She looked around the room. "Do you need anything? I can get you some dinner." She cast a disparaging glance at the tray on the nearby table. "Some real dinner."

"Actually, the food has been pretty good. I just haven't had much of an appetite."

"You need to keep your strength up." Camille paused, and a small smile etched the corners of her mouth. "I'm sorry. I got so tired of hearing those very words from people through the years. You'll eat when you need to. I always did." She made a face. "Why is it that in a crisis people always want to feed each other? Like a sandwich or a bowl of soup will make a difference."

Merry smiled in response. "I don't know. Maybe it's because we get frustrated that we can't actually do anything to change what's happening."

Both of their gazes moved back to Hunter, who snuffled in his sleep.

"Is he going to be okay? Really okay?" Camille asked.

Merry thought about giving her stock answer, the low-key reassurance she'd repeated to friends who'd stopped by the hospital, to her mother on the phone. But the stock answer wasn't the truth, not all of it. She could tell Camille the truth. Camille would understand.

"He may never be able to play sports," Merry said, the words tumbling out on a whoosh of breath. "Jeff refuses to acknowledge it, but that's what the doctor said. This disease can weaken the heart muscles, but there's no way to know—"

"Merry—"

"Jake plays every sport known to man and then some that he just made up." She felt pressure rising in her throat. "How will I tell Hunter that he can't do what his brother does?"

She knew she should simply be grateful her baby was alive, but he would also never be the same. What if he couldn't play soccer or basketball or even run—

"Merry." Camille grabbed her shoulders. "Stop. You have to stop."

Her knees buckled, and she slumped into the chair. "I'm sorry. I'm just so tired."

"It's okay." Camille knelt beside her. "You've been through the wringer. Look, why don't I stay for a while? You nap in the chair, and I'll keep an eye on Hunter."

Merry smiled through her tears. "Oh, Camille. Thank you, but I wouldn't want you to miss out on your dinner with Dante."

Camille returned her smile. "It's okay. He can grab something in the food court downstairs, and

I'm sure he can find a TV in a lounge somewhere and watch a football game."

"But—"

"Consider it a done deal. Just let me run down and tell Dante about the change in plans."

Merry nodded. "Tell him I'm sorry for ruining his evening."

Camille chuckled. "Are you kidding? He'd rather watch football than take me out to dinner any day of the week."

"That's a complete story and you know it." Merry paused. "But thanks for trying."

Camille grinned, waved good-bye, and disappeared through the door. Merry turned back to the crib and her sleeping baby.

The guilt had receded somewhat, but it still lingered at the edges of her mind, and she knew it would be back. For now, though, the care and concern of a friend would help her keep it at bay.

Camille found Dante already in the food court, eyeing the flavors offered at the Ben & Jerry's ice cream counter.

"Hey," he said when he saw her approach. "That was fast. I thought you might visit for a while."

Camille hesitated. Over the last few weeks, she'd let her guard down and let Dante into her life, but she'd kept their relationship carefully casual. Nothing serious had happened since that day in the movie theater parking lot. Until now.

"Um, look. There's been a change of plans." She wished she knew how he would react. So far he'd been pretty easygoing about their relationship, but he had an intense side as well. She'd seen it enough on the football field in high school, and more recently on the sidelines as a coach, to know he could be very focused on what he wanted.

"What's up?"

"I'm sorry, Dante, but Merry needs some company for a while."

He didn't hide his disappointment, but he didn't look angry either. "So dinner's off?"

Camille nodded. "I'm afraid so. I'm sorry. I know it's a long drive for nothing for you." He would be a good sport about it, but no doubt this would be the first nail in the coffin of his interest in her. In her experience, men had little patience for women who asked them to put their own desires on hold.

To her surprise, Dante reached out and pulled her toward him. She glanced around, but the food court was practically empty on a Saturday night. The girl behind the ice cream counter shot her a knowing look, but she was smiling too.

"Being with you is never for nothing, Camille." He leaned forward to whisper in her ear. "Besides, I get you to myself for the whole ride home." He stepped back. "How late do you want to stay with Merry?"

Camille looked into his eyes, and her stomach

flipped. At that moment she knew. Like a complete idiot, she'd fallen in love with Dante Brown.

Panic set in, washing over her in a flood of anxiety. "A couple of hours, if that's okay. I told her I'd watch Hunter so she could sleep for a while."

"Do you want me to come up with you?"

"You'd do that?"

Dante gave her a puzzled look. "Why wouldn't I?"

Her father had used every excuse he could muster to avoid being at the hospital when her mother was first diagnosed, and she'd gotten the message loud and clear. Illness was for women. Men didn't have time for it.

"Oh. No reason." She tried to sound nonchalant. "The room's not that big though. Would you mind finding a lounge to hang out in? I'm sure there's a football game on." She said the last part with a teasing smile.

"Sure. But you'll call me if you need me?" He tapped the BlackBerry he wore clipped to his belt.

Camille didn't want her insides to turn warm and mushy, but they did. "Okay." She kissed him, a quick brush of her lips against his that set every nerve ending she possessed to tingling. "Thank you."

He looked at her that way again, the way that said he'd do anything she asked. She tried to draw a breath and couldn't.

She had never wanted to be in love with him, but she was. Maybe she always had been.

"I'll see you in a little while," she said and turned on her heel, trying not to look like she was running for her life.

Twenty-Two

On Christmas Eve, Esther pulled her famous crispy roast duck from the oven and set it on the countertop. The smell, salty and sweet at the same time, teased her nostrils. Soft medieval carols played throughout the house, thanks to the expensive stereo system. A faint scent of evergreen from the seven-foot tree in the hallway mingled with the smell of the duck and the lemony counterpoint of wood polish. Every nook and cranny boasted candles, Santa figurines, or poinsettias. For this final Christmas Eve in her home, Esther had spared no expense.

"If you want to set those dishes on the dining room table," she said to the man standing at her side, "we're ready to eat."

Brody McCullough picked up the delicate china bowls—one heaped with brussels sprouts, the other with roasted potatoes. "Will do," he said with a grin before turning to carry the dishes to the dining room as instructed.

Esther swallowed past the nerves that seemed to

knot in her throat. Of all the people in the world, the last one she'd expected to spend Christmas Eve with was Brody. A few months ago, she hadn't even known him.

Her son, Alex, and his family had elected to spend the holiday in the Bahamas, leaving Esther to her own devices. When she'd mentally run through a list of friends and extended family she could invite for the holiday, she came up empty. Everyone else had a place to spend Christmas, it seemed, and someone to spend it with.

There'd been no one on her list until she'd run into Brody outside Vanderpool's grocery store the day before and they'd struck up a conversation that led to his presence in her house on Christmas Eve.

Inviting him had seemed like a good idea at the time.

Now that the meal was on the table and Brody was pulling out her chair, she felt foolish. Esther didn't like the feeling. She'd had little experience with it, but somehow, in the last few months, it had become her natural state.

She paused to admire the table. Her Wedgwood china, the gleaming family silver, tall crystal glasses of iced tea, and creamy linen napkins on an equally elegant linen tablecloth.

"Very nice," Brody said, as if he were reading her thoughts, "but you didn't have to go to this much trouble. I usually eat off a tray in front of the television."

Esther had no explanation for Brody's presence in her home, why he would be even remotely interested in spending the evening with her. A widow. Older. Destitute. Not even able to control her dog. That last thought at least made her smile.

"Christmas Eve is a special occasion." She pulled her napkin from under her fork and spread it in her lap. "We always—" Her voice failed her.

"You always . . . ," Brody prompted, his green eyes dark with concern.

"Holidays were always special occasions for the three of us." Her eyes drifted to the portrait on the wall above the buffet of Frank, Alex, and herself, taken a dozen years ago, when Alex was just about to leave for college.

Her family had meant everything to her, and now, inexplicably, it was gone. Frank was dead. Alex had his own life, and years of overindulgence on her part guaranteed that he put his own happiness and comfort first. That's why he'd left her home alone on the first Christmas Eve after her husband's death.

"My family did the holidays up pretty well too," Brody said, "but not so formal. Usually my mom burned the turkey or cooked the ham until it was dry as dirt. Don't get me started on my sisters' disasters in the kitchen."

As easily as that, he led her away from her grief-filled thoughts. Before she knew it, he was carving the duck, serving the brussels sprouts and potatoes.

They hadn't said grace. She thought of mentioning it, but decided perhaps Brody's presence was grace enough. An unexpected source of companionship, of comfort, to get her through the evening.

Before long, he had her chuckling over anecdotes from his practice, tales of everything from pet skunks who wouldn't stop spraying their owners to a horse that thought it was a puppy and kept trying to romp with a litter of black Labs.

She heard Ranger scratching at the back door. He'd been totally occupied in the yard, digging after something—a mole probably—and she'd been grateful for the respite while they ate dinner. She'd been worried about Brody seeing just how little progress she'd made with Ranger in the last few weeks. She'd bought a book on dog training and had even read a chapter. But as for putting any of it into practice . . .

"I'll get him," Brody said, rising on his considerably long legs and placing his napkin in his chair—a sign of good manners Esther hardly saw anymore. Most people didn't know you weren't supposed to place your napkin on the table until you'd finished your meal. Clearly someone had raised him right, burned turkey or not.

A moment later, the dog bounded into the dining room. He immediately started jumping in place next to Esther's chair, barking his demand for table scraps. Brody followed right behind him. Esther was about to reprimand the dog—for what little good that would do—when Brody's deep voice barked a command of its own.

"Down, Ranger." His words, as well as their no-nonsense inflection, brooked no argument.

Ranger stopped jumping, sat, and looked up at him. Esther couldn't tell whether the dog was surprised or cowed. Either way, she didn't expect it to last very long. Brody sank back into his chair, picked up his knife and fork, and began eating. Ranger whimpered from his prone position on the floor but otherwise didn't protest.

"How did you do that?" Esther asked, trying to keep the awe in her voice to a minimum. No sense letting Brody know just how impressed she was with him.

He laughed. "Years of practice. I learned early on that a vet's got to establish himself as the alpha dog. Otherwise, I'd be toast."

"That's what I need to know. How to make Ranger think I'm the alpha dog."

He shrugged. "It's easy really. You just withhold things. Food, affection." He shot her a sidelong look. "Sleeping on the bed."

Esther blushed.

"If you do that," Brody continued, "you've got the upper hand. You have what they want, but they only get it when you say so."

A chill, sudden and fierce, swept through Esther at his words. *You have what they want, but they only get it when you say so.* The forkful of duck she was chewing, which only a moment ago had tasted like heaven, now had the consistency and flavor of sawdust.

In that moment, with Ranger quiet at her feet and Brody happily consuming a heaping plate of her carefully prepared Christmas Eve dinner, Esther Jackson experienced an epiphany. Unwanted, unannounced, but an epiphany nonetheless.

"That's all?" she managed to choke out. Her voice sounded amazingly casual. It held none of the stark realization, the sudden avalanche of remorse that pinned her to her chair. "You just withhold?"

Brody nodded. "Works every time. Like everything else in life, it's about power. Dogs know that, just like people do."

Esther couldn't make a response. Years of behavior, her own behavior, were suddenly stripped of all the justifications and rationalizations. She'd wielded her power to withhold ruthlessly over the years. It had been for a good cause—or causes, to be more accurate. Frank's career, Alex's upbringing, social success, the betterment of Sweetgum. But when she'd had the power, she'd used it to further her own ends, demanding that others do everything her way, and now it was gone.

Which meant that whoever she had been, she couldn't be that person anymore. And if she couldn't be the person she'd always been, who was she now?

Esther had not planned on having an existential crisis in the middle of Christmas Eve dinner. She took a long drink of iced tea to cover her discomfort. "Why aren't you with your family this year?" she asked to divert her thoughts from herself. She had no interest in trying to reconstruct herself as a person, at least not until they'd had dessert. Better to deflect the conversation onto Brody. Only at her question, he started to look as uncomfortable as she felt.

"It just didn't work out this year."

When he didn't elaborate, she tried again. "I don't even know where you're from."

"Chattanooga." He didn't offer any further information.

"And will your sisters be at your parents' house?"

He shrugged. "Probably. They're not too happy with me at the moment."

"Why is that?"

"Because I'm here, on call for vet emergencies, instead of with them."

"But—"

"You do have a great house," he said, looking around the dining room and also changing the subject. "Still no offers?"

She shook her head. "I waited too long to put it on the market. This is the worst time of year to try to sell."

"I thought my friend James would make an offer." He shrugged. "Maybe he still will."

"You haven't spoken to him?"

"He usually spends the holidays skiing. But I thought, from what he said after Thanksgiving, that he wanted to be settled in Sweetgum by the first of the year."

"Why Sweetgum? He doesn't seem the small-town type."

Brody paused. He knew exactly why James Delevan wanted to relocate to Sweetgum. Esther could see it in his eyes, but she could also see he wasn't going to tell her. He would protect his friend's privacy. His discretion made her like him even more.

"It's okay," she said. "You don't have to tell me." What was it about Brody McCullough that made her want to be a different person? Kinder, more relaxed. Esther had never in her life wanted to be kind. Nor had she worried about being relaxed.

Her feelings toward Brody weren't wholly romantic in nature, either. At least, she didn't think they were. It had been so long since she'd had any experience with that kind of thing that she couldn't tell. She liked his company, in spite of her discomfort at some of his insights and observations, and he seemed to feel the same way. Drawn to her, yet wary. And, in an odd way, friends.

They had finished eating, so she rose from her chair and picked up their plates. He started to stand as well, but she waved him back to his seat. "Stay put. I'll get dessert and coffee."

He did as instructed, which gave her a moment to collect herself. As she used her kitchen torch to crystallize the tops of the crème brûlées she'd pulled from the oven, Esther thought of the book Eugenie had assigned them to read, *Gone with the Wind*.

Left to her own devices, she'd never have picked it up, but with so much time on her hands, and finding herself alone for most of it, she was making good progress through its pages. To her surprise, she'd found herself captivated by the story. Not so much by the tumultuous love between Rhett and Scarlett but by the blindness and stupidity of the heroine. Over and over again, she'd thrown away the love she could have had for the love she thought she wanted. Standing in her kitchen, with Brody and Ranger in the next room, Esther knew she wasn't much different from Scarlett O'Hara.

Was it too late? Were her life and choices so set in stone that she couldn't go back and change things? Not with Frank, of course. That part of her life was gone forever. But perhaps losing her husband and her home was more than twin tragedies. Perhaps those very losses held the seeds of some new beginning.

The idea both thrilled and terrified her, so she pushed it aside and attacked the crème brûlées with the torch until their tops were almost black and the smell of butane permeated the air.

Twenty-Three

"How could you forget the sage?" Althea Munden rolled her eyes at her daughter Maria in exasperation.

Maria took yet another deep breath. She'd taken a lot of them since they'd gotten out of bed that morning. So much for the joy of Christmas Day.

"I'm sorry, Mom. I'm sure if I run over to Vanderpool's—"

"You think the grocery store is going to be open on Christmas?" Her mother's pencil-thin eyebrows darted toward her hairline.

"I can't be the only cook in Sweetgum who's forgotten something. And I'm sure Mr. Vanderpool wouldn't mind. It would just take a minute."

As soon as she made this last statement, she realized her error. Mr. Vanderpool lived above his grocery store across the street from Munden's Five-and-Dime. Now that Maria and her mother and sisters lived in the rooms above their store, too, they were in the same class as Mr. Vanderpool.

"Why don't you just open the window and call across the street?" her mother said with a sniff. "Now that we live above the store, we might as well act like it."

Maria grabbed her wallet from the kitchen

counter and a jacket from the hook by the door. "I'll be back in a few minutes."

"C'mon, Mom." Daphne intervened. "We can start on the pecan pie while Maria's gone."

Stephanie, as usual, was still asleep in the other room with her comforter pulled over her head to drown out the rest of her family.

Maria slipped out the door and pounded down the narrow staircase. She let herself out the exit on the side of the building, around the corner from the square. At least they had a little privacy when it came to their comings and goings.

They'd only lived above the store for two months, but already the Munden women showed the strain of the close quarters. A combined kitchen/living/dining room and a shared bedroom—along with the world's smallest bathroom—were hardly enough space for one person, let alone four. But what choice was there? Daphne was desperately looking for a job, but she hadn't worked anywhere in years. Her major responsibility had been overseeing the farm. Stephanie was supposed to be looking for a job as well, but mostly she disappeared early in the day and didn't come home until late. Maria had no idea what she did with her time, but she doubted it was anything constructive. And as for their mother, a job was out of the question, but criticizing and nitpicking had always provided her with fulltime occupation.

Maria shoved her wallet in the pocket of her

jacket and looked both ways before crossing the street. There was little chance of much traffic this early on Christmas morning, but habit was habit. She jogged across the street to the store opposite, Vanderpool's Groceries and Sundries. Her father and Mr. Vanderpool had been cronies for as long as Maria could remember. They'd encouraged each other, extended each other credit, and generally kept each other afloat in the treacherous waters of the Sweetgum economy.

Maria ducked beneath the green-and-white-striped awning and peered through the door. The lights were on, which was a good sign, and then she saw Mr. Vanderpool's familiar balding head moving down one of the aisles. She rapped on the glass, softly at first, and then louder until he heard her and turned his steps toward the door.

"Maria! It's good to see you." He leaned forward and she gave him her customary peck on the cheek, a ritual they'd followed since she was a little girl and had developed a tremendous crush on him. The fact that he'd given her a lollipop whenever she was in the store had secured her affection from an early age. "What did you forget?"

Maria laughed. "Sage. The dressing's no good without it."

"Well, come inside and get it." He waved her into the store. "I thought I'd hang around down here for a while this morning in case anyone needed anything." He tilted his head and lifted his eyes to the ceiling. "Besides, I'm just in the way up there."

Maria knew that Mrs. Vanderpool and her daughters-in-law would be hard at work on their own meal upstairs. She could smell mincemeat pie baking.

"I won't be a minute." She dashed down the appropriate aisle and snagged a tiny jar of sage. As she headed back to the register, she heard the door open and someone else enter the store.

"Morning, young man." Mr. Vanderpool seemed pleased rather than perturbed to have customers this morning.

"Good morning, sir."

Maria would have known that voice anywhere. Her first instinct was to hide behind the shelves of cake mix, frosting, and flour, and she followed it. James Delevan. What was he doing back in Sweetgum?

Daphne had been hurt that Evan never called or contacted her after their night at the movie theater. Maria wasn't completely surprised. Evan seemed attracted to her sister, but he was old-money Memphis. He probably had women lining up outside his door. A sweet, gentle soul like Daphne wouldn't stand a chance against a cosmopolitan woman who ordered dirty martinis and shopped at designer boutiques.

"Maria? Are you okay back there?" Mr. Vanderpool's voice floated over the top of the shelves. From her crouched position, Maria cringed. Quickly, she scanned the shelf in front of her and grabbed a bag of mini marshmallows that rested at eye level. She lurched to her feet.

"Just grabbing some marshmallows for the sweet potato casserole," she said with a bright, forced smile. Like an idiot, she waved the bag in the air. "Wouldn't be the same without these." She paused, then acted surprised, as if she'd just noticed James Delevan. "Oh, hello."

Mr. Vanderpool gave her a funny look. Maria ignored it.

She darted for the end of the aisle and the cash register by the door. "I think that's all I need." She reached into her jacket pocket and grabbed her wallet, trying her best to ignore James Delevan. She could almost feel his gaze fixed on the right side of her face. If his look grew any more intense, he might laser her ear off.

"That'll be six dollars and forty-eight cents," Mr. Vanderpool said.

Maria grabbed a bill from her wallet and fished around for the correct change in the zippered pocket. All the while, James Delevan just stood there. Didn't the man have some emergency ingredient he needed to look for? No doubt Evan's sister was whipping up a gourmet meal right out of *Food & Wine*, although she was out of luck in Sweetgum if she needed something fancy like truffle oil or endive.

At last, purchase completed, she was forced to face him.

"Hello, Maria." He looked so grave that she wondered if someone had died. Mr. Vanderpool wandered off, leaving the two of them alone.

"Merry Christmas." She couldn't think of anything else to say.

"Yes. Merry Christmas."

"So you're back in Sweetgum." The brilliance of her conversation was second to none. What was it about this man that reduced her to bumbling idiot status?

"Yes."

"Spending the holiday with Evan?"

To her surprise, James shook his head. "I'm on my own."

If he wasn't staying with Evan, why would he come back? "Where are you staying?"

"Sugar Hill."

Again, Maria was surprised. "I thought the Parsons closed it for the holiday so they could go to their daughter's house in Louisville."

"They have. Gone to their daughter's, I mean. But they were kind enough to allow me the run of the place."

"But . . ." She didn't know what to add after that *but.* "You're celebrating Christmas alone?"

"I don't think *celebrate* is the right word. Let's just say I'm riding it out solo."

She noticed a funny look in his eyes, haunted

almost. *Riding it out solo.* Maria thought she'd never heard anything sadder in her life. Her own family was thoroughly dysfunctional—her mother drove her crazy, she despaired of Daphne ever being fully appreciated by a worthy man, and Stephanie couldn't be depended upon for anything other than converting oxygen to carbon dioxide—but at least they were together. At least they were a family, even if a rather warped one.

"You can't do that."

He lifted that eyebrow again, the one that went a mile high. He was almost as good at it as her mother. "I can't?"

"I mean, you shouldn't have to. No one wants to be alone on Christmas. Surely, someone asked you—" She stopped herself. What if she was wrong? What if no one had invited him to be a part of their holiday meal? She couldn't conceive how that might possibly happen to a man like James Delevan, but then again . . .

"My half sister's my only family," he said, looking grim. "She's skiing in Aspen with friends from boarding school."

"Boarding school?" Aspen? He really was rich.

"She's a junior. Seventeen." He smiled sadly, and Maria could tell he was fond of his sister, half or not, which made her feel even sorrier for him.

"And your parents?"

"They passed away a number of years ago."

"Oh."

A hollow silence fell. Maria swallowed and took a deep breath, knowing she had to follow the dictates of her upbringing in that moment, even though every shred of common sense told her to keep her mouth closed.

"Since you're on your own . . ." *Don't do it, don't do it,* a little voice chanted inside her head. "Since you're on your own, why don't you come have Christmas dinner with my family?"

His eyes widened, and for a moment he looked as if he'd been poleaxed. "With your family?"

"You're right. That's a stupid idea." Maria shifted the small paper bag in her arms. "I'd better run." She started to do just that, but his voice stopped her.

"I'd like that."

"You'd like for me to run?"

He smiled then. Grinned, really. She'd never seen that expression on his face, and it transformed him. Instead of dour, he looked relaxed and approachable.

"No. Well, I don't have an opinion on the running thing one way or the other, but if you meant it, I'd like to spend Christmas with you."

"Oh." She plastered a smile on her face that she hoped equaled his. "Okay. Follow me."

They exited the grocery store and stepped across the street to her door. As they climbed the steep flight of stairs, she half wished they would open up and swallow her. Their living quarters were a mess, and there was no telling what kind of reception he would receive from her mother or Stephanie, if she was even awake yet. At least Daphne would make him feel like a welcome guest.

Maria opened the door at the top of the stairs and stepped inside, James hard on her heels. "Mom, I'm back," she called. "And I've brought company."

Several hours later, when they sat down to eat, Maria couldn't believe how well the morning had gone. She also had no idea where the James Delevan she'd known before had gone.

Without even being asked, he had worked beside her, helping prepare the meal. As it turned out, he was a fairly experienced cook. He took over the sweet potato casserole and the green beans almondine while Maria made the dressing and Daphne finished the pies. The rooms above Munden's had once been leased by a caterer who'd eventually gone broke, but she'd left behind double ovens and an enormous range. With a little coordination and some good luck, they managed to have everything ready at the same time, the turkey browned and beautiful enough to be on the cover of *Martha Stewart Living.*

Her mother had greeted James cordially, if a bit stiffly, and then retreated to the bedroom to watch television. Stephanie eventually appeared and, under duress, set the table for the meal. For the most part though, Maria, Daphne, and James had been left to their work.

Now, as Maria sat in the chair James had pulled out for her at their small dining table, she felt a little like Alice in Wonderland when she'd fallen down the rabbit hole.

The James Delevan who'd spent the morning by her side in the kitchen, elbow deep in sweet potatoes and beans, was not the same stuffy stranger who'd first come to her store or attended that covered dish dinner at the church. And he certainly wasn't the same man she'd taken to the dentist that night. For one thing, he smiled quite a bit since all of his teeth were intact. And for another, he'd actually laughed at some of the jokes she and Daphne made. Something about him was different. The set of his shoulders was more relaxed, as was the line of his jaw.

"Thank you," Maria said as he helped her push her chair closer to the table. "You've certainly earned your share of the meal." She intended it to be humorous, but the words came out more seriously than she intended. "We don't usually turn our guests into indentured servants," she added, trying to lighten her tone.

"I enjoyed it," was all he said.

He'd already seen her mother to her seat, and now he turned his attentions to Daphne and Stephanie. His chivalry clearly pleased Daphne, and Stephanie looked over the moon. Maria could almost see her trying to calculate James's net worth in her head. Since Stephanie had never progressed much past long division, that was no doubt a feat beyond her abilities.

"Mama, would you like to say the blessing?" Maria asked.

Althea's head popped up. "The blessing?"

Maria felt the flush that rose to her cheeks throughout her body. She didn't want James Delevan to think they were total heathens. Not that they prayed before every meal, but her father had always done the honors on special occasions like this.

Daphne looked worriedly at Maria. "Maybe you should—"

"Dad always said the blessing," Stephanie blurted with her usual lack of tact or sensitivity. "A man should say the blessing."

Maria didn't agree with that statement for several reasons, not the least of which was that James again looked like he'd been poleaxed.

"I can—," she began.

"I'd be glad to," he interrupted, but then turned an apologetic look on her. "Sorry. Of course you'd rather do it. Your family. Your house."

Maria looked into his eyes, saw that haunted quality, and wondered again why he'd agreed to spend Christmas with them. He must have been really desperate or lonely. Or something equally awful.

"No. I mean, if you don't mind . . ." She cleared her throat. "It would be great if you said the blessing."

She wasn't expecting much, a few formal, ritualized words like her father had always said. It had never been about the content of the prayer, of course. The ritual itself provided the meaning, the acknowledgment of the occasion.

James did more than that. He invited them to bow their heads, and then he prayed. Not stiffly or formally, but not like some of the long-winded, self-important preachers Maria had heard either. His prayer was well-thought-out, reminded them of the bounty of their blessings, and asked for guidance and strength to live lives of gratitude.

When he was done, everyone sat silently for a moment, even Stephanie and her mother, until Stephanie said, "Who's going to carve the turkey?"

Her question made Maria's chest ache. Yet another of her father's responsibilities, yet another hole in their lives. But once again James stepped into the void.

"If you need me to, I can do it."

Maria looked at her mother, whose eyes were moist. The older woman nodded. "Please."

And that simply, that quickly, James Delevan found a place in the Munden family circle. It was the last place in the world Maria would have expected him to seem at home, but he did. He wielded the carving knife with experienced precision, and in another few moments all of the dishes had been handed around, the turkey had been distributed, and they were laughing and eating and squabbling as they had every other Christmas dinner of their lives.

Twenty-Four

"So what does Scarlett learn about love?" Eugenie asked the assembled members of the Knit Lit Society on the third Friday in January.

Esther looked around the table. The discussion would commence with one member notably absent. Although Hunter was much better, Merry still stuck close to his side. The baby's illness, along with the rest of the upheaval the women were experiencing, had put a cloud over the group.

"Love? Scarlett learns she's better off without it." Hannah's answer was immediate. "She should have hooked up with Ashley and left Melanie to fend for herself."

"Scarlett was too young to know what she wanted. It takes maturity to learn what you want. Or who you want." Maria shifted uncomfortably in her seat, as if she feared she'd revealed more than she'd intended. Esther thought she had. Maria wasn't much past thirty, but the gray streaks in her hair, the faded wardrobe, and her lack of makeup added another decade. Someone needed to give her a makeover.

"Do we ever really know what we want when it comes to love?" Eugenie asked. "Or do we come to understand that when it's too late?"

"It's not always a Rhett or Ashley choice though, is it?" Camille didn't look up from her needles. "The good guy or the bad boy. Life's not that simple."

"Or that complicated." Esther was weary of Eugenie's way of confusing the simplest question. "I think we make it too . . . what's the word? Messy, maybe. Or mysterious. We get carried away with our feelings."

"Scarlett was afraid of any man who was her equal," Hannah said with authority. "She just wanted to dominate and manipulate Ashley. Kind of like most of the cheerleading squad at the high school."

Esther pursed her lips to keep from smiling. Hannah always tried to shock them, but mostly her insights were amusing. And accurate.

"So how do we know if a man is an Ashley or a Rhett?" Eugenie asked.

For a moment, Esther resented Eugenie's analytical bent. The librarian had finally found the love of her life and could afford to be detached about the search for a mate. But Esther, having just lost hers, was at the opposite end of the spectrum. The prospect of finding another man with whom to share her life was so daunting that it made her want to run home, jump in bed, and pull the covers over her head. Especially when coupled with thoughts of Brody McCullough.

Thoughts that made her blurt out an answer.

"Frank was my Ashley Wilkes." Esther's words pierced the gloomy atmosphere, and the other women and Hannah looked at her as if she'd just sprouted another nose on her face.

"Esther, I know it's been a difficult time." Eugenie reached over as if to pat her hand, then stopped herself. "That is to say—"

"Then who's your Rhett Butler?" Hannah asked. Fourteen-year-olds apparently had fewer qualms than adults when it came to impertinent questions.

For once, Esther didn't resent the teenager's presence in the group. Hannah's honesty ordinarily irritated her, but today Esther felt like confronting things—the past, her feelings, and the other women seated around the table.

"I'm sure it's the shock of the loss—," Eugenie began, but Esther held up her hand and interrupted.

"No, Eugenie. It's the truth. I loved Frank, but was he my grand passion? I don't know." She felt her cheeks grow warm. Self-revelation was new to Esther, and she didn't like it one bit, but something was happening to her. Whether it was that dog or the loss of her lifestyle or Brody McCullough in his decrepit pickup truck, she didn't know. Whatever the cause might be, she couldn't stop what was happening.

"So who was your Rhett Butler, then?" Hannah asked again.

"She might not want to answer that." Maria laid down her yarn and needles and looked around the table. "We should respect her privacy."

Camille made a wry face. "A little late for that." The others laughed, and the tension eased.

"I'm just going to keep asking," Hannah said. "Who is your Rhett Butler?"

Esther paused and looked from one lady to another. Then she shook her head. "No. I can't tell you."

"You have to tell us." Camille leaned forward in her seat. "Come on. We deserve to know."

The others, except Eugenie, nodded in agreement. Esther suppressed a groan. Why had she opened her mouth to begin with?

"All right. If you must know, I think Ranger is my Rhett Butler."

"Your dog?" Eugenie peered at her over the top of her reading glasses, confusion pulling at the corners of her eyes.

"Yes. The dog." Esther wanted to slide under the table in embarrassment.

"He's the love of your life?" Camille said. Esther could see amusement in the younger woman's eyes.

"Yes, I think he might be."

She'd expected them to burst out into laughter. Instead they all looked at each other, then at the table, and finally back at her.

"Well," Maria said. And then smiled.

"Huh." Camille resumed knitting.

Hannah snorted. "The love of your life is a dog?"

The laughter did erupt then, but it was good-natured and Esther didn't take offense. She knew how strange it sounded, but it was also true. She only hoped none of the ladies repeated the story outside of their meeting. She'd fallen far enough in the eyes of Sweetgum as it was.

"On that note," Eugenie said, "perhaps we should share our projects."

"I'm guessing Esther knit Ranger a sweater," Hannah said with a teasing grin. Esther laughed along with the others, but only to cover up the rawness of her emotions.

Self-discovery should come with a first-aid kit, she decided.

As the end of January approached, Hannah practically barricaded herself in her room at the parsonage and read, dispatching *Wuthering Heights* in a matter of days.

She thought it was kind of a stupid story. All those people trying to be someone they weren't and making themselves miserable in the process. In her heart though, she knew she wasn't that different from the characters in the book. That had been her mistake with Josh. She'd tried to be someone she wasn't—the quarterback's girlfriend—and life, or fate or whatever you wanted to call it, had given her a major smack-down for her trouble.

Since that horrible Saturday by the creek, she had refused to take Josh's phone calls. Mrs. Carson looked at her with troubled eyes every time Hannah said to tell Josh she wasn't home. Mrs. Carson never told that lie, of course. She said Hannah was "unavailable," which was true. She didn't have time for jerks who treated girls like dirt.

One morning, though, when she turned up the walk that led to the front doors of the high school, Josh was sitting on the steps waiting for her. She almost pivoted on her heel and left, but she stopped herself and straightened her spine, hoisting her backpack higher on one shoulder. If she ran now, she'd be running the rest of the year.

"Hey." Josh didn't look good. His hair was mussed, and the collar of his polo shirt stuck up on one side. "I was waiting for you."

"I see that." She wouldn't make this easy for him, whatever he wanted to say. Not when just the sight of him made her want to burst into tears. Not when she could feel the eyes of dozens of other students on them, especially the heavily made-up ones belonging to the group of cheer-leaders and pompom girls milling around by the front doors.

"Why won't you talk to me?" He looked hurt, which sparked the latent anger in her heart.

"Why won't I talk to you?" She shook her head. "You really are a piece of work." That was an expression her mother had always used, usually in reference to Hannah.

Josh rose from the steps and towered over her. She wished he had stayed seated. It made it easier not to cry when she looked down on him instead of vice versa.

"Look, Hannah, I know I messed up. I messed up big time."

"Yes. You did."

He wiped a hand across his face and looked at the ground for a long moment. "I'm sorry." His eyes rose to meet her gaze. "I'm really sorry. I was stupid. I know that."

"That makes two of us." She refused to give a single inch. Why should she make this easy for him? He hadn't been humiliated in front of the entire school. Everyone knew. They looked at her with pity or laughter in their eyes, the slacker girl Josh Hargrove had led on, probably gotten what he wanted from, and then dumped. She knew what they were thinking.

"What do you want, Hannah?" he asked, his voice tight. "Do you want me to grovel?" He moved as if to go down on one knee. "If that's what it takes—"

"Stop it." She almost touched him, almost grabbed his arm to keep him from doing something that would draw even more notice than they were already getting. "You've humiliated me enough, okay? Just leave me alone."

That was the only way this would work. She had to cut him out of her life entirely, and he had to do the same with her. It was the only way for her to save face. They each had to pretend the other didn't exist. Romeo and Juliet they were not. More like the mismatched Heathcliff and Cathy, only Hannah was Heathcliff, the almost-beast, barely civilized.

Josh reached out and put his hand on her arm. Hannah forced herself not to jump, not to react.

"Don't touch me." She was proud of how calm her voice sounded. She refused to allow her heart rate to pick up. "Don't ever touch me again."

Josh dropped his hand. "Would you please give me a chance to explain?"

Hannah shook her head. "It doesn't matter, Josh. I don't know what I was thinking. Obviously, I wasn't thinking at all." Her throat tightened, and tears pricked at her eyes. "Go back to the football team and the cheerleaders and all of that, and just leave me alone. Leave me with at least a little dignity."

He dropped his hand, and his brown eyes filled with hurt. "So I'm not allowed to make a mistake?"

"It was a lot more than a mistake, Josh. A mistake is forgetting your homework or throwing an interception." She'd learned that much about football, sitting in the stands and silently cheering him on. "Everyone's laughing at me, Josh. Me, not you. You're still the great Josh Hargrove, football god, but I'm even more pathetic to all of them"—she waved toward the girls by the front doors—"than I was before."

"Hannah—"

She stepped around him and walked toward the building.

"I'm moving back to Alabama."

That stopped her, but she didn't turn around. "When?"

"Spring break."

Not that far away. Maybe after he left, the others would forget what had happened. Maybe they would let her return to her previous role as class loser instead of class laughingstock. She could only hope. Hope, and nurse a heart breaking at the news.

The only thing more painful than having Josh in her life was not having him in it at all.

"I'm sure they'll welcome you back with open arms," was all she could say before her voice broke. She raced up the steps, ignoring the curious looks from the other kids, and made a beeline for her locker.

One day at a time. One hour at a time. And soon, though not soon enough, he'd be gone and everyone would forget that brief period of time when Hannah Simmons thought she was good enough to date a jock.

• • •

During her break that morning, Eugenie left the library and walked up the street to the church. The winter wind, damp and swirling, chilled her before she'd made it halfway between the two buildings. Eugenie was determined to corner Paul in his study and set a few matters straight.

For more than two months, she'd held her peace about Paul's decision to cut back to part-time pay, just as she'd harbored the secret of her conversations with Hazel. Hazel had been right about one thing at least—for a minister, there was no such thing as part-time work.

What was Paul supposed to say to a parishioner who had an emergency late-night admission to the hospital? Or to the shut-ins he didn't have time to visit if he restricted his hours? His salary adjustment had begun only a few weeks before, but already Eugenie could see his head bowed just a little lower, his shoulders drooping the smallest bit. Over time, she believed, those signs would worsen. Eugenie, of all people, knew that being paid a fair wage for hard work was vital to a person's self-esteem.

Cora Lee, Paul's new secretary, waved at Eugenie from behind the plate-glass window that separated the church offices from the foyer. Ruthie Allen, Esther's sister, had been the church secretary until she'd left to do mission work in Africa last year. Eugenie missed Ruth a great deal. As unlike her sister as anyone could be, Ruth had provided the church with a calm, sensible presence. Cora Lee Bradford was more like a chicken on speed.

Eugenie admonished herself for the uncharitable thought and smiled as much as possible when she returned Cora Lee's wave. She opened the glass door and entered the office area.

"Hey, Eugenie." Cora Lee's bright red lips dominated her face beneath a shock of bleached blond hair. No one knew Cora Lee's age for certain. She'd hopped from job to job in Sweetgum for as long as Eugenie could remember. When Ruthie left last year, Cora Lee had landed in her chair before anyone could say anything. Paul never complained about her, though, so Eugenie supposed she must be a good worker.

"Good morning, Cora Lee. Is my husband in?"

"He'll be out in a tick. He's got Hazel Emerson in there." Cora Lee made a face. Eugenie had to school herself not to let her response to that bit of information show in her own expression.

"I don't mind waiting."

She didn't have to linger long. A few minutes later, after she and Cora Lee had chatted about the weather and the new specials at Tallulah's Café, Hazel and Paul emerged from the pastor's study.

"Your wife's here," Cora Lee said unnecessarily. Paul's face had lit up at the sight of Eugenie, even as Hazel's darkened.

"I don't want to disturb you," Eugenie began, but Paul waved her words away.

"I'm free. Let me just see Hazel to the door."

Hazel looked offended at the suggestion that she might need to be shown the door, but Eugenie recognized Paul's strategy. She'd often employed it herself with problematic library patrons. Under the guise of politeness, you could nudge your problems right out the door.

"Just remember what I said, Preacher," Hazel said, wagging a finger at Paul. "It's not too late."

"I'll consider it," was Paul's only response, and Eugenie couldn't tell what they'd been discussing. She was eager to know, though. Hazel certainly worked diligently to spread her poison around Sweetgum and its environs.

"Go on in and have a seat, Eugenie," Paul instructed her as he moved away with Hazel.

Eugenie did just that, closing the door to the pastor's study behind her so she wouldn't have to continue her conversation with Cora Lee. She needed a minute to gather her thoughts.

A moment later he was back. He took her in his arms and kissed her. Eugenie especially liked that part of marriage and could only regret all the years she'd missed out on such simple but enjoyable displays of affection.

"So what's on your mind?" Paul asked when he released her. He waved toward one of the chairs across from his desk. Eugenie sat down, and Paul lowered himself into the one next to her. "Must be important if you're here in the middle of the day."

His comment stung. It wasn't intentional, she knew, but was he implying, as Hazel Emerson had more than boldly stated, that her job was more important to her than her new husband?

"I wanted to talk to you about your decision to go part time."

He'd told her about it weeks ago, as part of a very brief, very casual conversation. She hadn't reacted then. Now, though, she didn't feel as if she had any choice in the matter. They might not be young and fragile, but their marriage was. Eugenie had kept her feelings for Paul a secret for forty years, from the moment they'd gone their separate ways after an early courtship. She didn't want to keep secrets anymore.

"I should have said something sooner." She tried to focus her thoughts so she could present a logical argument. "I guess I didn't realize the implications. Didn't *want* to realize them."

Paul arched an eyebrow in surprise. "What's bothering you about my decision?"

Eugenie took a deep breath. "I feel as if it's my fault."

"Your fault?" He looked even more surprised.

"The budget problems. They're because of me."

Paul looked at her as if she'd just sprouted a second head. "You think this is about you?"

"Hazel Emerson approached me last fall. She told me that many of the members don't believe I'm a Christian. She said it made the budget problems worse."

Paul was silent for a long moment, long enough to make Eugenie nervous. She'd hoped he would wave her worries away and assure her that Hazel was completely off base. Instead, he looked at his hands, clasped between his knees. Anywhere but at her.

"Why didn't you tell me?" Eugenie's question came out as a bark.

"Your faith is your business, Eugenie, and no one else's."

"Hazel says I need to prove I'm a believer."

Paul laughed. "Is that why you've been volunteering for everything in sight?" He shook his head. "Your relationship to the church, to God, isn't about me. It shouldn't be, anyway."

"But—"

"Look, Eugenie, I've dealt with far more difficult problems over the course of my career. I'll get through this."

"Yes, I'm sure you will, but it shouldn't be just you getting through this. I'm your wife. We're supposed to be a team now."

"So what should I have done? Told you that you had to stand up in worship and make a statement of faith?"

Eugenie pursed her lips. "Of course not. But you

had to have known how people felt. We could have at least discussed it."

"There's nothing to discuss." As quick as a wink, his eyes went blank, as if he'd pulled a set of window blinds closed. Eugenie had never seen him do that before.

"Paul? What's going on?"

"Nothing. You're making a mountain out of a molehill."

"Then why do you look like that? Sound like that?"

"I don't know what you mean." He turned away to shuffle some papers on his desk.

"You sound like I'm not allowed to know what you're thinking. To be part of your decision. Your life."

At that his face crumpled, as if a giant hand had wadded him up like a sheet of paper. "Eugenie—"

Just her name, but filled with anguish.

"Paul—" She reached for him, grabbing his clasped hands in hers. "Tell me."

He shook his head, and then his shoulders began to shake as well. Eugenie, for the first time in decades, knew pure fear.

"Paul, you have to tell me. What is it?"

He raised his watery gaze to hers. "It was my fault."

"What was your fault?"

"Helen's death. Helen's death was my fault."

Eugenie's head snapped back, as if he'd delivered a physical blow. "Your wife died of cancer." She gripped his hands more tightly. "How in the world could that be your fault?"

"I pushed her too hard, wanting her to meet everyone's expectations. The older I got, the more I tried to dictate to her."

Eugenie couldn't imagine Paul being dictatorial to anyone. "That's just survivor's guilt talking. I'm sure you did no such thing."

Paul laughed, but there was no humor in the sound. Only pain and loss. "I did. And eventually it killed her."

"So your solution is to not ask anything of me? Even if what you're saying is true, isn't that jumping out of the frying pan into the fire?" She paused. "Besides, I've heard you talk about Helen. She doesn't seem like a pushover from the way you describe her."

"She started to get tired, but I ignored it. Just kept encouraging her to play the piano for the children's choir, organize the fund-raising walk for steeple repairs." He freed his hands from her grasp. "None of which was a matter of life-and-death."

"People get sick, Paul. You can't control that."

"But I made her worse. Made it worse."

"How do you know that?"

And then, though she'd been afraid before, terror rose in her as she looked into his eyes, no longer blank but instead filled with anguish.

"I pushed her when she was sick, and she died. I'm not going to make that mistake again."

All her life Eugenie had thought preachers were a cut above regular people. She'd believed they had some special connection to God that insulated them from the vagaries of human existence. But since she and Paul had reconnected, she'd begun to see a new, clearer picture of the life of a minister. Now that Paul had revealed his secret fear to her, she could interpret his insistence that she not conform to the church's expectations in a whole new light. He wasn't being generous or tolerant or supportive. He was afraid.

"Paul, I'm not going to die just because I do a few things for the church. Or because Hazel Emerson and her ilk question my faith."

He shook his head. "I know that."

"But do you? Do you really? Or do you just know it without believing it?"

He looked at her. She could see that thought hadn't occurred to him before. "Maybe you're right."

"Of course I'm right. And it's not your job to sacrifice yourself at my expense."

"Eugenie—"

"That's why," she said, the words spilling out before she'd consciously formed them, "I've decided to stand up next Sunday and give my testimony."

Twenty-Five

Esther wasn't sure how it had happened, how she and Brody McCullough had come to eat dinner together numerous times over the course of several weeks. They certainly weren't dating, of that much she was sure. He was simply her friend.

Since Esther had left college to marry Frank and have her first child, she hadn't made many friends. She had her bridge club, her garden club, and the social committee at the country club. Funny how all those things had the word *club* in the name, but none of them had the word *friend*.

Sometimes she and Brody ate at Tallulah's Café after he finished at the veterinary clinic for the day. If anyone from her various clubs asked about him, she told them he was giving her advice on Ranger. Other times she cooked him dinner at her home. The house still languished on the market. The problem with owning one of the grandest homes in Sweetgum was that no one else could afford it.

During the second week in February, on a Friday evening, Brody appeared on her doorstep with a package wrapped in white paper. Steaks. Filets to be exact. Esther's favorite.

"We can grill them," he said, a twinkle in his eye that she was coming to recognize as a sign he was particularly pleased with himself. He must have had a good day at the clinic.

"I don't know if there's any gas in the tank for the grill," she said in mild protest. Grilling in February? Funny how Brody could suggest something and get her to go along with it in a way Frank never could.

Of course, she and Frank had shared a vested interest in maintaining their facade of perfection. With Brody, she was finding, she could just be herself. He never asked about her money problems, never hinted that he knew, but he invariably turned up with some sort of treat. Tonight it was steaks. On New Year's Eve it had been a bottle of French champagne. Even Ranger had shared in the bounty, as Brody brought several bags of the prescription dog food Ranger needed. It had turned out, of course, that the dog had an especially sensitive stomach. Esther was sure it came from eating so many of her hydrangeas.

"I can run to the hardware store for another tank of propane if we need it." He handed her the package and rubbed his hands together. "Let's see if we can fire that bad boy up."

Just last week he'd been eyeing Frank's massive outdoor grill. All Esther could do was laugh. That monstrosity was the dream of every man who'd ever gripped a barbecue fork. They might as well enjoy that ridiculous grill as long as they could. Surely the house would sell before spring.

After the proverbial dust had settled, Esther discovered that while her finances were bleak, she was not without hope. The sale of the house, when it finally happened, would provide her with a tidy nest egg. The hard part, of course, had been changing the financial habits of a lifetime.

She'd studiously avoided Maxine's Dress Shop and could only hope Camille wasn't offended. Esther knew she'd always been the store's best customer. She hadn't been to Nashville or Memphis in months—another way to save money. She wasn't exactly searching under sofa cushions for spare change to buy bread and milk, but now she had to think through every expenditure. On one occasion, at Vanderpool's Groceries, she'd even put an item back on the shelf rather than go over her self-imposed spending limit. Strangely enough, she'd found the whole episode empowering.

"Any word from your real estate agent?" Brody asked when they settled into their chairs in the breakfast room. Other than Christmas Eve dinner, they'd eaten more informally, just off the kitchen. The breakfast room's bay window boasted an expansive view of Esther's yard and garden.

Esther shook her head. "I feel as if I'm in a pit, and I have no idea how to climb out of it." As difficult as it would be to leave her home, she was ready to make the transition. This long, slow parting was worse than a clean, quick break.

"Have you considered lowering the price?"

Esther shook her head. "Not yet. Maybe in the spring if this goes on that long."

"It will sell soon," he said with calm assurance. "Then what will you do? What's next?"

Esther took a moment to slice off a bite of the delicious filet. She chewed thoughtfully and finally said, "I'll move to my condo at the lake. Beyond that, I have no idea."

Brody laughed. "Well, at least you've given your lack of plans a lot of thought."

Esther laughed, too, in spite of everything. He was good at making her see the humor in her difficulties.

"If you could do anything in the world, what would you do?" he asked. "No limits. Whatever your heart desired."

"No limits?" She'd never asked herself that before.

"Would you stay in Sweetgum?"

Esther nodded. "I was born and raised here. I've lived here most of my life." Unexpectedly, a small sob rose in her throat. It wasn't the first time grief had surprised her. She took a deep breath so she wouldn't cry. "I guess I never envisioned anything but doing what I've always done. Growing old with Frank. Doing my clubs. Spoiling my grandchildren."

"You can still do two of those three."

Esther shook her head. "Not without money."

And then she was sorry she'd brought up the subject. She didn't want to talk about it.

Brody took a sip of his iced tea. "If you could try something new, what would it be? What are you passionate about?"

"Passionate?" Esther had no idea. She never thought of herself or her life in those terms. Duty, social standing, family—those were the things she had always known. She shrugged. "I have no idea."

"What's your favorite thing to do?"

"Shop, of course." She smiled with more than a touch of self-deprecation. "I'm very good at that."

"So why don't you try the flip side of the coin?" Brody leaned back in his chair. "Why not open a store?"

"In Sweetgum? I'd be broke in six months."

"Not necessarily."

"How do you know that?"

Brody looked away, as if considering something, and then turned his attention back to her. "If I tell you something, do you promise to keep it confidential?"

Esther couldn't imagine what he could possibly tell her that would need to be shrouded in secrecy. "Yes. Of course."

"It's about the lake."

"The lake? What about it?" The ancient boat slips and even older clubhouse at Sweetgum Lake sat below the small condo development where Esther would live once her house sold.

"It's going to be redeveloped by some investors from Memphis. Upgrades to everything. New condos and lake cottages, retail, restaurants, the works." He put both hands palm down on the table. "It's going to be massive, Esther. And it's going to bring a lot of business to Sweetgum."

"Surely we would have heard about that. How do you know all this anyway?"

"Because my friend James is behind it all."

"The one you thought might buy my house?"

"Yes."

"But when—"

"They're going to announce it publicly in a few months." He stood and picked up their plates. "The influx of people will bring new life to Sweetgum and a lot of money to business owners."

"Oh."

"So if you decided to go into some kind of business for yourself, now would be the time."

"I can't. Not until the house sells."

"You could borrow against the equity in your home."

She suddenly found it very hard to breathe as panic spread through her. How could she possibly run her own business? She'd helped Frank from time to time with some aspects of his practice, but she was by no means well versed in things like inventory and accounting and payroll.

"I couldn't—"

"Your own clothing store. That's what you need."

"Sweetgum already has one." And she knew Camille struggled every month to balance the books. "Maxine's, on the square. My friend Camille runs it."

Brody scraped the plates and rinsed them before placing them in the dishwasher. They'd gotten so comfortable with this routine—Esther cooking and Brody cleaning up—that she hardly noticed it anymore. "Maybe you should offer to buy her out," he said.

"But what would Camille do?"

Leave Sweetgum. The answer popped into Esther's head immediately. The younger woman had been waiting for years to get out of her hometown, and now that Nancy St. Clair had passed away, Camille was free to go.

Brody poured them both a cup of decaf coffee from the waiting pot. He put sugar in his, sweetener in hers, and then brought the cups to the table. This time he took the seat next to her instead of across the table.

"What are you thinking?" he asked.

"I was thinking about Camille. She's always wanted to get out of Sweetgum. She never got to go to college because her mother fell ill."

"Maybe this is an opportunity for both of you."

To her surprise, Esther found herself nodding. "Maybe it is."

Then reality came flooding back. She had no

business borrowing money against her house for such a risky venture. Habit and instinct told her she needed to hoard every penny she could find. Now that Frank was gone, she was a widow. Alone. But the thought of a miserly, diminished existence depressed her more than the idea of taking a risk scared her.

"I don't know," she said, and Brody let the subject drop.

But the seed had been planted, and Esther couldn't quite put it out of her mind.

Maria couldn't figure out why James Delevan kept turning up—at the five-and-dime, at Tallulah's, even at church. She also couldn't figure out why he was still in Sweetgum. Since Christmas, she had seen him at least two or three times a week. Once, she'd even gone upstairs to find him drinking coffee with her mother.

Maria couldn't understand it. From the first, he'd made his contempt for her family clear. But now he didn't seem contemptuous at all. He was civil, polite. But why?

When she posed this question to Daphne, her sister only smiled.

"Surely Evan's told you what's going on?" Maria pressed. The only person turning up at the five-and-dime on a more regular basis than James Delevan was Evan Baxter. After that night at the movies, he'd disappeared, but not long ago he'd shown up at the five-and-dime with an apology and a dinner invitation for Daphne.

"Maybe he just likes the company," Daphne said evasively.

Friday evening, a week before the next meeting of the Knit Lit Society, Maria found herself closing up the store alone. Thankfully, business had been brisk that day, but it meant extra time dealing with the night deposit and balancing the register. By the time she finished and had the bank bag tucked under her arm, it was close to eight o'clock.

She let herself out of the store, locked the door behind her, and turned her steps toward the bank down the street, past Tallulah's Café and the post office.

"Would you like some company?"

The male voice, coming out of the darkness, startled her, and she gripped the bank bag with her free hand. Then the speaker materialized under the streetlight. James Delevan.

"Don't sneak up on me like that," she snapped and then bit her lip. "Sorry. But you scared me."

He stepped closer. Too close, really. Every nerve stood on end, not from fright but from her own unmanageable feelings. Feelings she'd not dared admit anywhere but the privacy of her own thoughts. She was far too old to play the fairy-tale princess in need of rescuing, and James was far too stiff and distant to be anyone's idea of Prince Charming.

"I didn't mean to alarm you." His eyes were dark and unreadable. He glanced at the zippered vinyl bag pressed to her side. "Are you headed to the bank?"

"Yes."

"Would you like me to walk with you?"

She nodded, not sure she trusted her voice.

He took her elbow, a proprietary gesture that should have irritated her. She was a grown woman, for heaven's sake. She'd been walking the side-walks of Sweetgum on her own for several decades. But strangely enough, she didn't resist, didn't even feel the urge to pull away. She just let his hand rest there.

"Do you always go by yourself to the night drop?" he asked, concern and a hint of disapproval in his tone.

She shook her head. "Not always. But Sweetgum's not exactly a hotbed of criminal activity. Besides"—she tapped the bag—"it's not like I've got a fortune in here."

"No one ever bothers you?"

"Only you," she said, smiling a little.

He took her teasing with good grace. "Still, you should be careful."

His concern was both novel and genuine, and it disconcerted her.

"Have you had dinner?" James asked as they passed Tallulah's. "We could come back." He nodded toward the café. Even after football season ended, Tallulah had kept the café open late on Fridays. The place was full but not packed.

"No, I haven't eaten." Did she really want to spend more time with James Delevan? Maria looked up at him, at the strong line of his jaw and the inky darkness of his hair. She was dangerously close, she knew, to falling in love with him. Pathetic, really. All it took was a handsome face and a bit of concern for her safety and well-being, and she was a goner. But then, spinsters were supposed to be easy pickings, weren't they?

"Then we should come back," he said, making the decision for her. Maria didn't object. How could she? She wanted his company. Not that it would last for long. She had no doubt that sooner or later he would tire of Sweetgum, or his role in the lakeside development would end.

In the meantime though, why shouldn't she enjoy herself? In the end, if she felt any pain when he left, she would have only herself to blame.

"Dinner would be nice," she said and fell into step beside him.

This time she shared a meal at Tallulah's with James Delevan and found it to be completely enjoyable. They talked easily, the food was delicious, and the other patrons looked at Maria with a new respect. Not that James treated her in any overtly romantic way. No handholding, no sharing bites off each other's forks, and certainly no kisses shared across the small, Formica-topped table. Not that people did that kind of thing in Sweetgum anyway. That was reserved for those Hollywood stars who hadn't been raised right, as Maria's mother would say.

After the meal he walked her back down the street and around the corner to the side door of the five-and-dime.

"Thank you for dinner," she said, suddenly unsure what to do with her hands. She thrust them in her coat pockets. Here, on the side of the building, the light from the streetlamps didn't penetrate the darkness. She could feel James standing next to her far better than she could see him.

"You're welcome."

She didn't know what to do next. Was it so wrong to think that the attention he paid her meant he was interested? At least a little?

"I'd invite you up, but—"

"I wouldn't want to disturb your family."

If they had still lived at the farm, she would have asked him in to sit in the living room. Offered him another cup of coffee. Kept him for a little longer.

Time to let it go, Cinderella, she admonished herself.

"Well, good—"

She never got to finish. Instead, she found herself pulled against James's chest. Somehow, in the darkness, his lips found hers.

In that short, thrilling moment just before he kissed her, when she felt his breath on her cheek, Maria thought her knees might buckle. Fortunately, he held her upper arms so she didn't slide to the pavement in a heap of ignominy.

Maria hadn't been kissed in a very long time. She was afraid she'd forgotten how, but it turned out it was like riding the proverbial bicycle. At least it was with James. And not just any bicycle. A very fast, racing bicycle.

After several enjoyable moments, he pulled away. "Maria . . ."

The tone of his voice should have warned her.

"I'm sorry," he continued. "I shouldn't have done that."

She was glad the darkness hid the heat that blazed across her cheeks. "No big deal." She didn't trust her voice enough to say anything more.

"I need to tell you—" He paused. "Look, I'm leaving town tomorrow."

"Oh." What was she supposed to say to that? "When will you be back?"

Silence. A long, painful moment of silence.

"You're not coming back." She said the words for him, without inflection. Without a hint of the pain they caused.

"I don't think so, no."

Suddenly, she was angry. "Then why did you do that? Why do you keep showing up here? Why take me out to dinner?"

303

"Because I felt sor—" He stopped himself, but not soon enough.

He felt sorry for her. Of course he did. Sad, prematurely middle-aged Maria Munden, who lapped up affection like a neglected puppy.

"Good-bye, James." It was all she could manage around the huge lump in her throat.

"Maria—"

He reached for her, but in the darkness his hand only brushed the sleeve of her coat. She turned, fumbled in her pocket for the key, and jammed it into the lock. *Hurry.* That was all she could think. *Hurry.*

"Maria—"

She didn't look back—just opened the door, stumbled inside, and slammed it behind her.

"Maria!" His voice, louder now, barked with impatience. "Let me finish!"

She didn't wait to hear any more. She scrambled up the steps, then paused at the top of the stairs to catch her breath and wipe the tears from her face. Two deep breaths, then another. She straightened her spine and reached for the doorknob.

Don't think about it, she ordered herself. *Don't think about him.*

By the time she swung open the door and stepped inside the living room, she had her expression under firm control.

If only she could have said the same about her heart.

Twenty-Six

At twenty minutes after eight on a cold February morning, Merry sat in the driver's seat of her minivan in the church parking lot. She'd been sitting there for half an hour, actually, but had yet to bring herself to get out of the car, much less take Hunter from his car seat in the back and carry him inside.

Other mothers and a few dads dropping off their children gave her curious looks. Some of them, when they realized who she was, made sympathetic faces. No one, however, came over to talk to her. No one, that is, until Eugenie pulled into the lot and saw her sitting there with her hands frozen to the steering wheel.

"How long have you been sitting here?" she asked when Merry rolled down the window.

The winter air, cold and damp, made Merry's eyes sting. "Awhile."

"Are you coming in today?" Eugenie asked in a neutral tone.

"Probably not."

Eugenie looked up, as if seeking divine guidance, then looked back at Merry with a pleasant but determined expression on her face.

"Hunter didn't get Kawasaki disease because you put him in day care."

Merry nodded. "I know that."

"Children have been coming to Mother's Day Out here for two generations."

"I know you're right."

"You know it, but you don't *feel* it." Eugenie's voice remained calm and even.

Merry could only nod in agreement. Somewhere along the way, probably about the time the doctor at the children's hospital looked at her with pity in his eyes, Merry had lost her ability to think rationally. Long days in the hospital spent soothing Hunter, trying to keep him from pulling out the IV pumping lifesaving medicine into him. Long nights alone, pacing his room because of what might happen if she fell asleep. Paul Carson had visited frequently, making the hour-and-a-half drive far more often than Merry ever would have expected.

"It's nothing," Paul had said, waving away her objections.

After her first visit, Camille came on Mondays, when Maxine's Dress Shop was closed, to give Merry a respite. Eugenie and Esther had both offered to come, but Merry declined their help. She didn't want to be away from Hunter. No need for them to drive all the way to Nashville just to sit with her.

The person she really would have liked to have by her side was Ruthie, Esther's sister. Ruthie had been a frequent babysitter at the McGavin house, especially for any overnight trips Merry and Jeff took. But Ruthie was practically on the other side of the earth.

Eugenie reached for the handle on the minivan door. The click when she opened it jerked Merry back to the present.

"Come on, Merry. You need to get to work. Hunter will be fine. The pediatrician cleared him to go back to the baby room. There's no reason to sit here."

No reason? *No reason?* Merry wanted to scream. Eugenie had not been the one sitting all those nights with nothing to do but knit and read. *Wuthering Heights* had been the perfect choice. She could lose herself in the melodrama of the Henshaws and the Lintons and, for a few moments, forget how close she'd come to losing her baby.

"I can't," she said to Eugenie and pulled the door closed. "I can't."

Merry didn't look at the other woman. She didn't want to see the pity in her eyes. She knew how pathetic she must seem. Her child was okay, but the fear that had seized her when she answered the phone that day at Jeff's office that was the kind of fear that never went away.

Elemental. That was the word for it.

"Maybe tomorrow," Eugenie said, smiling. "I need to get inside for my committee meeting." She paused. "You know, I can give you the name of a good therap—"

"No, thank you." Merry looked at her and grimaced a smile of thanks in return. "I'd better go."

She raised the window, started the van, and looked behind her to make sure Eugenie was out of sight before she backed out of the parking space.

Jeff didn't understand. He'd be furious, but Merry didn't care. She signaled a right-hand turn out of the parking lot and headed for home.

That same Monday morning, Camille and Esther met at Maxine's Dress Shop.

For the past several months, they'd been meeting this way—secretly, unbeknownst to the other members of the Knit Lit Society, in the back room of the small store. The only exceptions had been the Mondays when Camille went to stay with Merry and Hunter at the hospital in Nashville. Otherwise, they'd been regular as clockwork, although no one could have guessed the real purpose of their clandestine meetings.

"There. That's it. You're getting it," Camille said as she leaned over Esther's shoulder. Esther bit her tongue in concentration as she held the knitting needles, trying to keep the tension on her yarn, and attempted to execute a purl stitch.

"It's still lumpy," Esther protested.

Camille stifled a smile. "Keep going. It will get better."

"If you say so." She forged ahead, in a manner of speaking, working to establish a smooth rhythm of poking the needle up through the stitch, wrapping the yarn around it, and then pulling it back through.

"You could have been doing this all along," Camille said, but she wasn't criticizing.

"I wasn't ready to admit I needed help." She stopped and rescued a stitch she was about to drop. "Not until Frank died."

"The others never have to know," Camille said.

She was surprised that Esther had managed to conceal her inability to knit for so long. During the meetings, she usually held her work in her lap so no one would notice. Then, after the meeting, she would hand the project over to Camille, who completed it for her. She and Esther had agreed on a fair rate, which worked to both their advantages. Now, though, Esther no longer had the money to pay someone to do her knitting for her, and Camille was relieved. She would much rather teach Esther to knit than help her continue the subterfuge.

"I want to buy the dress shop," Esther blurted.

Camille's head shot up from her own knitting, and she looked at Esther in astonishment. "What?"

Esther set her knitting on the table. "I've given this a lot of thought. It solves both our problems. You'll be free to leave Sweetgum, and I'll be able to earn a living."

"I couldn't let you take the risk," Camille said, although she felt suddenly lightheaded. "Retail in Sweetgum will always be a struggle."

"It may not." Esther paused. "Can I tell you something in confidence?"

Camille nodded, unsure what else to do.

"A new development is going in at the lake. Sweetgum should see a huge increase in tourists, summer people. I might even open a small branch of Maxine's at the marina, maybe just accessories and boating wear."

"But I thought you were broke," Camille said. "Sorry, I didn't mean—"

"I'll borrow the money against the eventual sale of my house." Esther's voice thickened. "It's time to let go of the past. I'm sure we can agree on a fair price, and I'd pay you for your time while you showed me the ropes. You could go ahead and enroll at MTSU. Finally have your dream of going to college."

"Esther—"

"You've changed your mind. About leaving Sweetgum."

Camille nodded, unable to speak. Bitterness welled in her throat. Didn't her life always go like this? No matter how many Sundays she sat on a pew at the Sweetgum Christian Church, she'd never understand God. Or His sick sense of humor.

Be careful what you pray for. Her mother's favorite adage echoed in her head.

"I'm sure you and Dante could find a way to make it work."

"It's too far to commute," Camille said, misery

seeping from each word. "And I can't see Dante waiting four years for me to finish."

Esther frowned. "No. I guess not."

Camille looked up at the older woman. "It's too late for me."

Esther shook her head. "No, Camille. You're only twenty-four. You have an entire life ahead of you."

Camille twisted a skein of yarn in her hands. "I know I can be happy here with Dante. It's foolish to hang on to old dreams. They were never going to come true in the first place. I should have learned that lesson a long time ago."

Camille hated to see the disappointment on Esther's face, but if she stayed in Sweetgum to be with Dante, there was no need to sell. The store would provide a small additional income to supplement Dante's coaching salary.

"So you're not interested in selling?"

"I'm afraid not."

"Well, that's that then." Esther picked up her knitting and slid it into her bag. "I understand, of course. But if you change your mind . . ."

"I don't think I will." She paused. "Esther, I know we're not the best of friends, but I'd hate for this to come between us."

Esther leaned over and, to Camille's amazement, patted her hand. "I'm sure it will all turn out for the best. There's no need for anyone else in the Knit Lit Society to know about this. I'd appreciate it if you wouldn't say anything about the marina."

Camille smiled her thanks. "I don't think you're going to need any more knitting lessons. I think you've got it down pat."

"Finally." Esther looked softer, more vulnerable than Camille had ever seen her, even after Frank Jackson's death.

"So." Esther stood, brushing at the creases in her skirt. "I'd better be going."

It was too bad, really, that Esther Jackson wasn't the type of person you could hug, because Camille would have liked to at that moment.

"I'm sorry, Esther. You probably would do better with the dress shop than I ever could."

Esther waved a hand in dismissal. "It was just a thought."

Just a thought. Just everything Camille had ever wanted. Esther had just offered Camille her last chance out of Sweetgum, and she had turned it down. Because she loved Dante. Once again, the price of love would be her dreams.

Twenty-Seven

Hannah's heart was as heavy as her steps. She hadn't wanted to go to the Knit Lit Society meeting, but Eugenie talked her into it. They walked the short block from the parsonage to the church together without saying much. Hannah still hadn't told the librarian about her break with Josh.

Thankfully, Eugenie wasn't the type to pry. Other than to keep tabs on Hannah's schoolwork, of course.

The Pairs and Spares Sunday school classroom was cold. Rev. Carson had told her they were trying to conserve electricity because the bills were so high. Hannah was an old hand at that. When she'd lived with her mom in the trailer, they had their power cut off all the time. A little chill in a Sunday school room was nothing compared to seeing your breath frost in the air when you lay in bed at night.

Eugenie fiddled with the thermostat, and Hannah took her usual place at the table. This month's project had been to use the fan-and-feather stitch. The combination of decreases and yarn overs had confused her at first, but gradually she'd gotten the hang of it. She'd had plenty of time to work on it since she spent all of her free time holed up in her bedroom at the parsonage.

As much as she resented Josh's betrayal, she resented the freedom it cost her even more. Even all these weeks later, the popular kids still laughed and pointed at her. Josh had left a couple of notes in her locker, but she'd dropped them in the trash without reading them. And in honors English class, she'd taken to sitting in the front row, a move that kept her from having to look at the back of his head for an hour every day.

"It will warm up in here in a minute," Eugenie

said, setting her knitting bag on its wooden legs next to her chair and then rubbing her arms vigorously.

"Doesn't bother me," Hannah said. She hoped the rest of the women showed up soon. She'd managed to avoid being alone with Eugenie for extended periods, which helped the whole don't-ask-don't-tell policy succeed when it came to Josh.

Footsteps sounded in the hall, and Merry appeared at the door. She could hardly walk since she carried her purse, a knitting bag, a diaper bag, and Hunter's infant seat.

Hannah sprang to her feet. "Let me help."

She had missed the baby when Merry quit bringing him to meetings in the fall. Hannah hadn't seen him since he'd been so sick, although he looked pretty healthy now from what she could tell. She reached for his carrier, and Merry reluctantly handed him over.

"Thanks," she said, but Hannah knew she didn't really want to let go of him. She'd heard from Eugenie that Merry still hadn't taken him back to day care. Hannah wondered what that would be like, to have a mother who cared about you so much she was afraid to leave you alone even for a minute.

One by one, the others arrived. Maria looked out of sorts, so Hannah avoided her. Camille didn't look much better. Hannah thought she'd probably been crying, judging from the dark circles under her eyes.

"Let's get started, everyone," Eugenie said, calling them to some kind of order. "I'm interested to hear what you have to say about *Wuthering Heights*. I know, as a love story, it's not to everyone's taste."

There was a general murmur of assent to that comment.

"It was pretty convoluted," Merry said, leaning down to rock Hunter with one hand while trying to hold on to her knitting with the other. "Of course, I don't have the greatest powers of concentration these days. I may have missed the point."

Hannah was impressed she even had time to read the book, what with Hunter's illness and all.

"I've never heard of people who were so good at making themselves miserable," Camille said. "I don't think any of them really wanted to be happy."

Hannah bit her tongue. If ever she'd met anyone who ran away from happiness at top speed, it was Camille St. Clair. She'd been the golden girl in high school, not a loser like Hannah, but she was still miserable. Hannah couldn't understand why. If she'd been homecoming queen, prom queen, and head cheerleader—the perfect trio—she'd never know a minute of unhappiness the rest of her life.

"What kind of love would you say Emily Brontë was writing about in the novel?" Eugenie asked, keeping to her theme. "Try to describe it in one word."

"Obsessive." Camille's answer was as flat as it was succinct. "She's trying to show that you can love too much. That in the end it can destroy you."

Well, that was cheery. Hannah shook her head, then looked up to see if Camille had noticed.

"I disagree." Maria frowned. "That horrible old man, Cathy's father. What was his name? He couldn't love enough. Not real love. He wanted everything on his own terms. There was no room for anyone else's needs or desires in his mind."

Hannah nodded her agreement. Frankly, the old man had born a distinct resemblance to her mom. Self-centered, ruthless, and manipulative.

"I think Emily Brontë must have been haunted by love," Merry said. She reached down to adjust Hunter's blanket so he was fully covered while he slept.

Another pang shot through Hannah. She'd felt alone before the whole disaster with Josh. Now, watching Merry with Hunter, she felt even worse. It didn't help that Merry was Courtney's mother. She thought Courtney would have turned out nicer given how much love and attention she'd always had.

"So what can we learn about love from *Wuthering Heights*?" Eugenie asked. "What does Brontë say that's unique? Different from the other authors we've read?"

Hannah wanted to say she'd learned to quit thinking that one day she'd finally find someone

316

who loved her enough to put her welfare above his own. As nice as Rev. Carson and Eugenie were, they weren't family. They could change their minds at any moment and kick her to the curb without looking back. Not that they would—at least, she didn't think so—but the possibility still existed.

"Brontë's not much of a romantic," Maria said. "Her characters are all so mean to each other."

"But they're mean out of love, which is weird," Hannah couldn't help but add. "I thought love was supposed to make people nice."

Camille shook her head. "No. Sometimes love is the worst thing that can happen to you."

Hannah looked around the table, wondering what the others would say to that. As she expected, everyone was quiet. Eugenie tried several other questions to prompt more discussion, but there wasn't much energy. Hannah looked at Eugenie, at the lines of frustration around her mouth. Too bad that by making them read all these love stories, she'd made everyone less of a believer than they were before.

"All right. Well, what about the project then?" Eugenie asked. "What did you design with the fan-and-feather stitch?"

The majority were shawls for one of the Cathys. The colors and textures, though, ran the gamut from Camille's sparkly silver angora to Eugenie's sensible navy wool. Hannah's own project—a scarf for Heathcliff—looked a little strange. The lacy pattern was hardly masculine, but Eugenie said it was okay to experiment. Hannah thought she'd about had her fill of trying new things.

"You've all done a nice job," Eugenie said. "Next month we'll discuss *Pride and Prejudice*."

"Appropriate," Esther said under her breath, and Hannah chuckled at her sarcastic tone. After Mr. Jackson died, Hannah thought Esther might lose her edge, but she seemed to be returning to her usual prickly self. Hannah preferred people like that, because you always knew where you stood with them.

The group remained around the table for a while longer, chatting and knitting. Hunter woke up at one point, crying for a bottle. When Merry asked Hannah if she wanted to give him his bottle, she started to refuse, but before she knew what was happening, she had the baby in her arms and he was greedily sucking away.

"You're a natural," Merry assured her. Hannah looked down at the baby, touched that Merry would put him into her care. Hannah knew how distressed she'd been about his illness.

Looking at Hunter McGavin, Hannah wondered, not for the first time, why her own mother couldn't love her enough to stick around. Once upon a time, Hannah had been a baby like this. Her mother must have fed her, rocked her, changed her diaper. But somewhere along the way, that love had gone wrong, like in Emily Brontë's story. It had been twisted out of recognition and then abandoned.

Hannah bit back tears and hoped no one noticed the spots where some of them fell on the baby's blanket.

Twenty-Eight

Eugenie had never been given to rash actions. All her life she'd taken measured steps. As Jane Austen would say, she was a rational creature. Eugenie knew that sound, considered decisions yielded the best results, but her decision to speak in front of the church, as impulsive as it had been that day in Paul's office, wasn't one she wanted to change.

So the next time Hazel Emerson came into the library, Eugenie was prepared.

"About the concerns you've shared with me," she found herself saying to Hazel. "I've—"

"Made your position quite clear." Hazel sniffed. "I'm not here to pester you anymore. If you don't mind watching your husband's career implode, I'm sure there's nothing I can—"

"I've asked Paul if I can speak to the congregation."

Hazel's eyes widened and her jaw dropped. If nothing else, the decision was worth it just to behold that sight.

"I'm sorry?" Poor Hazel seemed quite disoriented.

"I've thought it over," Eugenie continued, "and I think the only way people's questions about my faith can be put to rest is if I address the church members directly."

"But—"

"Isn't that what you suggested? That I prove my faith to the church?"

"Well, I didn't mean it in exactly . . . that is, of course, it would be your decision . . ." For the first time since Eugenie had known her, Hazel Emerson was at a loss for words.

"Some people still won't be satisfied, I know." Eugenie paused. "But I can tell you what I will say."

Hazel stiffened. "It's not as if we're judging—"

"Yes, you are." Eugenie made an effort to keep her tone measured and even, although it wasn't easy. "Which is one of the reasons I stayed away from church for forty years."

"You can hardly blame the church for that." Hazel put her shoulders back and lifted her chin. "After all, if God is missing from our lives, it's because *we* turned away."

"Yes, yes. I've heard that one before." Eugenie wondered that people could find comfort in old chestnuts like that one. "That's the kind of belittling reprimand that passes for theology. Frankly, I don't think it's worthy of a loving God. I would think He'd have a bit more compassion for the lost."

"I'm sure I—"

"I'm sure you didn't." Eugenie didn't want to make any more of an adversary out of Hazel than she already had. "What I will say, when I speak to the congregation, is that they are certainly free to criticize my faith if they feel I've acted in an un-Christian manner over the last forty years. And they certainly have a point if they censure me for not being an active part of a congregation. But as to my relationship with God—" She drew a deep breath. "As to my status as a believer, they have no right to anything. While my practice may have been lacking in some people's eyes, my faith is a private matter."

Hazel didn't seem to know whether to look jubilant or disappointed. She'd gotten what she asked for, but not really. Eugenie was smart enough to know that what Hazel really wanted was to have Eugenie under her thumb as she'd had the last few pastors' wives.

"I'm sure you'll do as you see fit," Hazel said, but without her usual conviction in her own judgment.

"I'm glad that's settled then." Eugenie nodded at the library book in Hazel's hand. "Did you want me to check that out for you?" If nothing else, Hazel's quest to make Eugenie prove her faith had turned the other woman into a library regular.

Perhaps one day she'd even open one of the books she checked out and start reading it.

That evening after supper, when Hannah had drifted off to her room and Eugenie sat with Paul in the living room by the fireplace, she broached the subject of her testimony.

"I told Hazel I would speak to the congregation," she said to Paul.

He lowered his book and looked at her over the top of his glasses. "I still want you to reconsider." He'd been putting her off over the last few weeks, hoping she would change her mind. "Are you sure that's what you want?" Paul's mouth drew down. "You know that I—"

"Have never pushed me to be the traditional pastor's wife. Yes, I know." She stopped, laid her own book in her lap, and sighed. "Much as we both might want to pretend it doesn't matter, it does. How people perceive me affects you and your work."

"But—"

She held up one hand. "I made this choice because I want to, Paul. Not because of Hazel Emerson or anyone else."

He paused, then took off his glasses, rose from his chair, and came toward her. With one hand, he reached out. She clasped his hand in hers, and he drew her to her feet, into his arms.

"I should have prepared you better, given you more of a chance to turn me down," he said.

"When you marry a minister, you're taking on a lot more than just one man."

Esther rested her hands on his shoulders and looked him in the eye. "I've learned how true that is, thanks to Hazel." She lowered her gaze and studied the buttons on his shirt for a long moment. "It's been a long time, Paul, since I had much use for church. Or God. I'm a little rusty."

"I think you bring a fresh perspective."

She laughed. "That's one way to put it."

"Eugenie, I don't want you to think your actions are going to make or break what happens financially with the congregation."

She shook her head. "I don't. But it can only help, as far as I can tell." She kissed him on the cheek. "Besides, if the ship is going down, my place is with the captain."

"Thanks for that image." Paul's laugh always made her heart jump a little.

"Everything will be fine," she reassured him.

"I know that. I've always known that. I just forget to believe it sometimes."

Eugenie was glad Hannah was in her room. She was certain the teenager would have been horrified by the kiss that followed.

This time, when Merry pulled into the church parking lot on an early March morning, Jeff sat beside her in the passenger seat. Hunter babbled happily in the back, unaware of his mother's turmoil.

After the last meeting of the Knit Lit Society, she'd done a lot of thinking—about what it meant to love Hunter, but also what it meant to love her family. And then they'd gone straight on to *Pride and Prejudice*, and now everywhere Merry turned, all she could see was how difficult it was to be a parent, to manage a family, to choose the needs of one child over the needs of the others.

Love was not always the clear-cut choice people wanted to believe. Or as Merry had believed, until those long days in the hospital when she'd felt a fierce desire to protect Hunter but also longed for her other children. Somewhere in the days since the last Knit Lit Society meeting, Merry had accepted that she would never be the mother she'd thought she was supposed to be. She would have to compromise, over and over again.

And today that compromise meant taking Hunter back to day care and heading for Jeff's office.

Her other realization had been that she shouldn't have tried to shoulder this burden alone. Jeff worked hard, but so did she, and when it came to placing an infant in day care, it wasn't the mother's job to go it alone.

Jeff had balked the night before when she'd told him she expected him to come with her the next morning.

"I've got a lot to do tomorrow, honey, and I don't think it takes two grownups to carry one baby to day care."

But Merry had been adamant. Jeff humphed and grumped about it until bedtime, then fussed a little more that morning, but he was here beside her.

And suddenly looking white as a sheet. She knew she should feel sorry for him, but his pallor made her feel a lot better.

"Maybe you're right," Jeff said when she pulled into a parking place.

Merry switched off the engine. "Right about what?"

"Maybe it's better if Hunter doesn't go to day care."

Somehow she kept the corners of her mouth from tugging upward into a smile. "On a scale of one to ten, how nauseated are you?"

He turned toward her and grimaced. "There's nothing higher than a ten?"

Like a lot of men, Jeff dealt with difficult emotions by pushing them to the side. Merry wasn't trying to inflict additional pain or stress on him. She just needed him to understand why she'd been having such a hard time with the whole Hunter-in-day-care thing.

"I'm sure there's something higher, but I try not to think about it," she said. "Come on. It doesn't get any better if we sit here waiting."

"You sure?" He gave her a ghost of a smile.

"Believe me. I know that for a fact."

Getting out of the car was both easier and more difficult than it had been the last time. Easier because Jeff was there. More difficult because she knew this time she was actually going to leave Hunter in the infant room with Sandra.

Merry took the diaper bag while Jeff wrestled Hunter's car seat free. Together they turned and crossed the parking lot. They were ten feet from the door when Merry saw Eugenie approaching from the opposite direction.

"Good morning," Eugenie called, smiling kindly.

For once, Merry didn't have tears in her eyes when she spoke to the other woman. "Hello, Eugenie."

"Big day today?" There was no censure in her expression. Just encouragement and maybe a bit of humor.

"Finally," Merry answered. "It's been a long time coming."

Eugenie nodded toward the car seat in Jeff's hand. "Hunter will do fine. And so will you."

"I know." When it came to children, there were no guarantees, no infallible choices or perfect scenarios. Life happened, even to your kids. The most frightening thing was accepting that. Ironically, it was also the most liberating.

Someday Hunter would grow up and leave her. As possessive as she felt toward her children, she'd come to realize that they weren't really hers to keep. God had given them to her on loan, like the master in the parable who entrusted his treasure to his servants when he went on a journey. Parents had a choice. Merry had a choice. She could let her children breathe freely and thrive, or she could try to protect them so much that they suffocated. While the first one was more painful for her, it would be far more beneficial for her kids.

"We can do this," she heard Jeff mutter under his breath as they walked down the hall toward Hunter's classroom.

"Yes," she reassured him. "We can."

Sometimes letting go was the most loving thing to do. But it was also the hardest lesson Merry had ever learned in her life.

Camille and Maria met at Tallulah's for an early lunch. Camille knew that Maria was curious why she'd invited her, but she hadn't wanted to give any hint of what she had planned. Her decision was too new, too painful, but Maria could be trusted to keep Camille's secret in confidence.

"Hey." Camille greeted Maria, who had arrived first and already sat at a table by the large plate-glass windows at the front of the café. "Sorry I'm late. I had to get someone to cover the shop for me."

Maria smiled in sympathy. "I was afraid I might not make it at all, but Stephanie put in a rare appearance."

"I'm glad it worked out." She slid into the chair opposite Maria. "I hope this doesn't seem weird."

"I have to admit I'm curious."

Tallulah appeared, sliding menus in front of them and taking their drink orders. When she'd retreated, Camille proceeded straight to the matter that had troubled her so much over the last few weeks.

"I've made a decision," she told Maria, "and, in a way, it involves you and your family."

Maria arched an eyebrow in surprise. "That's intriguing."

Camille paused, unsure how to share what she wanted to say to the other woman. She didn't want to hurt Maria's pride or offend her. "I need to swear you to secrecy," she said. "At least for a little while."

"Are you sick?" Maria's question was immediate and anxious.

"No, no. Nothing like that."

Maria sank back in her chair, clearly relieved. "I was afraid that—"

"Sorry. Didn't mean to alarm you. It's actually a good thing. For you, I mean."

"Now I really am intrigued."

"I was wondering—"

Tallulah interrupted her as she set their glasses of iced tea on the table. "What can I get for you ladies today?"

Maria ordered the meat loaf special. Camille opted for the diet plate.

"I feel like a glutton next to you," Maria said, her words lighthearted.

"I'm still trying to make up for all those casseroles and brownies people dropped by after my mom's funeral."

Maria nodded. "It's been a tough year, hasn't it?"

"Yes. That's why I thought of you."

"Thought of me?"

"I'm going to leave Sweetgum." There. She'd said it. Made it real.

"You're kidding."

"No. I'm not."

Maria sank backward in her chair. "But what about—"

"Dante." Camille felt the familiar wave of grief rise up within her. Would she ever come to a place in her life where loss didn't threaten to overwhelm her on a regular basis? First her father, then her mother. Now Dante.

"I thought you two were—"

"I'm going to break it off."

"Wow."

"I've been accepted at Middle Tennessee State. I want to start as soon as possible. In the May summer session."

"What about the dress shop?"

"I'm going to sell it."

Maria frowned in confusion. "I still don't understand what this has to do with me and my family."

Camille fought the knot in her stomach. "I need someone to live in my mom's house. I'm not ready to sell it yet, and if I rent it, I won't have any place to stay during semester breaks."

"You're going to live in the dorms?"

Camille laughed. "Yeah. I may be the oldest freshman on record."

"I don't know." Maria looked at the tabletop, studying her flatware intensely.

"You'd be doing me a favor."

Maria shook her head. "Not really." Now her eyes were blinking back tears, Camille saw. "Look, I couldn't afford to pay any rent. We're barely making ends meet as it is, living above the store."

"I don't want rent. I want someone who'll look after things, take care of them." She paused, trying to get the words past the lump in her throat. "Even though I'm leaving Sweetgum, that house is still my home."

"Are you sure?" Maria looked at her with cautious optimism. "We'd pay the utilities, things like that."

"We'll work something out." Camille wasn't concerned about minor issues like gas or water bills. "It would only be for the time I'm in college. I'm not sure what I'll do after that."

"Of course." Maria reached across the table and laid her hand on top of Camille's. "You don't have to do this though. My family, we'll get by. You should find someone who can pay you—"

"You can't buy family." Camille smiled at the other woman, willing her to understand. "Now that my mom's gone, the Knit Lit Society's the only family I have left. Please say you'll do it."

Maria nodded. "Of course we will. You're being far too generous."

"No. Just practical."

"When will you leave for Murfreesboro?"

"In early May."

"We can manage over the store until then." Maria paused. "When are you going to tell Dante?"

"Soon," Camille said. "As soon as I get my courage up, anyway."

"It's a shame that you two found each other right when you finally get a chance to follow your dream."

"A shame?" Camille laughed, wishing it didn't sound so bitter. "No, I just think God has a sick sense of humor."

"You're sure you don't want to stay?"

"I can't." Camille was as sure of that as she was of her own name. "I just can't."

"It will be okay." Maria squeezed her hand. "I'm sure it will. Maybe you can have a long-distance relationship."

Camille wished she felt a tenth as optimistic as Maria seemed to be. "No. When I leave Sweetgum, I don't want to still be tied to it. Otherwise, what would be the point?"

"You're really sure?" Maria asked.

Camille nodded. She was very, very sure, and it was breaking her heart.

Twenty-Nine

Maria stared through the plate-glass window of the five-and-dime at the gray day. The sky hung low and heavy, as if threatening a rare March snowfall. Well, that was one advantage to living above the store. She never had to worry about getting to and from work during bad weather. Soon, though, she and her family would be in a house once more. Maria smiled, the thought of Camille St. Clair's generosity warming her despite the chill in the air. She'd never imagined when Eugenie Carson invited her to join the Knit Lit Society that it would turn out to be such a saving grace.

Her mother had been pleased at the prospective arrangement, if a bit critical of the location of their home-to-be. She would have preferred something in Esther Jackson's neighborhood to the modest bungalows along Camille's street. Daphne had been delighted, of course, and even Stephanie had shown some maturity for once. She'd stopped by Maxine's Dress Shop to thank Camille in person. Maria had been astonished at the news. Perhaps her younger sister wasn't a complete disaster.

Maria looked down at the counter in front of her. Business had been slow that day, mostly due to the weather, so she'd settled on a stool behind the register and alternated reading for the Knit Lit Society with working on the assigned knitting project for *Pride and Prejudice.* The subtle pattern of the moss stitch looked sufficiently old fashioned to have been worn by the Bennett sisters. After much thought, Maria had decided on a pair of stockings. Well, more like socks, really. But the double challenge of the stitch and the sock ought to keep her mind off her troubles for a while.

The bell over the door, the one she'd installed right before Christmas, jangled, and a *whoosh* of cold air filled the store. Maria set her book on the counter and looked up. She froze. Not from the cold but from the sight of the man standing ten feet away from her.

"Hello." James Delevan was as tall, handsome, and arrogant-looking as ever.

"Hello." She didn't trust herself to say anything more.

He unwrapped a navy blue scarf from around his neck, then tucked it into the pocket of his dark wool overcoat. "How are you?"

"Fine." Could their conversation be any more stilted? "How are you?"

"Fine." He stepped forward, then stopped. "Actually, that's a lie. I'm not fine." His eyes, as indecipherable as ever, seemed to pin her to the stool where she sat.

"I'm sorry to hear that," she lied. After that last evening, when he'd taken her to Tallulah's and then later expressed his regret at having kissed her,

333

as well as the pity he felt for her, she'd imagined a thousand torturous endings for him, even though she knew her humiliation had been her own fault. Why had she ever imagined a man like James Delevan would be interested in her?

"Are you really sorry to hear that?" He took a step closer. "After what I said the last time . . . Well, I thought you'd be happy to see me miserable."

She certainly would be, but she wasn't about to admit it to him. After their last encounter, she'd learned her lesson. She would not show that kind of weakness again.

"I guess I haven't given you much thought." She flipped her book closed. He moved forward again and looked at the cover.

"*Pride and Prejudice*?" He raised one eyebrow, which immediately put Maria on the defensive.

"What of it?" As if he had any right to criticize her reading material. "It's for my book club."

"And the knitting?" He eyed the half-finished pale blue sock that hung from a circle of double-pointed needles.

"It goes with the book." She wished her cheeks wouldn't redden, but even she could see how hokey that was, knitting something to go with the selected title. With one hand she scooped up her yarn and needles, and with the other she snatched the book from the counter. She shoved all of it into the basket at her feet. "Did you need something today? Pens, maybe?" she asked, hoping to remind him of his boorish behavior the first time he'd come into the store.

"I came to talk to you."

"I can't imagine what about."

"I owe you an explanation." He took another step toward her, and Maria was thankful for the width of the counter between them. Whenever James Delevan came too close, she behaved like an idiot. Better to keep him at arm's length.

"You don't owe me anything."

"I intended to stay away. To avoid Sweetgum at all costs."

He would certainly never be known for his flattery, Maria thought with a wisp of a smile. Despite the pounding of her heart, she could see the humor in the situation.

"So why did you come back?"

"Like I said, I have something to tell you."

"I can't imagine what you could say to me that would be worth the drive from Memphis."

He slipped off his overcoat and laid it over the counter. The movement stirred the air, and Maria caught the clean, crisp scent of his aftershave. It was as no-nonsense, and as attractive, as he was.

"You're the hardest woman to read I've ever met."

"That's a laugh coming from you, the king of inscrutable."

He sighed. "I lied to you." His gaze caught hers. "I lied to you about something very important."

"Look, James, I barely know you. Whatever you were untruthful about, I'm sure it doesn't matter. And it certainly didn't merit a trip from Memphis."

"My sister's dead."

The words didn't make sense at first, and she looked at him in confusion. "I'm sorry?"

"I lied to you at Christmas when I said my sister was skiing with friends. That she was at boarding school." His voice broke, jagged as glass and raw as the March wind. He wasn't inscrutable now. Grief etched his face in deep lines, around his eyes, across his forehead. Maria had no idea what to say.

She said the first thing that popped into her mind. "Why did you lie about that? Why would you need to?"

He looked away. "I didn't want your pity." He paused, then turned back to her. "I didn't want anyone's pity."

"What makes you think I would have pitied you?" Of all the things he might have said to her, this admission was the last thing she would have expected.

"Because you have a good heart. Because you recently lost your father, your home. You know about grief." His voice wavered on the last words before he caught himself, stood up straighter, and banished the emotion from his voice. "That night we ate at Tallulah's, after I kissed you, you thought I was going to say I paid attention to you because I felt sorry for you."

"I didn't—"

"You did. And I let you think that. I walked away and left you believing that was my motive." He moved to the side and stepped around the end of the counter. Two short steps, and he stood directly in front of her. Her heart pounded as ferociously now as it had the last time he'd been so close.

"I don't understand." She wasn't sure whether the conversation or his nearness scrambled her brain more.

"That night, I wasn't going to say I felt sorry for you."

"You weren't?"

"No. I was going to say that I kissed you because I felt sorry for myself."

"Oh. Well, that makes me feel much better. Better to be the nearest warm body than an object of pity." If he'd wanted to offend her on purpose, he hardly could've been more effective.

"No." He clasped her upper arms with his hands and drew her toward him. "I wanted to say I felt sorry for myself . . . except when I was with you."

Maria hadn't seen that coming. "But—"

"Why do you think I stayed in Sweetgum so long? I used every trick in the book to keep running into you."

She shook her head. "I don't believe—"

"You should. You should believe it." His hands moved upward, skimming her shoulders, and then cupped her face. "My sister, Kimmy, died in a car wreck last summer." Sheer emotion twisted his features. "I didn't think I'd ever feel anything but grief again. Never. Until the day I walked into this store. I behaved like a jackass that day, and you let me know it. You looked at me as if I was a bug you should squash under your shoe." He leaned down, ever closer. "You irritated me. You challenged me." His lips were a breath away from hers. "You made me feel something again."

"James—"

"No. Don't say anything. Please."

Her heart raced so fast she thought it might explode.

"Just kiss me," he said.

Maria wanted to, more than anything, but she was too fragile to risk her heart on a man as difficult and withholding as James Delevan.

"I can't." With one quick move, she pulled free and stepped back, bumping into the display shelves behind her. "I'm sorry about your sister. I don't know exactly what that's like, to lose a sibling, but I've done enough grieving in these last months to know a little about loss." She kept moving backward, intent on putting distance between them. "But I can't—"

"Why not?" His expression turned thunderous, as black as his hair. "Fine. Punish me for being an idiot. Just tell me how long I have to suffer before you're satisfied."

Maria's mouth fell open in shock. "That's what

you think of me? That I'm the kind of woman who would enjoy seeing you suffer?"

"I wouldn't have thought that until now."

"You are the most arrogant man I've ever met." The pinpricks of guilt that had stung her disappeared. "Not everything is about *you,* James Delevan. I know that may be a hard concept for you to grasp, but other people have actual lives, actual problems."

"I know that," he snapped back. "Give me a little credit."

"What do you want from me?" she demanded. "Other than to soothe your grief?"

He ran a hand through his hair, causing it to stand on end. Finally, James Delevan looked less than perfect. She should have found more satisfaction in the sight than she did.

"I want—" He broke off, shaking his head in exasperation. "I don't want anything *from* you," he said. "I just want *you.* To be near you, with you. To talk to you as much as possible." The last words came out in a whoosh of breath, leaving him almost gasping for air.

"But why me?" His words set loose that traitor hope in her heart. "Of all the women you must know, why in the world would you want to be with me?"

James looked down at the knitting basket at his feet. He leaned over and retrieved her book. "How did Darcy know Elizabeth was the one for him?"

"This," she said, waving a hand between them, "is hardly a Jane Austen novel."

"Why not?" He moved toward her again, but she was almost to the end of the counter. Plus she hated to keep giving ground. "How are we so different from them?"

Maria bit her lip. She could definitely see him as Mr. Darcy. But her as Elizabeth Bennett? She almost laughed. For one thing, she was way too old. And for another . . .

The almost-laugh died on her lips. She was a spinster, like Austen's main character. She was poor. She had an obnoxious mother and two of the requisite four sisters. Maria put a hand to her mouth, unsure whether to laugh or cry.

"Weird, isn't it?" James said. He, too, looked as if he didn't know whether to be amused or worried.

"I never thought—"

"I guess there's a reason people still read her books." He shook his head. "Darcy was a fool for most of that novel, but maybe I can learn from his mistakes."

"I can't believe you've read it."

He stopped, his cheeks pale. "My sister asked me to a couple years ago."

"I'm sorry." She reached out and put her hand on his arm. Beneath her fingers, the wool of his expensive suit was as soft as the cashmere she'd been using to make the socks.

His free hand covered hers. "I'm not usually so

incompetent when I try to tell a woman I like her."

"And I'm usually much more receptive to compliments."

"I'd say we've both behaved less than heroically."

Maria nodded. "Yes. I'd agree."

"Do you want to change that?" His eyes filled with a kind of earnest enthusiasm she'd never seen before.

It took her a moment to find her voice. "Yes," she said. "I do."

Fortunately, it was a slow day at Munden's Five-and-Dime, so when James Delevan took Maria Munden into his arms and kissed her quite thoroughly, no customers stood in the aisles to be outraged by the shocking display.

Thirty

Hannah hadn't ditched class at all as a freshman, although it had been a regular habit in middle school. That morning, though, she just couldn't bring herself to face it.

Posters for the freshman spring dance had gone up the Friday before, bright pink and purple reminders of how alone she was. Josh no longer even tried to speak to her in the hallway. She told herself that was what she wanted, that it was the only way to get over him. She just didn't know why it still hurt as much as it had that day by the creek, when he'd told her he was taking Courtney to the winter formal. She had no doubt he'd already asked Courtney to go with him to the spring one too.

Instead of crossing the street east toward the high school, Hannah headed north, ducking behind cars and trees so that Rev. Carson and Eugenie wouldn't see her. A block over, she reached the edge of the trees that bordered Sweetgum Creek. A few steps down the steep bank and she stood at the edge of the water and out of sight from the street above.

Ten minutes of walking and she reached the wide sand where the creek narrowed. Without the coming spring rains, the water merely trickled beneath the bare branches that arched above it. Dry winter grass on the bank above rustled in the swirling breeze.

Hannah zipped her coat up to her chin and thrust her hands in her pockets. When she'd decided to play hooky, she hadn't considered the weather. A long, cold day stretched before her. When she lived in the trailer with her mom, she'd just stayed at home and watched television when she ditched school. She couldn't do that at the parsonage. Too many neighbors, and Rev. Carson had a habit of stopping by the house to get some lunch or fetch a book he'd meant to take to the church with him.

Hannah sank down onto the sand. A moment too

late she realized it was damp beneath the top layer. The cold seeped through her jeans in an instant. She tugged the tail of her coat lower and tried to sit on it.

This place held a lot of memories, but the last terrible one overwhelmed the good ones. Josh, the one person she'd thought she could trust, breaking her heart. It just proved she should never let anyone get close, because it was only a matter of time until they betrayed her.

With a sigh, Hannah reached into her backpack and pulled out her latest knitting project. She could work on it until her fingers got too stiff from the cold. Then she could read some. She'd just gotten to the part where Lydia Bennett runs off with the scoundrel Wickham, ruining Elizabeth's chances with Darcy.

Hannah could identify with Elizabeth Bennett on that score. She knew what it was like to have her own chance for happiness squashed like a bug beneath the shoe of other people's bad behavior. That last thought caused a sob to rise in her throat. She let it escape, wiping at the splash of tears on her cheeks with the back of one hand. She was so tired. Not trusting anyone was exhausting. Always keeping her guard up, never a moment to relax.

She picked up her needles and opened the book she was using for the knitting project. The diagrams for the moss stitch baffled her, but she was determined. She concentrated so hard on the movement of her needles that she didn't hear Josh until he plopped down next to her in the wet sand.

"Hey."

Her head snapped up, and she dropped her knitting. "What the—"

"It's just me."

Hannah scowled. "You really can't take a hint, can you?"

"No. Not really." He grinned.

If he had apologized again, continued to grovel, she could have kept up her defenses. But that lopsided smile pierced her where she was weakest, right in the vicinity of her heart.

"Won't you get suspended from the team or something for cutting class?"

Josh leaned back in the sand on his elbows, his long legs stretched in front of him. "What are they going to do to me? I'm moving in a few weeks."

"Good point." She had to be cool, not let him see how much he got to her. She picked up her knitting and dusted the sand off of it.

"What are you making?"

"A sweater." At least, it would be a sweater someday. No way could she finish it by the Knit Lit Society meeting next week.

"My mom made me a sweater like that once. It has those bumps in it," he said, examining the soft green wool.

"It's called a moss stitch."

"Didn't know that."

"There are a lot of things you don't know, apparently." The sarcasm slipped out against her better judgment.

"You know, I'd think that living with a preacher you would have learned to be a little more forgiving."

"I'm forgiving. I'm just not stupid."

"Touché." He looked up at the branches above them and didn't say anything else.

"What would you have done if you were in my shoes?" Hannah asked when Josh remained silent. "I don't know anyone who gets all warm and fuzzy about being humiliated."

Josh rolled to his side, propping himself up on one elbow. "I've already told you I'm sorry. I was stupid and wrong and idiotic and everything else you can think of. I messed up, Hannah. Now I'm asking for forgiveness." He softly touched the back of her hand with the tips of his fingers. "I'm asking if we can start over."

She refused to flinch at his touch or let him see that it in any way affected her. "Why bother? You'll be gone soon." The moment she said it, she realized she'd betrayed herself.

Josh raised one eyebrow. "So you might forgive me? If I can convince you it's worth it for the next month?"

"That's not what I said."

"But that's what you implied."

"Josh—" She sighed, then looked him square in

the eye. "How could I believe anything you say?"

"You'd have to make the choice to trust me again." He wasn't smiling now. His eyes pleaded with her.

"Yeah, well, that's the problem. I don't trust you anymore. No, it's more than that. You took away any reason I had to trust you in the first place. It's gone, Josh, and trust isn't something you just whip up out of thin air."

"Actually, it is." He levered himself into a sitting position. "That's all it is, really. If you think about it, none of us has any reason to trust anyone else."

She let out an exasperated sigh. "Of course you'd say something like that. You're the one who screwed up."

"I may be a partial idiot but not a total one. I have been known to learn from my mistakes."

"And I've been known to be humiliated by them."

"All right, then think of it this way. If you go to the spring formal with me, you'll have the best revenge of all."

"What?" The knitting needles in her hands jerked so that several stitches slid off the end of one of them. "Not funny, Josh." She scrambled to get the stitches back on the needle.

"I wasn't trying to be funny. I want you to go to the dance with me." He reached into his back pocket and wiggled something free. "Here." He thrust two pieces of pink paper toward her.

"So you bought tickets. What does that prove?"

"Look at the names on them."

Reluctantly, Hannah did. She saw Josh's name on one. And hers on the other.

"Josh—"

"We don't have a lot of time, Hannah. Every minute you won't forgive me is a minute we lose."

"But you're leaving. There's no point."

"Just because you can't have everything, you don't want anything?"

"Josh—"

He reached over and gently lifted the knitting needles from her grasp. He set them aside, and took her hands in his. "Please, Hannah. I really need you to forgive me." His eyes sparkled with moisture. No macho football player. Just her friend Josh. "I need something to hang on to when I go back to Alabama." He shook his head. "I know I don't deserve it, but none of us deserves to be forgiven. That's what they always say in church."

"I don't know—"

He kissed her then, simply leaned forward and pressed his lips to hers as he had that night after the football game. Unexpected, warm, and everything she missed, everything she needed.

"Please, Hannah," he murmured against her lips, and she couldn't hold out against him any longer.

"If you hurt me again"—she pounded his chest with her fist for emphasis—"I will hunt you down like a dog. Do you hear me?"

His hand reached up to grab hers. "You won't have to. I promise."

Hannah still didn't know if she could trust him. She only knew she couldn't *not* trust him. To banish him from her heart forever would hurt far more than his betrayal had.

"I don't have a dress," she said.

"What?"

"I don't have a dress for the dance."

Josh chuckled. "I bet Camille St. Clair would hook you up. If she doesn't, we'll skip the dance and just hang out together."

"Okay."

He slid an arm around her, and she tucked her head into the crook of his shoulder. "Josh?"

"Yeah?"

"Do we have to go back to school?"

He nodded. "If we get suspended, we can't go to the dance."

She lifted her head. "How did you know I was here?"

Josh squeezed her shoulders. "I didn't. I just needed someplace to think. It never occurred to me to go anywhere else."

At that moment, Hannah knew everything would be okay. At least until spring break.

Esther stood in her backyard and eyed the small stone angel in the flower bed. Frank had placed it there under her direction when they'd first moved into the house. She'd had no idea how heavy it was—she couldn't lift it herself. The movers had already left, so there was no help from that quarter. She glanced around the yard and considered her options. The buyer would be pulling up any minute. She had to take the statue with her now.

Beside her, Ranger barked for her attention.

"Not now," she said to the dog. "It's a shame I don't have a harness for you. You could help me get this to the car."

"Maybe I could give you a hand." Brody's voice came from over her shoulder. She swiveled toward him and almost lost her balance. "Steady, there," he said, catching her arm to keep her upright.

"I didn't hear you," she said, pushing a strand of hair out of her eyes. She was dusty and dirty from the last-minute packing and cleaning—not to mention the effort of digging up two of her prize rosebushes to take with her to the condo on Sweetgum Lake.

"Didn't mean to sneak up on you." He grinned. "You have dirt on your nose."

Esther swiped at her nose. "What are you doing here?"

"I came to see if you needed help." He shrugged. "It's my day off."

"This statue's too heavy for me. I should have asked the moving men to help."

Brody moved closer and leaned over the stone

angel. In one quick motion, he bent at the knees, grabbed the angel, and hoisted it in his arms. "Where do you want it?"

"The car." She nodded toward the garage.

"Last time was easier," he grunted and took a few stumbling steps toward the garage. "At least with Ranger we had a blanket to carry him in."

Esther suppressed a laugh. "True. But this thing won't bite us."

"C'mon, woman," Brody growled as he walked. "Open that door for me."

Esther did as instructed, opening first the garage door and then the passenger door of her Jaguar. Brody managed to wrestle the angel to the floorboard.

He groaned and straightened, one hand to his back. "What are you going to do with it when you get to your new place?"

"I'll bribe one of the maintenance men or something."

"Seems like a strange thing to take with you. Where are you going to put it? You won't have a yard."

"I have a little patio. It will go there."

"What's so special about this statue?"

Esther paused, unsure if she should or even could answer him. For decades, being Esther Jackson had meant keeping her own counsel, never letting her guard down. This angel represented perhaps her darkest secret, one she'd never shared with anyone but Frank. She looked Brody up and down, as if sizing him up.

"Why are you looking at me like that?" he asked.

"Nobody but Frank knew about this angel."

"Didn't everybody who set foot in your backyard notice it?"

Esther shook her head. "I don't mean its existence. I mean its purpose."

Brody nodded. "It marks something important."

"Yes."

"Are you going to tell me what?"

Esther didn't know what to do. "I'm not sure where to start."

"The beginning's usually the best place."

"That might take awhile."

He nodded. "Why don't I help you finish here? Then I can follow you to the lake and help you unload that thing."

Esther refused to cry, but she couldn't avoid the mixture of gratitude and relief that rose in her throat. "I would appreciate that very much."

Brody shrugged. "What are friends for?"

Esther bit her lip "I don't know. It's been a long time since I had one." The confession sprang out of her before she could stop it. "I'm a little out of practice."

"Yeah," Brody said agreeably. He put a friendly arm around her shoulders as they turned back toward the house. "But you're getting better at it. Pretty soon you'll be a pro."

Esther laughed and felt a weight slip from her shoulders even as they were encircled by Brody's arm. Change was inevitable as the tides, and she'd been forced to make the choice between allowing it to drag her under or fighting her way to the surface and swimming for the shore. For now, at least, her head was above water, and she could see dry land in the distance.

"I've got coffee on," she said to Brody.

"I'd love some."

Later she would tell him the story about the stone angel. How it had marked the place in the yard where she'd sprinkled the ashes of her first child, the little girl who died only hours after her birth. The little girl no one knew about, because she and Frank had lived in Nashville at the time.

But that was later, not now. For now, she would simply enjoy the company, and the comfort, of a friend.

Thirty-One

At five o'clock on Saturday, Camille closed the door to the dress shop behind her and then reached up to put the key in the deadbolt and turned it with a click. She stared for a long moment at the sign that still swayed gently on the other side of the glass.

Closed.

Her past, her time in Sweetgum, her memories. All that would change soon. She would take only essentials—dorm rooms were small. She'd need to work, too, when she got to Murfreesboro, but she could easily find something as an assistant manager at a retail chain store. Beyond that, she didn't have to worry about anyone or anything else, except getting as far away from Sweetgum as she possibly could.

"Camille."

Dante's voice startled her, and she turned to face him. He stood on the sidewalk not ten feet away, still dressed in his coaching clothes even in the off season—anorak emblazoned with the Sweetgum High School mascot, those knit pants coaches always wore, and running shoes. The brim of a Tennessee Titans baseball cap shaded his eyes.

"Hey."

"I saw Natalie Grant at Tallulah's." He stared hard at her. "She said Esther Jackson bought your shop. When did this happen?"

Of course Natalie had found out. Camille nodded, her throat tight. She thought she'd have more time to prepare for this conversation. "I'm on my way to drop the keys off at her condo at the lake."

Dante continued to regard her steadily, and that very calm made her nervous. She felt moisture breaking out across her forehead.

"I'll drive you," he said.

She started to protest, but before she could get the words out, he took her arm and hustled her toward his car.

"There's no need—"

"We have to talk. Might as well tie up all your loose ends at the same time."

She had known he'd be angry, which was why she hadn't told him about the dress shop. Or about college. His hand on her arm was insistent but not controlling, like Dante himself.

"I'm not sure this is a great idea," she said.

He stopped, turning her to face him. "Right now, I'm not sure you would know a great idea if it ran over you."

Camille bit her lip and slid into his car when he opened the door for her. She would just have to ride out the storm. She was an expert at that by now. Heaven knew she'd had enough practice over the years. What couldn't be cured had to be endured. She'd heard someone say that once, and it had become her personal mantra. But she wasn't sure that advice had ever been intended to cover a situation like this.

"When were you going to tell me?"

Dante kept his eyes on the road as he drove away from the town square, and so did she. She couldn't afford to look at him now, not if she wanted to keep her composure.

She also couldn't answer him. The silence stretched out between them.

"You weren't going to tell me."

She shrugged. "You would have found out."

"From who? Tallulah, the next time I had lunch at the café? Esther Jackson, when I went in the shop looking for you?"

"Yes."

He took his foot off the accelerator, and Camille's heartbeat sped up even as the car slowed. When he hit the brake, she clutched her purse in her lap and felt her pulse pounding in her neck. Dante swung the car onto the shoulder of the road and stopped.

Camille felt the tears pressing against the backs of her eyelids, but she refused to let them fall. He had a right to be angry. She was a coward.

Dante turned the key, shutting off the engine. Then he turned toward her.

"Do you know what I thought freshman year, the first time I saw you?" he asked.

That was the last thing she expected to hear. She'd thought he would yell at her with the same deafening roar he used on his football players, but Dante was as cool and calm as if they were discussing the weather.

"Freshman year?"

"My family had just moved here from Nashville. As far as I knew, my life was over, stuck out here in the middle of nowhere. But there was football. And there was you. When I saw you, I knew why God had brought me to Sweetgum."

Camille stared at him, dumbfounded. "But—"

"That's not something you say to a fourteen-year-old girl. I kept it to myself. But I knew."

"Dante—"

"I still know."

"Don't bring God into this. That's not fair."

"Then tell me you don't love me, and I'll shut up."

"That's even less fair."

"You think life is supposed to be fair? After all you've been through, you still haven't let go of that?"

"I have to leave, Dante. I'll suffocate if I stay here. As it is, I've been on life support for the last six years."

His hands clenched around the steering wheel. "We'd be worth it, Cammie. We'd be worth your staying here."

"It's too high a price." She wished she could wrap her own hands around something, anything to hang on to. "If I don't go now, Dante, I never will. And I'll always regret it. Always."

She knew that with bone-deep certainty. And as the silence lengthened between them, anger, fierce and low, kindled in her midsection. Why couldn't she get just one break? One time when things went her way?

Dante took his hands from the steering wheel and retrieved something from the front pocket of his pants. A box. Small, black, and velvet.

"Don't."

Her command didn't stop him. He opened the box.

The ring was breathtaking, a square-cut diamond in an old-fashioned platinum setting. "It was my grandmother's," he said. "She left it to me."

Camille couldn't stop the tears. "Put it away." Instead, he took it out of the box and reached for her hand. She jerked away. "Dante, put it away."

"Just let me see it on your finger. Just once, Cammie. You can at least do that much."

With her right hand, she wiped away tears while he took her left and slid the ring onto her finger. It fit perfectly. The weight of it terrified her.

"That's where it belongs," he said. He reached over and cupped her chin, turning her face toward his. She didn't want to look in his eyes, but she made herself. The love she saw there frightened her even more than the feel of the ring on her finger.

"No. It doesn't belong there." She started to take the ring off, but he stopped her. She looked at him in confusion. "What?"

"It's yours," he said.

"Dante, I can't marry you. This belongs to the woman you'll spend the rest of your life with. Not me."

"No, Cammie. That ring's meant for you."

"I can't keep it."

"You don't have a choice."

"Of course I have a choice."

"Camille, you can leave Sweetgum. You can go anywhere in the world, see everything there is to see. But no matter where you go, I'll still be here, loving you. And that will still be your ring."

She didn't know what to say. He reached for the key and turned the ignition. Before she could gather her thoughts, he had the car in motion, gliding down the road.

"I'll drop you off at your house. I don't think driving you to the lake right now is a good idea."

"I'm not keeping the ring, Dante."

"Yes," he said without looking at her. "You are." He turned, and their eyes met for a brief second. "You owe me that much, Cammie."

She cried in earnest then, her heart breaking, torn in two by her love for Dante and her fear of being trapped in Sweetgum.

When they reached her house and pulled into her driveway, she didn't wait for him to get out of the car and come around to open her door. She clambered out as fast as she could, and then stood there, twisting the ring on her finger.

"Please take it back," she said.

He shook his head. "If you won't stay, then at least take part of me with you." He paused, his voice choked with emotion. "I love you, Camille. Maybe someday you'll understand what that means."

He leaned across the seat and grabbed the door

handle to pull it closed. Before she could say anything, he had the car in reverse and was pulling out
of the driveway.

She watched him drive away, feeling like the
worst sort of traitor, knowing there was nothing
else she could do. She couldn't help how she felt
about Sweetgum any more than she could help
whom she loved. She hated Sweetgum as much as
she loved Dante, but there was no room for compromise. It had to be one or the other. She had
dreamed of escaping Sweetgum far longer than
she'd loved Dante.

In the end, she'd really had no choice at all.

Thirty-Two

At the March meeting of the Sweetgum Knit Lit
Society, Eugenie looked at the assembled group
and wondered, not for the first time, if she'd made
a critical error in judgment with the reading list.
Although they still had two months and two books
left in the year, she felt somehow that they were
coming to an end. She wasn't sure "Great Love
Stories in Literature" had been much of a success.

"Where's Hannah?" Merry asked, nodding
toward the empty chair next to Eugenie.

"She's at the freshman dance at the high school."

At long last, Hannah had broken her silence and
told Eugenie the whole story of her troubled rela-

tionship with Josh Hargrove. Eugenie hadn't done much but listen and nod in the appropriate places. Hannah appeared to have worked out the problem for herself.

"I helped her pick out a dress from the shop," Camille said. She glanced toward Esther. "I forgot to tell you. I don't usually charge Hannah for clothes since she's been so good about helping out. I hope you'll keep that arrangement in the future."

Eugenie looked from Camille to Esther in surprise.

Esther saw her confusion and smiled. "We were going to tell you all tonight. I've bought Maxine's Dress Shop from Camille."

Exclamations of surprise sounded around the table.

"I'm leaving to go to school." Strangely, Camille didn't look as happy as Eugenie would have expected. "I'll be around for a few more weeks, helping Esther learn the ropes. We don't have to say any big good-byes yet."

"I'm speechless," Merry said with a laugh, because clearly she wasn't. She, too, looked from Camille to Esther in both delight and surprise. "You two sure can keep a secret."

"I wasn't certain I'd be able to do it," Esther admitted, "but my house finally sold. To that James Delevan from Memphis."

Maria gasped. "What?"

"We closed on it last week. I'm living in the condo at the lake now."

"James Delevan?" Maria said. "Are you sure?"

"I think I know who I sold my own house to." A bit of the old Esther reappeared in her pursed lips and short answer.

"What about Ranger?" Merry asked. "Do you have room for him at the condo?"

"He'll have to adjust," Esther said. "But Brody tells me that as long as I walk him twice a day, he'll be fine."

"Brody?" Eugenie was confused.

"The new veterinarian who took over for Dr. Everton. We're . . ." Esther paused, as if searching for the right word. "We're friends."

No one seemed to know what to say to that. The new veterinarian must have something to do with the new, improved Esther Jackson.

"How's Hunter, Merry?" Eugenie asked.

"Doing well. We have to take him back to Nashville periodically to the pediatric cardiologist. There may be some long-term effects on his heart, but we won't know for sure for a while." She looked around at the group. "Any and all prayers would be appreciated." Her words were greeted with nods and murmurs of assent.

"Of course we'll continue to pray for Hunter." Eugenie decided she'd better steer the conversation back to the purpose of the meeting. "So what about the book? I thought *Pride and Prejudice* would be a group favorite. What did you all think?"

361

"It's certainly the most traditional romance," Maria said.

Merry nodded. "You know, for the first time I actually sympathized with Mrs. Bennett. After the last couple months . . ." She paused and took a deep breath. "Well, let's just say I understand her anxiety about her children's futures."

"So love makes mothers anxious?" Eugenie asked, only partly in jest. Now that she was responsible for Hannah, she, too, had a newfound understanding of the scattered Mrs. Bennett.

"Ninety percent of the time," Merry said with a smile. "The other ten percent it just makes us pushovers."

"I thought Austen made a good argument that love means compromise," Eugenie said. "Both Elizabeth and Darcy have to change before they can be together. What did you all think?"

Camille shook her head. "Happy endings are an illusion." She tapped her copy of the book where it lay on the table. "There's a reason they call it fiction. Even Jane Austen herself never married."

"Yes, but she didn't give up her belief in happy endings either," Maria said. She looked younger for some reason, Eugenie thought. Then she realized that the streaks of gray in the other woman's hair were gone. She wore lipstick too. A very pale pink, but definitely there. "Sometimes love is totally unexpected," Maria added.

"Well, I, for one, have given up trying to understand anything about love," Esther said, but her words held a note of humor rather than the defeat that hung heavy in her voice last fall. "All I can say is that I've learned that endings, painful as they are, can be beginnings in disguise. Someone taught me that these last few months." She paused. "Maybe that's what love is. Helping other people see what they need to see."

Eugenie pondered that for a moment. "So have any of you changed your mind about your original definition of love?"

Maria nodded. "I guess I believe now that love doesn't always have to be painful. Sometimes it's nice."

"I always thought love meant sacrificing everything for other people." Camille laid her knitting on the table, her hands suddenly idle. "But there's another kind of love. Self-love. Sometimes"—her voice trembled—"sometimes you have to love yourself before you can love someone else."

Clearly she was thinking of Dante Brown. Eugenie felt a wave of sympathy for the younger woman. She'd been in a similar situation years before with Paul, when they'd been young sweethearts. She hoped Camille wouldn't need four decades to find her way back to love as Eugenie had.

"I always thought love was about doing your duty," Esther said, "but now I wonder if love isn't more about what you give because you want to, not because you have to."

Merry nodded in agreement. "I think I said love was overwhelming." She paused, biting her lip, and Eugenie could tell she was struggling to control her emotions. "After the last few months, I'll never take love for granted again."

"What about Hannah?" Camille asked Eugenie. "Would you say her definition has changed?"

Eugenie nodded. "Yes. Although I'd say Hannah's relationship with love is still a work in progress."

"What about you, Eugenie?" Esther asked. "Have you changed your definition?"

Eugenie thought of the words she'd spoken before the congregation two weeks before. Her testimony had been disguised as a Minute for Mission, a regular part of the service. She'd talked about the tutoring program she ran at the library and how books had been an important part of her journey. She'd talked about how they could help an individual grow spiritually. And without saying it in so many words, she'd asked the congregation to remember that she'd been a faithful citizen of Sweetgum, if not of a particular congregation, for many years.

She hadn't known if it would work, but the next Sunday the offering had been up ten percent. A coincidence, most likely, but more rewarding had been Paul's appreciation of her decision. She had accepted that in marrying a preacher, she'd com-mitted herself to a church as well. She wasn't naive enough to think there wouldn't be more rough patches in the future, but she and Paul would work it out, one day at a time.

"I've always believed that love means doing for others. That hasn't changed," Eugenie said. "Although I think I have changed my mind about what I'm willing to do for the people I love."

The others looked at her in confusion, but Eugenie decided not to offer any clarifications. It was enough that she knew what she meant.

"So let's see your projects," she said, ready to turn their attention to a new subject. "I thought the moss stitch had that old-fashioned feel of a Jane Austen novel. What did you think?"

The last thirty minutes of the meeting were spent admiring one another's work. As Eugenie listened to the women's chatter and observed their ani-mated, smiling faces, she decided that maybe "Great Love Stories in Literature" hadn't been a complete failure after all. Its success had come in the unexpected. In Hannah's willingness to forgive Josh. In Esther's choice to embrace a new life. In whatever—or whoever—had invigorated Maria. In Camille's difficult choice to follow her dream. In Merry's acceptance of her imperfections as a mother. And even in Eugenie's own willingness to sacrifice a little of her privacy for the sake of her husband.

Perhaps that was all any of them could ask of love, really. That it would help them to grow and change as their lives took them in unexpected directions. And that it would open their hearts and minds for the journey that lay ahead.

Readers Group Guide

1. What is your favorite love story in literature? in real life? What do you find most compelling about the story?
2. Does a great love story have a happy ending or a tragic ending? Why?
3. Over the course of the novel, each character's definition of love undergoes a change. How do you define love? What specifically led you to this understanding?
4. Are we ever too young or too old to fall in love? How does falling in love change as we move through the different stages of our lives?
5. Do you think that Camille makes the best choice for her at the end of the novel? Why or why not? Is it ever the best thing to walk away from love? Why or why not?
6. Hannah learns to practice forgiveness so that she can continue to have a relationship with Josh. Did she do the right thing in forgiving him? Do you think they will ever reconnect in the future?
7. Where is God moving in the life of each character?
8. How is knitting a metaphor for the presence of the divine in our lives?

About the Author

Beth Pattillo loves knitting and romance and enjoyed combining the two in *The Sweetgum Ladies Knit for Love.* She is also the author of *The Sweetgum Knit Lit Society.* She won the RITA Award from the Romance Writers of America for Best Inspirational Romance for her book *Heavens to Betsy.* Beth lives in Tennessee with her husband and children.

Center Point Publishing
600 Brooks Road • PO Box 1
Thorndike ME 04986-0001 USA

(207) 568-3717

US & Canada:
1 800 929-9108
www.centerpointlargeprint.com